Death in the Kitchen

A San Amaro Mystery

Marnie J Ross

Death in the Kitchen
A San Amaro Mystery
Marnie J Ross

MEERSCHAUM PRESS

Editor: Leighton Wingate
Cover: Bart Hopkins

© 2024 by Marnie J Ross

ISBN 979-8-9860071-3-7 Paperback

For Tricia

Contents

Prologue

Eduardo Escamilla, short in stature with sturdy limbs, wore a wide-brimmed straw hat above his round, brown face. He possessed the aura of age beyond his forty-two years. Pulling a midsize, dirty-gray wheelie bin and carrying a push broom, he opened the back gate to the San Amaro pickleball courts and stopped abruptly. His usual morning routine of sweeping the courts and inspecting the nets was forgotten.

In the predawn haze, his eyes had been drawn to an unusual sight—a heap of discarded garments strewn carelessly about one of the courts. The murky atmosphere compelled him to switch on the court lights before he entered to investigate.

Two minutes later, having locked the gates, he was on his cell phone dialing the police.

When the league players started arriving a few minutes before seven, they encountered a hand-written sign. *Cerrado* (closed), it said in Spanish. Eduardo's English was negligible, but among the early arrivers, Willie Platz had some rudimentary Spanish. Through Eduardo's rapid-fire, impassioned explanation, Willie identified the fateful words: *hombre* (man), *muerto* (dead), and *policia* (police). A collective sense of foreboding descended on the assembled group as it absorbed the gravity of the situation.

"Revenge is a sorrow for the person who has to take it on. And the person who is rash enough to think it's going to help a situation is always wrong."

Louise Erdrich—*The Round House*

Chapter One—Three Days Earlier

"I have a Range Rover reserved for three weeks. The name is Stephanetti, Rudy Stephanetti." The well-dressed, handsome, middle-aged man with sandy-brown wavy hair spoke as he swaggered toward the car-rental counter at the Yuma airport.

"Yes, sir, I see your reservation. Where will your trip be taking you over the next three weeks?" the young rental agent asked in a friendly tone.

"I don't see that's any of your business," Rudy answered abruptly, pulling his shoulders back.

"I'm not trying to pry, sir. I'm required to ask that question of everyone who rents from us. Being so close to the Mexican border, we must know whether you'll be taking our vehicle across the border. Special restrictions apply. Will you be spending any time in Mexico?" the agent asked matter-of-factly.

"I see. We will be spending two weeks in Mexico, but we're just going to San Amaro, on the Baja. I understand it's three hours from here. It's not as if we're driving to Mexico City and back. What kind of special restrictions apply for such a short trip?" Rudy asked, slightly less gruffly.

As the young man explained the need to pay with a corporate credit card and buy additional insurance, he watched his customer. The man's face started to get red, and he appeared to be preparing himself for an argument. "Do you have a corporate card, Mr. Stephanetti?" the agent asked with some trepidation.

Rudy was unexpectedly caught off guard by the restrictions governing car rentals for a journey from the United States to Mexico. And it pissed him off. He didn't like it when unexpected obstacles occurred in the roadway of his life. He had an inherent expectation he'd get what he wanted when he wanted it, and so was often pissed off.

His wife, Gloria, seeing the signs of her husband's darkening mood and having overheard the conversation, approached the counter beside him, leaving their two adult children guarding their luggage.

"Aren't we lucky you have a corporate card, honey," she said sweetly to her husband. Rudy, an executive in a medium-sized company, was provided a credit card issued in the business's name. Then turning toward the rental agent, Gloria thanked him for explaining it to them.

Behind her, she could hear their son, Logan, sigh loudly and hoped Rudy was paying more attention to providing the agent with the specific dates of their time in Mexico than his kids. Rudy had no patience for insubordination from his family, as the sigh would surely have been considered. She observed Rudy's posture and saw his shoulders relax. A good indicator that his temper was also calming.

Ten minutes later, the requisite insurance bought on Rudy's corporate credit card, the family of four loaded their suitcases and pickleball gear into a blood-red late-model Range Rover. Rudy, feeling back in control, entered their destination into the vehicle's GPS. Three hours and twenty minutes, not including the border crossing. They'd be there before it got dark, something he'd been told was wise.

By the time they set off, the feeling in the Rover was one of excitement. This was their first time going to the small town on the Sea of Cortez, and a sense of adventure enlivened each of them. An easy hour's drive later, they had arrived in Calexico, California, where they grabbed some fast food before heading to the border crossing. Everything was going smoothly, and Rudy was jovial, though he was slightly uncertain about crossing the border. All his previous trips to Mexico had been by air, so driving across was something new.

Soon, however, he was laughing at himself as they cruised across the border with no problems. He'd been told they would need to get visas at the border and easily found the building housing immigration on the Mexican side of the border. Another easy process, but one that took $120, thirty dollars each. He hadn't anticipated the cost. Not that it was a problem, just a surprise. Rudy again checked their estimated arrival time given by the GPS and was pleased to see they'd still arrive well before dusk.

As they made their way through Mexicali, a city of over a million people, the quality of some of the roads made Rudy glad he'd gotten such a rugged vehicle. But, as soon as they reached Highway Five, the main north-south road on the east side of the Baja peninsula, the road improved immensely. Their southward journey took them first through agricultural and farming communities, then gave way to salt flats, deserts, and mountains. It was a pretty drive.

Logan, his red hair curling over his earphones, listened to whatever was passing for music to a twenty-year-old these days. Brianna, also a redhead just three weeks from her eighteenth birthday, was engrossed in a game on her iPad. Gloria and Rudy were lost in their thoughts. It was a quiet drive.

Once in San Amaro, the quest for keys, wristbands to access the facilities, and an orientation to their condo was a time-consuming affair. They were staying in the gated community Cortez Oasis, which they were told everyone calls The Oasis.

On the drive from The Oasis security office to the condos, they passed pickleball courts, a swimming pool, and a restaurant. They were delighted to see that their condo was a short distance from these amenities.

The Stephanettis were relieved to be at the end of an extremely long day of travel that had started in their home in Newark at three-thirty that morning. Though they had all dozed on the long flight, all they wanted was something to eat and a good night's sleep.

Gloria traversed the short distance to the nearby restaurant and bought a dozen tacos and four sodas. It was the first few moments alone she'd had since they left home that morning. Certain she was unobserved, she pulled out her phone and sent a text, then anxiously waited.

By the time their food was ready, she still hadn't received a reply. Disappointed, she returned to their condo. After their simple meal, not even the nearby sound of waves lapping on the moonlit beach could entice them. Bed called. Tomorrow would be soon enough to explore the area and start an adventure none of them could have imagined.

Chapter Two

"Zero, zero, start," called Stella Monroe to begin her first pickleball game of the day. It was early spring, warm, and, judging by the wind sock above the main gate to the courts, the wind was light. Playing with Stella was Pippa Drummond, her longtime friend, and a relative newcomer to San Amaro. They were both beginners at this fast-growing sport.

The San Amaro Pickleball Club courts were located in the gated community of The Oasis. Neither Stella nor Pippa was a resident of The Oasis, but their friend Molly was, and she got them in the gate and stayed to watch them play. Their opponents for this game were Nancy and Helen, a recently retired lesbian couple newly moved to San Amaro, and relatively new to pickleball.

They were a well-matched foursome, and there were much laughter and many "sorrys" coming from their court as they all did their best to adhere to the rules. Like all newcomers to the sport, they were all challenged by trying to call the score properly before their serve, get the ball across the net into the proper court, and get out of the kitchen immediately upon hitting a ball that bounced there.

Sandy McLean had just arrived at the courts and stood leaning on the top crossbar of the chain-link fence that separated the courts from one another watching the four women play. Sandy had been playing pickleball for a couple of years and, while not one of the more competitive players, could hold her own with the intermediate-skilled players.

When Nancy returned a serve from Pippa before it had bounced, Sandy reminded the newbies of the rule disallowing her action. Pippa and Stella got a point. She also mentioned that in tournaments, the starting serve must be called as "zero, zero, two." Using "zero, zero, start," she said, was fine when playing with friends, but is not strictly correct.

The four thanked her and commented, not for the first time during their game, that remembering all the rules was much harder than playing the game. Sandy chuckled and said in a soft Texan drawl, "Don't worry. It's the same for everyone when they start playing. But, there truly aren't many rules, and after a few more games, they'll be second nature."

As Pippa served again, Sandy moved into the center area between the courts, pulled her paddle and water bottle from her pack, grabbed a ball, and asked one of the other women there whether she'd like to help her warm up. They chose a corner court and gently tapped the ball back and forth across the net to each other, a type of play called dinking. After two or three minutes of that, another couple joined them, and they began a game.

Pickleball is played on a court less than one-third the width and four-fifths the length of a tennis court. The paddles are slightly reminiscent of ping-pong, and the hard plastic Wiffle-like balls used are a bit larger than a tennis ball. Pickleball is a whirlwind of hand-eye coordination and not much running. Perfect for retirees, yet popular with all ages.

The court's kitchen delineates a seven-foot-deep area on either side of the net within which a player can hit the ball only once it has bounced. Given the game's fast-paced nature, new players frequently find themselves illegally hitting a ball midair while standing in the kitchen, or the no-volley zone, as it is sometimes called. When it happened to Helen and she lost her service, the group laughed as she cursed jovially, and tossed the ball to Pippa.

San Amaro, Baja, basked in the deceptive beauty of the day. The breeze was light, and the sun shone brilliantly in the cloudless azure sky. Nature's façade was impeccable. But appearances, as they say, can be deceptive.

Imposing palm trees bordered two sides of the courts, like sentinels, their fronds harboring a murder of crows. The persistent presence of one of the beady-eyed black birds, like a voyeur, watching the daily games had earned it the moniker Mayor of Pickleball. Today was no exception. The mayor was in position. The rest of the murder remained concealed. At least for now.

Chapter Three

It was a weary Stephanetti family that rose late that morning. Jet lagged from the three-hour time change and the previous day's travel, they learned restaurants at The Oasis were closed on Mondays.

If they wanted food, it was time to explore.

Brianna located a tourist map of San Amaro on her iPad showing restaurants, grocery stores, and local attractions. They learned from the security guard at the gate as they left The Oasis they were about seven miles from the actual town of San Amaro and got directions. *Turn left at the stop sign just ahead and keep going until you're in town.*

As Rudy drove, Brianna pointed out various places shown on her map. Originally, they'd planned to find the first open restaurant on the road into town and eat. They quickly discovered this part of Baja was nothing like the resort areas Gloria and Rudy had previously visited in Mexico. There were no high-rise hotels, no Señor Frogs. To the eyes of these first-timers, the small restaurants they did see looked a bit grim from the outside. They carried on into San Amaro.

Things didn't look much different in the little town, but as they drove to the end of the road, they found themselves on the Malecon, the street fronting the beach. This looked more inviting. The three-block-long street was packed with restaurants, open-fronted stores selling tourist souvenirs, and street vendors selling everything from sunglasses to silver jewelry.

Stepping from the Range Rover, their senses were assaulted as in any foreign place. Rich cooking smells from different spices had their mouths watering and mingled with the salt-sea air wafting to them on the ever-present breeze. They walked past several restaurants perusing the menus before deciding to try an open-air place with plastic tables and chairs no more than a hundred feet from the beach. They had an unobstructed view of the fishing boats, called pangas, in the bay and the screeching seagulls circling the ones on which fish were being cleaned.

"¿Quieren algo tomar?" a middle-aged Mexican woman asked the four as they took their seats.

"Sorry, we don't speak Spanish," Rudy said while Gloria smiled and shrugged.

The server looked flustered for a moment, then placed menus on the table and pointed to the section showing drinks. Fortunately, they were listed in English and Spanish. Ordering was handled with much pointing. When she left to gather their beverages, they read the offerings for "Brekfast" and laughed at the Spanglish prevalent throughout the single-page menu.

Most of the items offered were unfamiliar, and their bewilderment must have been obvious, because a woman who was not dressed like the servers approached their table. She was wearing slacks and a sweater that spoke of money, as did her simple but classy open-toed flats.

"Can I help you make sense of the menu? I am Estephanie, and this is my restaurant. Is it your first time in San Amaro?" The woman's English was strongly accented.

Gloria beamed at her. "Thank you so much. Yes, it's our first time. And yes, we'd love some help with what these things are."

Several minutes later, Estephanie rattled their orders in machine-gun-fast Spanish to their server and then left the family to enjoy its first day in her beloved town. While they waited for their food, they watched the boats in the bay and the everyday activities taking place on the Malecon. In the restaurant, there were a couple of tables with other Americans, but the majority of customers were Mexican. *Another thing,* Gloria thought, *refreshingly different from the Mexican cities where they'd previously vacationed.*

Gloria noticed bathrooms near the back of the restaurant and headed toward them. She had felt her phone vibrate, indicating a message, while they were driving and was eager to see whether it was the one she impatiently awaited. It was.

She spent a couple of minutes texting but knew she couldn't be away from the table for long without Rudy getting suspicious. He had semi-jokingly said recently he was starting to suspect she had a secret boyfriend. She didn't have a boyfriend, but she still harbored secrets.

Brianna and Logan had both chosen huevos rancheros. A fried-egg dish served on tortillas and refried beans with chili sauce. When it arrived, the savory aroma drifted enticingly, inviting them to dig in. Gloria wanted to keep things in the food department as close to the familiar as possible and had opted for a cheese omelet. She'd once suffered Montezuma's revenge on a trip to Cancun and was nervous about trying anything sounding too Mexican.

Rudy thought he took the opposite approach to his wife's, selecting molletes. When they arrived, he realized this typical Mexican breakfast was just an open-faced sandwich made on the two halves of a bread roll. His was topped with over-medium eggs, a dusting of cheese, and fresh pico de gallo. Estephanie came by their table once they'd all been served and had had a moment to taste their food.

"How is everything? Do you have any questions about your food?" she asked.

Gloria answered for everyone when it appeared her family members was deeply enjoying their food. "Everything tastes great. Thank you. How do you get your omelets so fluffy?"

The owner explained the secret. "We whip the yolks and the egg whites separately, then fold them together to cook. The cheese is added a couple of minutes before serving, and then a lid is placed on the pan. I'm glad you like them. It's an old trick I learned from my father. He started this restaurant. I've been running it for the last five or six years. *Buen provecho!*" Estephanie wished them the Mexican version of "bon appetit."

On their drive back to The Oasis, they stopped at a grocery store on the main drag reminiscent of supermarkets back in the States. Gloria bought some staples to keep them fed for the next few days, a couple of bottles of wine, and some snacks. They all commented on the great selection of food the place carried.

In the checkout line, Gloria struck up a conversation with an American woman behind her and learned they had chanced upon the best place to shop for "back home" experience. "Don't expect to find this familiar layout at other stores in San Amaro," the woman admonished. "But, please, don't bypass the local grocery stores. They have their charm and all the staples you'll need. And, they're fun to look around in."

The remainder of their return trip to the condo was spent discussing how to spend their day. Rudy had cautioned the kids that today would be their one day to relax. They hadn't come here for a vacation. This trip was all about getting Logan ready for a pickleball tournament in Palm Springs two weeks hence. "Have fun today. Tomorrow we all have work to do," he said.

The decision was to spend the day enjoying the beach. Brianna and Logan sat in the back seat, texting each other rather than openly discussing their dad.

Logan:
Dad thinks he's the best coach in the world. That is
such bullshit.

Brianna:

When are you going to tell him you've hired a new coach?

Logan:
While we're here. That should be fun! When are you telling him your plans?

Brianna:
Never, if I can get away with it. I'll be eighteen in three weeks.

Logan:
You think that will change anything?

Brianna:
Yes. Then I can do what I want and he can't stop me.

Logan:
Good luck with that.

Brianna simply sent a meme of a not-so-smiley face throwing up.

Chapter Four

The sun cast a honey glow across the bustling pickleball courts. All were in use, and more members kept arriving to play during the morning's league play window between seven and ten o'clock. One court had what appeared to be a family group, parents and their young adult son and daughter, playing game after game. They were all extremely good players, though the father was constantly yelling criticism at his kids. The son's patience with all his father's coaching was fraying.

A group of waiting players congregated to watch their games. The family was not involved in the club, and the consensus among those watching was the family must be visitors renting one of the condos across the street from the courts. League rules and common courtesy dictated any foursome finished with a game would move to the seating area so another group could play.

Clint Brayer, the league's president, waited until the family finished their latest game and then strode over to their court. "Hi, folks, I'm Clint, Clint Brayer." He approached the father with his hand out in greeting. The father hesitated a moment then shook it.

"Rudy Stephanetti. This is my wife, Gloria, and our kids, Brianna and Logan. Is there some reason you've interrupted our play?" he asked in a gruff, impatient voice.

Clint was taken aback by the man's tone but carried on genially. "Nice to meet you, Rudy, and your family. I'm the club president, and as you can see, there are lots of members here to play this morning. League times are from seven to ten. Nonmembers are welcome to play when league play is finished for the day, after ten.

"You are all great players, and I know some of our better players would enjoy the new competition, so if you want to stay and keep playing now, all I ask is that you split up and join in the rotation of players so everyone gets a chance to play." His manner was friendly, conciliatory, and open, yet observers felt a crackle of tension in the air.

"Your league is not my concern. My son is a professional player. We came here to San Amaro because you have good courts, and he needs to get ready for an upcoming tournament. You people can play whenever you want. You're all retired. And I don't want Logan wasting his energy playing substandard players. Will you let us get on with playing?" Rudy voice was raised, and his last sentence was more of a demand than a question.

Many of the other players had stopped their games at the loud, angry voice and were watching the interaction with interest and concern. One person watching had blanched and remained pale. Clint, though not used to encountering such vehemence on the courts, had previously needed to enforce the daily three-hour window of club play with nonmembers. He took a deep breath and straightened himself to his full six-foot-one height. An ex-cop from Saint Paul, he was not a stranger to confrontation.

"I'm going to have to ask you to leave, then. This is league play time, as posted on the board by the gate, and you're not league members."

Logan stepped over to his father's side and spoke quietly. "Dad, I'd rather play with this group than not play at all. Let's just split up and play with the members as the man suggested."

Rudy's wife, Gloria, also moved closer to her red-faced husband, placing a hand gently on his arm. "I think that's a great idea, Rudy. Logan can always benefit from playing other people. If you prefer, you can coach rather than play. It might even be better for you. What do you think?" It was clear to those watching that being a mediator was a frequent role she played with her hotheaded spouse.

After a moment of grumbling to his wife and son, Rudy acquiesced. He moved to the side of the court and grabbed his water bottle. The anxiety in the group caused by the altercation soon dissipated. But not for one of the players. For that person, the anxiety was just beginning.

Gloria and Brianna joined a small group of women waiting for an open court, and Logan was joined by three of the club's best players, two men and a woman. At age twenty, Logan was a similar age as the other three players' grandkids. Still, the young man soon realized they played well. The players else hurried back to their games. The questions "Whose serve is it?" and "What's the score?" were heard from several of the courts. Those watching chuckled. They were questions often voiced during games.

People waiting for their next game all gravitated to the court where Logan was engaged in an exciting game in which the action alternated between frenzied smashes with seemingly impossible returns and gentle dinking of the ball back and forth across the net right at the kitchen lines. The watchers were mesmerized by the play but aggravated by Rudy's almost constant yelling at Logan. His coaching style verged on abuse.

The final score was eleven to seven, with Logan and his partner, Suzanne, winning. As Logan walked to the waiting area while a new foursome took the court, he grabbed his dad's arm and led him out of the court area and into the parking lot behind the bleachers. It was clear an argument was underway, but the other players were out of earshot.

In an electrifying moment, Logan raised his paddle over his head poised like a weapon aimed at his father. But instead of releasing his fury upon his dad, he relaxed his grip on the paddle and allowed it to fall to the sandy ground at his feet. With simmering resentment in every step, Logan turned and stalked off in the direction of the condos.

Rudy stooped to retrieve the paddle and then returned to the courts, his gaze oscillating between the games his wife and daughter were playing. Observers would later admit to the police they couldn't tell whether the man's mood was anger or frustration.

As the morning league play window drew to a close and players were gathering their belongings, Logan returned and retrieved his paddle. He was ready to continue training now the league was done.

Rudy surprised everyone by clearing his throat and saying, "Hey, folks, before you take off, I just want to apologize for being abrupt earlier. I embarrassed my son and was confrontational with you, Clint. I'm sorry. You have a nice club here, and I appreciate you including us in your league play time." He stretched his hand out to Clint. "No hard feelings, I hope." Clint shook the offered hand and nodded.

Many of the onlookers smiled and nodded to themselves, glad the man had redeemed himself somewhat after his earlier rudeness. One person, however, was not appeased and simply stared at Rudy with loathing. And something else. Fear.

Then in the next moment, another man, big and burly, said loudly, in a rough voice, "Don't forget the Rattlers are organizing a poker run this Saturday morning. If you like going into the desert in your off-road vehicle and you wanna participate, be at the main gate of The Oasis with your seventy-five bucks at eight that morning. If you've already registered, be there at nine. And if you're not playing poker, the fee is thirty bucks."

Suzanne was next to address the group. "One more thing before you all head home. I just wanted to remind you, Edie and I are hosting the monthly pickleball potluck at six thirty tonight at our place, condo twenty-seven-A. Bring whatever you want to drink and finger food to share. Rudy and Gloria, you and your family are welcome to join us. It's not every day we have a professional player on our courts. I hope you'll all come," she said. "My great-niece and her boyfriend are visiting, so there will be some other young folks there, too." Suzanne stepped over to Gloria and described how to get to their condo.

No one noticed one person in their midst whose happy world was on the brink of collapse.

Chapter Five

Stella Monroe's arrival in San Amaro ten years before marked a new chapter in her life. Widowed several years before and recently retired, she'd rented a cozy casita. It was nestled on the lot of a home near downtown. Her landlord was the good friend of another San Amaro resident, Rick Whorton.

As Rick was a frequent visitor at the main house, he was one of the first people Stella befriended in her new little town. Their close friendship had been forged over the decade they'd known each other, and Stella considered Rick one of her inner circle of amigos.

So, when Rick phoned her just two hours after she'd returned home from a morning of playing pickleball and asked whether she would be willing to show him and Troy, a visiting friend, the courts and maybe give them a quick lesson on how the game was played, she agreed. Needing a fourth for the game, she called Pippa and cajoled her into returning to The Oasis for more pickleball that afternoon. Her next call was to Molly to see whether she'd get them onto The Oasis. Molly, also a great friend of Rick's, agreed.

When Rick first expressed his curiosity about pickleball, Stella had warned him, as she had been told, he needed the proper footwear. Court shoes rather than running shoes were essential; otherwise, the possibility of tripping was too great. Thus, Rick had equipped himself with court shoes and a couple of paddles. Troy said his basketball court shoes should be fine.

At three in the afternoon, the five met at a coffee shop near The Oasis and piled into Molly's minivan to drive to the courts. On the way, Stella gave them a quick explanation of how the game was played. Since she was new to it and didn't feel confident in remembering all the rules, she'd printed a summary she found on the USA Pickleball Association's website.

Troy's first comment upon seeing the courts was how great they were. Having seen the dilapidated condition of so many places in San Amaro, his expectations for the courts were low. Pippa explained she'd recently heard on National Public Radio that pickleball was the fastest-growing sport in the US, and the majority of regular players were over sixty-five. "This is mostly a retirement community, and the facilities at The Oasis are all geared to things we young-at-heart old farts like to do," she said.

Molly perched herself on the bleachers, and the foursome of players took the court directly in front of her to entertain their friend. The first-timers quickly learned pickleball is nothing like tennis, a game with which they were both familiar. Holey yellow plastic balls littered the nearby courts in no time as they tried to learn the proper force needed to get the ball over the net and into the proper court.

Molly thought it was a good thing they were the only people using the courts at that time of day. When the courts were full, an errant ball interrupting play on another court, while sometimes unavoidable, could disrupt a game. The frequency of wayward balls from this novice foursome would have miffed even the most affable of players had there been any.

After twenty minutes, however, the fellows had gained a modicum of control over their shots and were starting to have some fun. Stella and Pippa had taught them the process of dinking and then moved on to show them how to serve the ball. Recent changes to the rules now allowed two different types of serve. Pippa preferred the new drop serve, where the ball is dropped, allowed to bounce, and then hit across the net on the up bounce. Stella used the traditional serve, in which the ball is dropped and hit in the air before it bounces. As first-timers, the guys chose the traditional serve, as it seemed easier.

Before they called it a day, the foursome played one game. Stella teamed with Troy against Pippa and Rick. Molly was thoroughly regaled with their antics, curses, and laughter. They ended with a close score of eleven to nine, with Pippa and Rick being victorious. As they drove back to their cars at the coffee shop, Rick suggested they stop at the brewery for a pint. The idea received universal agreement. Rick also ordered buffalo wings from the food truck on location, and they relived each failed shot and gawky move they'd made on the court.

As they parted company, Rick and Troy admitted they were hooked, but not yet ready for games with the league's serious players. They made a date to meet for another afternoon in a few days. Stella mocked being insulted, saying *she* was a serious player, then tempered it by adding *serious but not very good*. They all laughed.

Chapter Six

The sea-fragranced evening air was starting to cool as the sun caressed the tops of the Sierra de San Pedro Mártir, the mountains to the west. The cloudless sky was fading from deep indigo to dusty purple, the mountaintops edged in orange as the sun set behind them. A family of four strolled along a brick-cobbled lane from their condo toward the sea on the evening of February 24 and spoke of the beauty of the night.

Music and laughter could be heard through the door of condo 27-A as the Stephanetti family arrived. Rudy rang the bell, and a second later, an attractive young woman about Logan's age opened the door. She introduced herself as Tiffany, Suzanne's great-niece, and invited them in.

Gloria scouted for a place to put the stuffed mushroom caps she had brought and found a vacant spot on the marble-topped kitchen island. Next, she went to say hi to Edie, Suzanne's partner of thirty-two years and co-host of the potluck. Brianna and Logan followed Tiffany to the upper-level den, as did Rudy's eyes. *Nice ass,* he thought, watching Tiffany on the stairs.

Realizing he was momentarily stranded by the door holding a bottle of Mexican red wine he hoped was drinkable, Rudy quickly moved into the kitchen to find a corkscrew. Scanning the kitchen and great room, he realized he and Gloria, aged fifty-seven and forty-nine, respectively, were likely ten to twenty years younger than most of the others there. No attractive ladies in the thirty-to-forty age range, he thought glumly.

Having spent almost three decades working in marketing,

Rudy was never a wallflower. After supplying Gloria with a glass of what he discovered was an aromatic, palatable red and armed with one himself, he headed toward a group of men standing in the living room near the main floor deck.

These gals have some money, Rudy thought as he took in the luxurious furnishings and one of the best sea views at The Oasis. Clint was among the group to which Rudy headed and spoke as he approached, "Hey, Rudy, you decided to join us. Let me introduce you to these fellas."

Clint believed Sun Tzu's admonishment to keep your enemies even closer than friends. From his years in policing, he was not taken in by Rudy's apology on the courts that morning. He wanted to keep an eye on him. See how he reacted in a purely social setting.

Since Rudy was the new guy, he became the center of attention. In his head, he rehearsed the names and key attributes of the people he'd just met. It was his process when introduced to new people: Willie Platz, short, stocky, real estate agent; Dean McLean, fit, barrel chested, ex-union steward, not a pickleball player; Glenn Wilburn, blond, brush cut, quiet; and Norm Webster, medium height and stocky, whom Rudy knew from his job.

Someone asked Rudy about his work. "I'm VP of marketing for Pickleball Pro Gear. We make paddles, clothing, and paraphernalia. We also sponsor the big tournament in Fort Lauderdale every year. I first encountered the sport in the late 1990s through a coworker in Seattle. The guy was friends with the kids of one of the men who invented the game. I started playing shortly after, so I've been playing for over twenty years. I love it, and I'm lucky my family does, too.

"Logan started playing professionally last summer, and I'm hoping Brianna will follow in his footsteps. And I know this guy." Rudy clapped Norm Webster on the shoulder and explained to the others. "Norm is a rep for our paddles, as you probably all know.

He's how I found out about San Amaro. Logan normally trains on indoor courts this time of year, which is mandatory when you live in New Jersey as we do, but he needs more practice on outdoor courts, with wind and sun. This seemed a perfect training spot for a couple of weeks before the Palm Springs tournament. The weather is similar, and the courts are in good shape."

Gloria, too, was the center of attention in a group of women who were gathered in the kitchen. She was introduced to Pippa Drummond, Stella Monroe, Nancy Pillard, Helen Nobel, and Sandy McLean. "I'm a nurse at an adult care facility in Newark. That's where we live these days," she said to Sandy, who had asked the question.

"Oh, I've heard the Cherry Blossom Festival there is beautiful. Where were you before Newark? Sounds like you move around a bit." Sandy continued the conversation.

"Yes, Rudy's work does seem to involve moving. That's how you climb the corporate ladder, I guess. Now he's with the Pickleball Pro Gear company, I think we'll stay put for longer. Their headquarters are in Newark. And, since they sponsor Logan, I know Rudy will think twice before changing companies again.

"But, to answer your question, Sandy, we lived in Seattle for about three years, back when the kids were still in preschool. Logan is twenty, and Brianna will be turning eighteen next month. After that, we were in San Diego. It was so expensive there, so we moved to Dallas, and then Saint Paul, Minnesota. And before moving to Newark we were in Pittsburgh, Pennsylvania. Thank goodness, as a nurse, I can always find work pretty easily. How about you? Where are you from? Are you still working? You look too young to be retired." Gloria put Sandy's age in the midfifties.

Sandy, her bright green eyes momentarily gazing into space, hesitated for a second, as though her thoughts were elsewhere, then looking Gloria in the face, she smiled tightly and said, "Wow, you've lived all over. Dean and I are from Fort Worth. I guess we were almost neighbors then. When you lived in Dallas, I mean. I was an admin assistant for the same company for my whole career. I started in the general pool, then was assigned to the marketing department, and later to the IT department before becoming executive assistant to the CFO. The only reason I left was because Dean retired last year and decided we were going to spend seven or eight months a year here."

As Edie questioned their new acquaintance, asking about her kids, Sandy moved closer to the food and placed a couple of Gloria's stuffed mushrooms on her plate along with a deviled egg. As she continued to chat with Edie, Gloria's gaze caught Sandy a few times. She noticed Sandy was frequently glancing at the group of men by the French doors to the deck.

Rudy and Clint were talking with a few other men. One of them Sandy had pointed out as being her husband, Dean. *Hmm, she seems preoccupied with him,* Gloria thought idly. The look on Sandy's face was not a happy one. *Maybe they've had a squabble,* she speculated to herself.

Moments later, the kitchen was invaded by the four young people looking for food. Gloria smiled at her two as they filled their plates and bantered with their new friends. They seemed to be having fun. Then she caught a snippet of Brianna's conversation with Tiffany and was saddened.

"I like pickleball, too, but I don't want it to be my life. Not like loopy Logan, here. I just graduated from high school at the end of the winter semester. I'm going to work with the Peace Corps as soon as I'm eighteen, next month. I've already completed the application process. I'm just waiting for my assignment. I'm going to start college when my two years is up, no matter what my pigheaded dad says."

Brianna and her dad argued endlessly about pickleball. He believed she was a better player than Logan and needed to explore her options in the professional arena before traveling to Guatemala or wherever or going to college. He contended both those options would still be there in a few years, but her athleticism should be exploited now. Brianna thought he was trying to manipulate her life to match his vision, and it made her furious. Her temper matched her dad's, and they had flaming rows about it almost daily.

Gloria tried to stay neutral. She knew from experience that siding with either of them could lead to disaster. She prayed Rudy would concede, but advocating for Brianna would not produce the desired result. *Best keep her thoughts to herself,* she had decided long ago.

As the evening progressed, the group of men in the living room morphed several times with different people joining and leaving the group as the evening ensued. At one point, Rudy and Norm wandered off to a nearby couch when Norm produced a flask of brandy. The two enjoyed the aromatic warmth of the amber liquor and chatted about pickleball.

After a couple of snifters, Rudy pulled a cigar case from his breast pocket, and the two men headed outside to smoke. Several people noted their departure, but none could provide the police with information on the men's movements later in the evening.

Chapter Seven

Julia Garcia embarked on her run, her thoughts steeped in contemplation. The pensive mood had begun during her sojourn in Ensenada and enveloped her still. She'd taken a few days off to visit her favorite uncle, Victor, in Ensenada, a city on the Pacific side of Baja. Self-reflection was her companion on the three-hour drive back to San Amaro the previous day and persisted this morning as she got back into her usual daily routine.

Her uncle, though her mother's brother, reminded Julia more of her father than she could fathom. Julia had shared a profound bond with her dad. It eclipsed her connection to her mom. Since she'd lost her dad to a fatal car crash when she was sixteen, she cherished her relationship with Victor. He made a wonderful surrogate dad.

Though unplanned, his daughter, Alma, Julia's cousin, had also been visiting Ensenada at the same time. Her presence added an extra layer of sweetness for Julia. The two were seven months apart in age. Victor and his now-deceased wife had been living in San Amaro during the girls' growing-up years, and the cousins were kindred spirits, almost sisters.

While Victor was at work, Julia and Alma had taken walks on the beach, enjoyed coffee or a glass of wine at outdoor cafes, and reconnected. It had been almost five years since they were face-to-face, at a family affair. This was the first time in almost a decade since it had just been the two of them. Alma, a librarian with the National Library of Mexico in Mexico City, had wanted to know everything about Julia's life including her work with the state police in San Amaro, and Julia now realized those conversations had sparked her current introspection.

Their grandparents, Juan and Elda Pérez, formed the bedrock of their shared heritage. As they reminisced about their grandparents, both discovered Papito Juan, as they affectionately referred to him, deserved credit for their academic pursuits. His encouragement and his focus on scholastic achievement had shepherded both women to English fluency, good grades, and taking an active role in their community.

Alma had gone to Mexico City for her master's degree in library science. Julia had gone to Arizona for her master's in criminology. Both had received scholarships. And, both decisions had been promoted by Papito Juan, yet neither Alma nor Julia had thought they'd been pressured by him. Together they marveled at how instrumental their grandfather had been in helping them mold the lives they now lived, their careers, and their values. Julia made a mental note to thank him.

Julia quickly realized her cousin's profession had some similar aspects to hers. While Alma was an expert at teasing out every detail when doing research, Julia dug deeply for details to unearth criminals. And Julia experienced firsthand Alma's effective probing.

For example, when Julia had given her pat answer of "Because Grandpa and Dad were cops" when asked why she'd gone into policing, Alma had explored further. She did not accept the glib response as the real reason. Under her cousin's probing, Julia had reflected on her reasons then, and their conversation became visceral, more meaningful to both of them. Twenty minutes later, under Alma's continued questioning, Julia finally admitted or perhaps finally realized she was driven by an innate need to try to make the world fair.

They talked about their undergraduate studies together in Mexicali, where Alma began preparation for her desired career, to be surrounded by the amassed knowledge of the world. Julia said she'd picked psychology to gain a better understanding of human behavior. "Why not sociology?" Alma had asked. Julia conceded she was far more interested in the intricacies of individual lives than groups. Why? Why? Why? Alma's mantra of curiosity eventually led to the revelation of Julia's deepest motivations.

Ultimately, Julia excavated the truth, not because she'd been hiding it from Alma, but perhaps because she'd been hiding it from herself. She'd simply not ever explored her deepest motivation: psychology might help her make sense of herself, especially the almost total devastation she experienced at her dad's death and why it still so deeply affected her life.

Julia was enthralled by her time with her cousin and uncle. On one hand, she believed several layers of self-protection or self-delusion had been scraped away from her soul. On the other, she believed she'd been truly seen, understood, and fully loved.

Now the self-discovery can of worms was open, she found it hard to close and get back to the norm of her life. She hoped it would make her a better detective and person, and suspected it would. She also pondered why she'd needed her cousin's questioning to bring about this contemplation and vowed to continue it on her own.

She was so immersed in these thoughts she ran almost three miles farther than usual. By the time she returned home, she was later than normal. She would still make it to work on time, just not as early as she'd hoped. After showering and dressing, she grabbed a tortilla, warmed it on the stove burner to eat in the car, and made it into the station by a quarter to seven.

She'd finished a big case just before taking her trip to Ensenada and hoped her inboxes, email, and the one on her desk wouldn't be very full. Her heart sank upon seeing a formidable mountain of paper awaiting her. However, on a quick review, much of it was general, internal mail she could read at her leisure. Her email box was in better shape. Amid the digital clutter, one message marked urgent grabbed her attention. It was from the officer in Flagstaff with whom she'd worked the last case.

An American man wintering in San Amaro from Flagstaff had defrauded people in both places with a scam involving dog rescues. In Flagstaff, he used forged paperwork indicating he represented a nonexistent Mexican dog rescue needing money to save dogs. In San Amaro, he did the same in reverse, saying the Flagstaff rescue needed money to expand its kennels to enable it to take dogs from the dog rescue in San Amaro. He'd defrauded gringos in Mexico of several thousand dollars and five times that amount from folk in Flagstaff.

Because of her fluency, she'd been the police boots on the ground in Baja and had provided her Arizona counterpart with the information he'd needed to make the arrest. The urgent email was simply a request for an electronic copy of the information she'd mailed before taking her vacation, and she easily dispatched it.

Her partner, Ricardo, whistling a barely recognizable version of a popular song, had no sooner arrived at his desk than the desk sergeant was calling them with a new case.

There had been a murder.

Chapter Eight

At seven thirty, an old, brown Honda Civic arrived at the pickleball courts. As Sergeant Julia Garcia had recently passed her detective exam, her personal car was doing double duty as an unmarked police car. She and her partner, Detective Sergeant Ricardo Hernandez, exited La Chica—as she called her trusty, rusty, old car. They were surprised at the number of off-road vehicles in the parking lot. Everything from lifted Jeeps and RZRs to sand rails and barneys—homemade buggies with seats, wheels, and an engine held together with tubular steel—was on display.

There was a crowd gathered around the courts. The detectives quickly understood these people were all pickleball players expecting to play. And it appeared many were also members of one of the local off-road groups, Baja Rattlers, judging by the curled rattlesnake bumper sticker on many of the vehicles.

Julia addressed the gathered players before entering the courts. The desk sergeant had given she and Ricardo the briefest description of the scene they were attending—a dead body at the pickleball courts at The Oasis.

"Hi, folks, I'm sorry to inform you there will not be any pickleball games today. We are here because the body of a man was found on one of the courts. I want to talk with all of you, so please don't leave and be prepared to give me your name, address, and contact information. Once I have your information, you are free to go. If it's necessary, I'll contact you later, either this afternoon or in the next few days to speak with you."

As Julia informed them a man was dead on a court, she heard

a woman in the crowd gasp, and watched as she was helped to the bleachers by two young adults. She went to the three of them and introduced herself. Julia learned that Rudy Stephanetti, woman's husband and the father of the young woman and man, may not have returned home last night.

His wife explained her husband wasn't in their condo when she had gone to bed nor when she awoke. She suggested he may have slept under the stars or simply gone out early, while the family still slept. Now, however, she feared the body on the court could be their missing family member. Julia did not yet know the identity of the victim but promised to speak with them again as soon as she knew something.

Julia's curiosity was piqued by the wife's assertion her husband had slept on the beach and wondered what the real story was. *A question for later,* she thought.

While Julia was cautioning the gathered onlookers not to leave until she spoke with them, Ricardo had gotten Eduardo Escamilla to unlock the back gate. He was taking pictures of the scene on his cell phone and trying to determine what had happened.

Julia joined him. It was obvious from the first glance at the body they were investigating a murder. The man, lying in a heap beside one of the nets, had been beaten and now lay in a large pool of congealed blood. Beside him lay a bloody, broken paddle. The dead man was wearing pressed khakis and a blue, button-down shirt. A light beige linen sports coat lay on a chair in the area between the courts. In his left back pocket, Ricardo found a wallet.

The dead man was Rudolph Stephanetti, of Newark, New Jersey, aged fifty-seven.

Before she started collecting the gathered players' details, Julia familiarized herself with the court area. She had never been on a pickleball court, and so acquainted herself with the layout. While she looked about, she idly wondered whether all pickleball courts bore the same surface colors as these did. The nonplaying areas were all green. The lines around the courts were white. The main playing areas were blue, and the smaller playing areas nearest the nets, which she later heard referred to as the kitchen, were red. The colorful symmetry of the courts was marred by the grotesque tableau before her.

The body was lying in the red area of court seven. Around his head and overlapping the blue of the court's playing area was the blood pool. The head of the paddle, cruelly detached from its handle, lay near the corpse. The wooden handle eerily jutted from the lifeless man's neck.

The face and head appeared to have been hit repeatedly. It was a grisly scene. Before Julia turned away and returned to the group waiting outside the chain-link fence surrounding the courts, she observed her partner for a few moments. Ricardo photographed the body and surrounding areas from every imaginable position and documented each picture he snapped on his phone. She admired and appreciated his thoroughness.

Leaving the macabre tableau, she spoke briefly with the family of the deceased. Their worst fears were confirmed. From the son, she got their contact information. She sent the family home, saying she would go to their condo in the next couple of hours. First, the scene needed to be processed and the names of everyone assembled to be gathered. The son and daughter took control and helped their shocked and weeping mother to their condo on foot.

With Eduardo's help, Ricardo ran crime-scene tape, which he pulled from a cardboard box in the trunk of Julia's car, around the fence enclosing the courts. He left the locks on all four of the gates into the courts and obtained the keys from Eduardo. With the scene secured, he awaited the arrival of Dr. Emilio Serrano, a local general practitioner, who also acted as the San Amaro coroner.

Ricardo and Julia, friends as well as work partners, had investigated another murder case together under the direction of Inspector Detective Martinez, almost a year before. But this was their first big case working without an inspector actively investigating the crime with them. They were still reporting to Martinez, but he had sent them out without him to see how they performed. Both had recently completed the detective exam and were filled with anticipation at undertaking their first murder since passing that milestone event.

Ricardo, five ten and extremely good looking, had a tiny lexicon of English words, so Julia took the lead when dealing with the expat community. In this situation, that appeared to be the entire group assembled outside the courts. Ricardo would take the statement from Eduardo, the maintenance man.

Julia had collected the names and addresses of twenty-six people, all of whom revealed they were regular players in the club. Three people from whom she needed to gather contact details remained. As they approached her, Julia was surprised to realize she knew them.

"Mrs. Monroe, what a surprise it is to see you again. How are you?" Stella Monroe, a longtime resident of San Amaro, had been the suspected murder victim in the case Julia and Ricardo had investigated just under a year ago. Stella, however, had survived, another woman having been the victim in that case.

Her friend Molly Lopez, also a longtime San Amaro resident and one of the people in the hiking group from which Stella had gone missing on that fateful trip, though present, was not there to play pickleball. Dressed in her signature flouncy turquoise layers and bejeweled sandals, Julia correctly surmised she was there to watch her friends play. The third woman, Pippa Drummond, a close friend of Stella's who had moved to San Amaro about ten months prior, after the death of her husband, was dressed in sportswear. Julia had spoken to Pippa on the phone during the investigation into Stella's disappearance but had not met the woman in person.

"I'm doing very well, thanks, Sergeant Garcia. It's nice to see you again, though not under these circumstances. Do you know yet who it is?" Stella asked.

"I'm sorry, I'm not prepared to release that information yet. Are your address and phone number still the same?" Julia asked.

"Oh, of course!" Stella said quickly, then gave Julia a nod of affirmation regarding her contact information.

Julia turned to Molly. "And how about yours, Mrs. Lopez?"

Molly stated she still had the same contact information, so Julia moved on to Pippa, documenting her particulars and telling the women she'd be in touch in the next day or so to ask them some questions.

By this time, the doctor had arrived. He was a short, slim, handsome man in his forties wearing green scrubs. As he viewed the remains, Julia and Ricardo took notes on his preliminary findings. They were straightforward. There was a single slice to the back of the head, presumably caused by being struck in a downward motion, most likely with the paddle lying near the body. Then the man had been punched repeatedly in the face while he was in a supine position. It was most probable the wooden paddle was broken by the force of hitting the man's skull. Nearly all the blood loss had occurred from the head wound, and based on the skull fragments visible in the lesion, it would have been sufficient to cause death, though not immediately.

The corpse did not have any defensive wounds. They surmised the victim was likely bludgeoned with the paddle from behind, causing him to fall, and the beating, most certainly fist punches, followed while the victim lay bleeding on the court. Two voids in the blood spatter were visible and appeared to be where the killer knelt, straddling the victim while delivering the beating. The killer's pants would surely have been splattered with blood.

There was a lake of blood from the most gruesome injury. The broken handle from the paddle protruded from man's neck. The doctor concluded that jamming the broken end of the handle into his neck was the coup de grâce. The victim would have died quickly.

Apart from a couple of car accidents she'd attended, this was the most horrific sight Julia had seen. *How brutal and vicious,* Julia thought. *An act of deadly passion.*

Chapter Nine

The gentle wind off the sea, bringing with it the tangy smell of salt, caressed the cheeks of the police detective as she made her way to the Stephanettis' rented condo. Ricardo remained at the courts to assist the doctor.

It was the son, a young man of about twenty, who answered the door when Julia knocked shortly before ten that morning. The young man's grief was visible. His face was blotchy and his eyes red rimmed. Standing in front of Julia now, however, he was composed as he led her into the living area, where his mother and sister sat huddled together on a long couch. Julia took a chair opposite the couch, declining his offer of water or coffee.

"I'm very sorry for your loss. And I'm sorry to tell you your husband"—Julia dipped her head toward Mrs. Stephanetti, then looked directly at Brianna and then Logan—"and father was murdered."

Gloria wailed and then quickly placed her hand over her mouth and shut her eyes tightly as though to keep from absorbing the information. Logan embraced her, and she sobbed into his chest. Brianna folded in upon herself with her head on her knees and her hands cupping the back of her head. She rocked for several moments and then dragged her torso upright, looking intently at Julia. "What happened?"

Julia explained what she and Ricardo had learned from Dr. Serrano. She wished she could shield them from the brutality of the attack, though she hoped their shock might numb them to some of the horrors. Julia knew from experience it would be better for the family to hear the gruesome truth from her now than learn the details sensationalized later from some other, possibly less sensitive source.

The horrific details brought on a fresh wail from Gloria and more tears from both her and Brianna. Logan sat as though in a trance through her explanation, staring at nothing in particular, except when she mentioned the paddle-handle strike to the neck. Then he scrunched his eyes shut and looked decidedly ill.

When the women regained some of their composure, Julia began. "I know this is a hard time for you all, but I do have to ask you some questions." All three looked at her through masks of anguish. "When was the last time you saw your husband, your father?"

Logan was the first to respond. "We all attended a party last night at a condo near the beach. The women who hosted it are part of the pickleball club here at The Oasis: Edie and Suzanne. I don't know their last names. Many of the pickleball players were there, and most had brought their spouses. Dad gravitated to a group of men, some of whom we'd met earlier in the day on the courts. He was talking to a man from pickleball on the front steps when I went out to our condo for a few minutes, later in the evening. It was the last time I saw him."

"What time was that?" Julia asked.

"I'm not sure. Maybe ten or ten thirty," Logan answered. "I suppose it could have been later, maybe even eleven. I wasn't paying any attention to time."

Gloria spoke next. "Rudy went outside with another man, Norm Webster, to smoke cigars. I'm not sure when. He and Rudy knew each other slightly because Norm is a representative for the pickleball paddles sold by Pickleball Pro Gear. That's the company where Rudy works."

Julia noticed Gloria used the present tense. Reality had not fully hit her. After a pause to collect herself, she continued. "I didn't see him after he and Norm went outside."

Julia's astute mind quickly grasped a possible lead. "What was the relationship between the two men?"

"Oh, it was a casual, working connection. They didn't know each other well. But they seemed to get on just fine," Gloria said.

"Did you see Norm come back into the house? And if you did, do you remember the time?"

"Well, I think it was possibly a little less than a half hour from when they went outside. I didn't notice the time," Gloria said. "And Norm and his wife left a few minutes later."

"How about you, Brianna? When did you last see your dad?"

"I was mostly upstairs with Tiffany, Suzanne's great-niece, and her boyfriend, Todd. We all came downstairs to get some snacks at about eight thirty. Dad was standing with a group of men in the living room. I didn't see him after that." The young woman answered without looking at Julia.

Julia continued. "Had Mr. Stephanetti had any arguments with anyone recently?"

No one spoke for several moments. Finally, Brianna took a deep breath and blew it out quickly. "Dad argued with a guy at pickleball yesterday morning about us being on the courts when the league was playing. I think the other man's name was Cliff or Clint. But it ended okay. The guy decided to let us play so long as we rotated on and off the courts with all the other players. And I saw them chatting at the party. Plus, Dad apologized to all the players yesterday before they left the courts." She glanced at Logan, holding his gaze for a moment, then looked at her lap.

"Was his name Clint Brayer?" Julia asked after looking at the list of names she had collected earlier.

Gloria answered. "Yes, that's him. You need to understand, Rudy was used to getting his way. He wouldn't have seen his actions as being argumentative—he was just firmly stating his case."

Julia noticed another brief look pass between Logan and

Brianna. *Hmm,* she thought, *there is more going on here than they're saying.*

"How were things between you and your dad, Brianna?"

"As Mom told you, Dad liked getting his own way. He wanted me to try going professional in pickleball. I have a high enough rating, but it's not what I want to do with my life. I want to work with the Peace Corps and then start university the fall I'm released. It was something we talked about a lot recently."

"And by talked, do you mean argued?" Julia asked in a gentle voice.

"Sometimes, I guess. It never got crazy, though. We just disagreed. I turn eighteen soon, so there wasn't much he could do. I can make my own decisions. He knew that!"

In the dance of father-daughter relationships, the steps could be frustratingly intricate, as Julia knew from personal experience. Brianna appeared to be self-assured and independent, which could be a sign of a healthy relationship with her dad. Equally, her intention not to follow her father's desire for her future could be defiance rather than independence. Something to keep in mind.

"How about you, Logan? How were things between you and your dad?"

"I play pickleball professionally. I'm sponsored by the company Dad worked for *and* he was also my coach, so there were several dynamics between us apart from father-and-son stuff. Sometimes we got on great and sometimes, we disagreed. No big deal, right?"

Julia's attention was piqued by the young man's last word. He was trying to get her on board with his idea that arguments between his father and him were a normal part of father-son dealings. She found it suspicious, and it made her wonder. She made a notation in her notebook and moved on. "Did your husband have any enemies here? Or other friends, for that matter."

Gloria responded, "I'd love to be able to say everybody liked

Rudy. He could be charismatic, but he was also stubborn and had a short fuse. Sometimes it got him in trouble, but no, I can't think of any reason someone here would be so angry with him. Isn't it possible someone beat him to rob him?"

"His money and credit cards were still in his wallet and he was wearing a watch and rings, so we have ruled out robbery as a motive. Also, the violence of the attack makes it seem personal. I hate to have to ask, but was there another woman in your husband's life?" Julia asked.

"I don't think so, and certainly not here, if there was." She was looking at the couch seat, at the space between herself and Logan. Julia recognized the body language of shame. Also, Brianna had stiffened at the question, so Julia strongly suspected infidelity played a role in the dynamics of this family. Something else to keep in mind.

"Were you aware your husband didn't come home last night, Mrs. Stephanetti?" Julia asked. She could understand that the kids might not know that their dad hadn't returned to their condo after the party.

"No, I'm a sound sleeper."

"What did you all think when Mr. Stephanetti wasn't home when you got up?" Julia asked.

Both Brianna and Logan simply shrugged as though they hadn't given it any thought. Gloria looked pensive for a moment before answering. "As I said earlier, he could have decided to sleep on the beach. The other possibility I considered was that he'd risen early and was out for a run or a walk on the beach. I just figured we'd see him at pickleball. It may seem strange to you, Detective, but my husband wasn't in the habit of checking in with me about his comings and goings. And I wasn't in the habit of expecting it."

Julia absorbed this new information skeptically but carried on. "Is there anything else you think I should know, that might help us find his killer?"

All three shook their heads.

Just then, Gloria's phone, which was sitting on the couch between her and her daughter, dinged. Without looking at the phone, she placed her hand over it and tucked it under her thigh. "I can't think of anything else," she said, looking at Julia, a sad smile crossing her face briefly.

"Okay, thank you. Here's my card. And, if you think of anything else that could be useful to our investigation, please call me. I will be back in touch as things progress. Again, I'm sorry for your loss." Julia stood and showed herself out. The remaining members of the Stephanetti family stayed immobile on the couch.

As Julia walked back to the courts, she wondered again whether Rudy had perhaps arranged for a mistress to join him in San Amaro. If so, was she married—to a jealous husband? This crime was personal. It screamed of pain and anguish long contained, now released as murderous fury and hatred, its roots in the past; its poisonous fruit, the mutilated corpse lying now in the morgue.

Chapter Ten

Back at the courts, Ricardo had just finished getting Eduardo's statement. He turned toward the old Honda in which they arrived and saw Julia walking their way.

"Did you learn anything useful from the family?" Ricardo asked, walking toward his partner.

"I got the impression Rudy Stephanetti was a hard man to live with, and he was probably unfaithful to his wife. I think there's more to learn from them, but they are all in shock right now. We can try again tomorrow. Today, I want to start interviewing the people who were at the party last night. Let's start with the hosts. They live close by in the condos, unit twenty-seven-A. Did you learn anything from the maintenance guy?"

Ricardo nodded his head. "Yeah, I did. Seems yesterday, the victim argued here. It was with another male player, the club's leader, Clint. It got heated and loud enough for the other players to stop and watch. And, just before the club players left, the victim spoke to the group. Of course, Eduardo doesn't speak any English, so he couldn't give me any idea what the argument was about or what Rudy said to the group. Still, it will give us some good questions to ask the other players. Right, Lucy?"

This evoked a wry smile from Julia. She knew Ricardo was a good cop and serious about his profession; still, he loved to joke around. The two had been in police training together nine years before and had been dubbed Lucy and Ricky by their fellow cadets. Their jovial banter throughout training reminded their cohort of the lead characters in *I Love Lucy*. Ricardo bore a marked resemblance to Desi Arnaz.

Upon their graduation, they had both been hired by the San Amaro State Police. Their banter just continued as they teased and kidded each other and used their nicknames. They had a solid friendship and were good work partners. Ricardo would have liked it to be more than friendship, but Julia firmly maintained the friend boundary.

"Right, Ricky!" Julia winked. "I heard about the heated interaction between our victim and the club leader. It's interesting, for sure," Julia said and drove them the short distance to condo 27-A.

On the way, she mentioned her speculation about a possible mistress, with a jealous husband. "There's no evidence to support it yet, but the murder was impassioned, personal. It makes me wonder."

Ricardo had also been musing on the kind of anger that resulted in hitting a man hard enough to crack his skull, followed by a vicious beating, and finally a stab to the neck with a piece of broken wood. Rage. He wondered—*Why would someone have that kind of fury toward a person who had been in San Amaro for a couple of days only?* It made him wonder about the family and whether there was someone else in San Amaro who might have known this man before his recent arrival.

Edie answered the door moments after Julia knocked. She invited them in and called for Suzanne to join them. The couple's gray hair and wrinkles placed their age in their early seventies. Everything else about them, however, spoke of internal youth. Both moved with agility. They were lean, fit, and deeply tanned. Edie was taller than Suzanne by about three inches. Julia gauged Edie to be about her height, five nine. The aroma of coffee was very appealing, and Julia said yes to the offer of a cup. Ricardo, always a coffee hound, also requested a cup.

As they waited for the coffee, Julia took in the condo. The

main door was at ground level and opened into a large living room with what appeared to be twenty-five-foot ceilings. To the left of the entrance, a staircase with wrought iron balusters and a brass handrail led to the second level. The living room was furnished with a sumptuous black leather couch and settee. Two wingback chairs in rich teal and sea-green upholstery echoed the same tones in the curtains. *Beautiful room,* Julia thought.

Once seated with their drinks, Julia took the lead. She mentioned Ricardo was not fluent in English, so she would be speaking to him in Spanish during the coming conversation to help him stay abreast of the information they provided. The women nodded their understanding.

"I heard you had a party last night, which the victim attended. How did that come about? The Stephanettis have just arrived in San Amaro."

"The party was a potluck with the pickleball club members, and since they were playing with us yesterday, we invited them to join us," Edie answered and then continued. "They arrived shortly after seven last night. Suzanne's great-niece, Tiffany, let them in and took the kids upstairs to meet her boyfriend, Todd. Tiff and Todd are staying with us for a couple of weeks, and the kids are all about the same age. Gloria came directly into the kitchen with their potluck dish, and Rudy stood at the door for a minute or two, surveying the place before coming into the kitchen, pouring himself and his wife glasses of wine, and then returning to the living room.

"He spent most of the evening talking with a group of guys, mostly players from the club, but there were a couple of non-pickleball-playing husbands, too. I've written their names for you," she said, passing a slip of paper to Julia. "On one side are the names of the people Rudy was chatting with, and on the other is a list of everyone else who was here last night."

"Wow, Edie. You're certainly organized. Have you done this before?" Julia asked.

"I was a detective in Wichita, Kansas, for most of my career. It's been almost two decades since I retired, but I remember the drill," Edie replied.

"Okay, great. Were you playing pickleball yesterday morning?" Julia asked, and seeing both Edie and Suzanne nod their heads, she continued. "Can you tell me about what happened with Rudy and your club leader?"

"Ah. Yeah, it was a bit tense. The Stephanettis were playing on one of the courts as though it was theirs. Normally, when there are more players than courts, foursomes play a game and then relinquish the court to another group. Everyone gets to play when there is a constant rotation of players. Clint, the league president, walked over to let the Stephanettis know they were on the courts during league play time and asked them to leave.

"Rudy instantly got angry. He was almost yelling at Clint. In the end, they struck a deal. Clint offered to let them stay if they rotated on and off like all the other players. Rudy agreed. Just before we all left for the day, Rudy apologized to the entire group for his outburst. That's mainly why Suzanne invited them to last night's potluck," Edie said. Suzanne nodded her agreement.

"Father and son had a bit of a disagreement as well," Edie said, seemingly as an afterthought.

"Oh? Did you see any of their argument?" Julia asked, looking from Edie to Suzanne.

Suzanne answered this one. "I was Logan's partner when it started. Rudy was Logan's coach, not just his dad, and he was what I'd call a bully coach. He pointed out only the things Logan did wrong, and never suggested other strategies or praised him for the good plays he made. In my opinion, Logan reached a point where he'd had enough of being yelled at and criticized in front of everyone. After our game, he took his dad's arm and led him off the courts. I couldn't hear their conversation, but it looked as though Logan was angry. He threw his paddle at his dad's feet and left. Logan was gone for a couple of hours. He returned just about the time we were all packing to leave. He didn't talk with Rudy, so I guess he was still mad, but I didn't see them interact again until they arrived at our house."

"Did you see them together at all during your party?" Julia asked.

Edie said no, and Suzanne shook her head.

"When was the last time you saw Mr. Stephanetti?"

"Rudy and Norm Webster headed outside about ten thirty or eleven with cigars in their hands. I don't remember seeing him again," Edie answered.

Suzanne chimed in. "The last time I saw him, he was on the couch with Norm, and they were drinking brandy from Norm's hip flask. It would have been about a quarter after ten. I saw Gloria and the kids leave sometime after eleven thirty or maybe eleven forty-five, but it was just the three of them."

Ricardo, who had followed most of the conversation, helped by Julia's Spanish interjections to him, spoke rapidly in Spanish to Julia. "*Sí, sí,*" she responded and then turned back to Suzanne and Edie. "Did Mr. Stephanetti have any arguments during your party?"

"No. He was charismatic if a little boastful whenever I was near enough to hear any of his conversations. Typical marketing person, jovial, boisterous. Edie, what about you?" Suzanne answered and asked.

"The same. I chatted with him for a minute in the kitchen when he came in looking for a corkscrew, and he was pleasant. It almost made me forget how *un*pleasant he was on the courts yesterday morning."

"Is there anything else you think we should know for our investigation?" Julia asked.

Edie chuckled. "I always used to ask the same question at the end of a conversation with a witness. But no, I can't think of anything. Though I am curious. Did Rudy know anyone here in San

Amaro, other than Norm, I mean?"

"Not according to his wife," Julia said.

"And I was also wondering whether Gloria was involved with anyone else. A man with a motive to get Rudy out of the way?" Edie asked.

Julia gave her head a mental shake. It was a question she hadn't asked Mrs. Stephanetti when she spoke with her. It was a rookie mistake. She wrote a reminder to ask the next time she met with them. "Not that we know of," she answered evasively.

During these interviews, Ricardo focused on body language, tone of voice, and shared glances, anything to help him get a sense of the person speaking and how others with them reacted. He spoke some English, but not enough to lead an interview or even understand much of the conversation. The word *detective*, though, is the same in English and Spanish, so he had understood Edie had been a cop, a detective, one of them. It explained her even, forthright demeanor in speaking with Julia. Most people were intimidated by the police. These women were not. Though he appreciated the brief input from Julia during the interview, he was eager to learn the details of their answers to Julia's questions. During the interview, Julia noticed how intently Ricardo had been observing the couple. She valued his insights. She was interested in hearing his input on the interview.

When Suzanne declared she didn't have anything to add, Julia continued. "I'd also like to speak with your great-niece and her boyfriend if they're around."

"They are at the beach at the moment. They should be back later this afternoon."

"Okay, thank you, ladies. If you do think of anything else, here's my card. We'll stop by another time to speak to the kids." Julia and Ricardo stood to leave.

Suzanne stopped them. "Oh, I have a question for you. Will the pickleball courts be open tomorrow?"

Julia assured them the courts would be open. They had cleared the site and given Eduardo the go-ahead to clean the blood.

Back in Julia's trusty, rusty chariot, Ricardo debriefed Julia on her meeting with the two women to see whether he'd missed anything important. He observed that the victim sounded as though he were a bit of a chameleon in how he presented himself to those around him. *Manipulative* was the word he used, and Julia concurred. They were both interested in hearing other people's impressions of Rudy Stephanetti. She also admitted her earlier mistake of not asking Gloria Stephanetti an important question.

She and Ricardo did not spend long with the grieving widow. When asked whether she had a boyfriend who might have come to San Amaro on the sly to be with her, Gloria shook her head and firmly stated she didn't have a boyfriend, nor had she ever through her marriage.

Ricardo asked Julia to clarify something with Gloria. Julia did. "Didn't you think it unusual your husband wasn't around when you were ready to leave? Or that he hadn't told you he was leaving earlier? Or even when he didn't come home last night?"

Gloria looked flummoxed for a moment, during which she blushed deeply. "No. I thought I explained when you were here earlier. It wasn't unusual for Rudy to go his own way at parties. He often left when he had had enough socializing." Gloria said no more, but Julia noticed Brianna shift uneasily.

Julia didn't let it pass. "Brianna, did you have anything to add?"

"No. As I already told you, Dad liked to do his own thing," she said. Then she turned toward the kitchen and left the others standing at the door.

"Logan, tell me about your argument with your dad yesterday at pickleball," Julia asked pointedly.

"It was nothing. I just suggested he not coach me so loudly. I was concerned it was bothering the other players."

Julia didn't believe him, but let it go. For now.

In the car, Ricardo said, "I'm not sure I believed her when she denied ever having a boyfriend while married. Her eyes became almost hooded as she said that. She may have been lying." Then he voiced what they were both contemplating. "What weren't they saying? He went his own way at parties. He liked doing his own thing. What do they mean by 'his own thing'?"

Julia speculated. "I think they might be trying to tell us Rudy was a philanderer."

Chapter Eleven

As it was nearly noon, Julia and Ricardo decided to return to the station and their bagged lunches before beginning the interviews with all the people from the pickleball club. It would also allow them to check in with Inspector Martinez about the case. Deciding to do the latter first, they climbed the stairs of the San Amaro State Police office to the second floor, where the senior officers had their workspaces.

They both wanted to remain in charge of this case and knew keeping their boss informed was the only way to make that possible.

"*Buenos días,* Inspector Martinez." Ricardo, being slightly senior to Julia, announced their presence at the door to his office. After they'd graduated as police officers, Ricardo became a sergeant in just a few years. Julia, being a woman, didn't get the same opportunities as her male colleagues. It had taken her several more years to make it to sergeant level one. By then Ricardo had already progressed to level two. Now they were both detectives, but Ricardo maintained his level-two sergeant status as a detective.

"Come in. And it's Hector, or sir, if you feel the need for more formality," Inspector Martinez said. He was a striking man. Nearly six feet tall, he had brown hair and hazel eyes and was often confused by expats as being one of them, rather than Mexican. "So, tell me about the dead person at The Oasis."

Though he often appeared to be lackadaisical to casual observers, Ricardo was dedicated and earnest about his job. With complete professionalism, he started the update. "The murder occurred at The Oasis at the pickleball courts. A visiting American named Rudy Stephanetti was brutally murdered sometime between ten thirty last night and six this morning. He had been hit on the back of the head with a wooden paddle used in the sport of pickleball and then punched repeatedly while supine. The final act of brutality was a stab to the neck with the jagged end of the broken-off handle of the paddle. He died instantly from the final stab." He looked at Julia as if to pass the rest of the update over to her. Ricardo had the utmost respect for Julia as a police officer and a person, and he gave her every opportunity to shine.

"Mr. Stephanetti was visiting San Amaro with his wife and two adult children to prepare his son, who is a professional pickleball player, for an approaching outdoor tournament in Palm Springs." Julia took over seamlessly from Ricardo. "Where they live, in New Jersey, they can't play on outdoor courts this time of year.

"His wife admitted he had had an altercation yesterday on the pickleball courts, with a local expat, Clint Brayer, but confirmed it was resolved before they left the courts.

"Also, the victim and his family joined about twenty-five other people at a party last night with many of the same people who were on the pickleball courts that morning. As far as we know at this point, the last time anyone remembers seeing him was around ten thirty or eleven last night when he left the party with another man, Norm Webster, to smoke cigars." Julia paused briefly.

"We have spoken with the victim's family and the maintenance worker who found the body. Plus I have a list of everyone at the party last night and all the people who came to play pickleball this morning. We will continue getting their statements this afternoon and tomorrow." Finished with her update, Julia leaned back in her chair.

Julia was an attractive thirty-three-year-old, five foot nine, with a statuesque body. Today she was wearing a long-sleeved, collared pale-patterned blouse and dark slacks. She was still trying to get used to being out of uniform, now that she was a detective, thanks to Inspector Martinez.

Hector had sponsored her for the detective exam even though she wasn't high enough in the police hierarchy to sit the exam based on position. Hector based his sponsorship on her excellent work on a murder case the previous year.

Ricardo, because of his seniority, was able to take the exam, too, without the need for a sponsor. As they had been at the academy, they again became study buddies while they prepared for the test. Unlike the majority of senior officers in the San Amaro State Police, Hector recognized and promoted talent unhindered by the typical Mexican male sex bias. He recognized her ability to do more than answer phones and file reports, as was the lot of most female officers in Mexican police departments.

"Do you have any suspects yet?" Detective Inspector Martinez asked.

Ricardo answered. "On our list at this point are Logan, the son. Clint Brayer, the man with whom the victim argued. Norm Webster, who, at this early juncture, is the only person we know of who previously knew the victim and was the last person with whom the victim was seen. And Eduardo Escamilla, the man who found the body. It's unlikely he had anything to do with it, but since he found the body, we will look into him."

"Okay, what's next?" Martinez asked.

"Both Stella Monroe and Molly Lopez were at the pickleball courts yesterday," Julia said, referring to two women the three officers were familiar with from the previous case they'd worked together. Hector nodded to indicate he remembered them. "I'm hoping to talk with them before we interview any of the others. They know us and will likely be more forthcoming. We're hoping they may have useful perspectives on the arguments Mr. Stephanetti had with the club president and his son."

Ricardo filled in the final details. "Dr. Serrano has the body and will do a postmortem today, time permitting. We may learn more then, and hopefully, get a narrower time-of-death window from him. Currently we are working with a window from about ten thirty to six, when the body was found by the maintenance man. For now, we will begin interviewing the pickleball people, as Julia indicated."

"Ricardo, would you please close my door? There's one more thing I want to talk with you both about."

The inspector, clear the update on the murder case was complete, moved on to a new topic. "How well do you know Constable Javier Bustamente?"

Julia answered first. "I've never worked directly with him. So, I don't know him well." She wanted to add that he was particularly unpleasant to the female officers but didn't. Hector was one of the good guys and didn't need to be told how women in policing were treated. She didn't want to sound as though she were whining.

Ricardo answered next. "He and I worked on a robbery case a few months ago. The owner of a restaurant in Calle Guadalajara, the main road into town, had some equipment stolen. Javier seemed competent. It turned out the guy's son had taken the equipment to sell to support his drug habit, but we found it before the son could unload it. And, since then, as you likely already know, Sergeant Dueñas is working with the son as a civilian informant in hopes of getting some new intel on the local meth trade. But, other than that, I don't know Javier well. He seems a bit of a loner. What's up?"

"You remember how the garage housing the stolen RZR from our case last year was burned just minutes before you arrived to investigate it?" the inspector asked. Both Julia and Ricardo nodded glumly. "Well, young Mr. Bustamente may have been the leak. The comandante wanted you two to know because if he is selling information to people outside the police, your case might be one he could profit from. Please be on alert when he's around and don't share any details of the case with him. You understand?" Both sergeants nodded.

"Also, I have made Javier and Luis Flores work partners."

They were both constables and had known each other at a station in Mexicali. "It was Luis who helped us determine Javier may be our mole. We senior officers have been trying to keep an eye on Javier, but haven't gotten any information confirming he may be dirty. So, Luis has agreed to work with him and report any improper behavior. Julia, I know you and Luis have a good working relationship, so I'm hoping you can mentor him if he finds this task difficult."

"Certainly, sir. I'd be happy to."

Before they left the inspector's office, Martinez informed them he had commandeered the senior officers' conference room for them to use as a war room during their investigation. So, after grabbing their lunch bags from downstairs at their desks, they started to document what little they knew so far on one of the many whiteboards in the upstairs conference room.

Chapter Twelve

As Ricardo and Julia were finishing their lunch, there was a knock at the conference-room door. Julia opened it to see Luis poised to knock again.

"*¡Hola!* Julia, can we talk for a minute?" Luis asked, looking a little sheepish.

"Certainly, Luis. Come in," Julia said.

Luis entered the room and said hi to Ricardo, then took a seat. It looked to Julia as if he weren't sure how to begin. Ricardo also clocked the young man's concern and made an excuse to leave the two to talk. Julia, assuming why Luis was there, opened the conversation.

"I understand you're now partnered with Javier. How are you feeling about it? Is he downstairs right now?"

"That's why I wanted to talk with you. But no, he's getting back later today. He was helping with a prisoner transport to Mulegé. We become partners tomorrow. And, I'm concerned, I have to be honest." Luis spoke rapidly, with obvious stress in his voice. "We did our police training together in Mexicali and, while I wouldn't say we're friends, we've always been friendly. I have reservations about spying on him and reporting back to Detective Inspector Martinez. I've never thought of myself as a snitch." He stopped and looked beseechingly at Julia.

"I understand how you might feel. It may seem as though you've been put in a difficult position. Martinez told me he's asked you to keep an eye on Javier in case he's the person in the station leaking information to outsiders. But, rather than going into this new situation with the idea of trying to catch him doing something bad, perhaps you could consider yourself as the person who can clear him if he's got nothing to hide.

"You're a good cop, Luis. And, if Javier is a good cop, too, you can let Martinez know. If he's not, then you're simply being a good cop and catching someone breaking the law."

Luis considered this for a few moments before replying, "Yes, I see what you're saying, and it does help a bit." He paused for a few more moments with a pensive look. "I think what I'm most worried about is if Javier is leaking information and I turn him in, what will the other cops here think about me? Am I going to be a pariah? I don't want to ruin my career before it gets started."

Ah, thought Julia, *this is the real reason he's concerned.* "That's a valid worry, Luis. We both know there is some corruption in every police force. Usually nothing major, but it's there, nonetheless. Those officers who are not always on the right side of things could present a challenge for you if it's obvious you're the one who informs on him.

"However, I haven't witnessed any overt corruption in our station, and our comandante is a pretty straight arrow. Are you asking me for advice on what to do, Luis, or do you have some thoughts on how you want to proceed?" Julia asked, not wanting to tell him what to do unless he desired her input.

"Yes, I'd be grateful for your suggestions."

"Okay. Well, as I already stated, Javier may not be our leak, but if he is, see whether you can have another officer or outside witnesses observe him, in the act. You have good instincts about people and situations. Trust yourself. If Javier is a bad cop, you'll see it. You'll get a sense of the kind of situations in which he is not acting in the spirit of law enforcement. If he is acting outside the law, tell Martinez, Ricardo, or me and ask for help in catching him. That way, no one will be able to point a finger at anyone in particular. Do you think you can do that?" Julia asked.

"I think so. I guess it's pretty much what the inspector told me, too. I may have other questions for you as Javier and I start working together. Is it okay if I ask for more advice later?" Luis asked.

"Of course, you can. I'll help in any way I'm able. Okay?" Julia was hoping to calm his nerves. It appeared to help. Luis took a deep breath and rose from his chair.

"Thank you, Julia. I appreciate it. I should get going. Thanks again."

Julia pulled La Chica to a stop in front of Molly Lopez's house. It was almost a year since Julia had last visited the Lopezes' home. Seeing again the profusion of garish hand-painted pots full of plastic flowers, she smiled to herself as they walked through the yard. *What an eclectic sense of style Molly has,* she thought. Her knock on the turquoise front door was answered by Molly's husband, Jaime. By the time he'd led them into the living room, Molly had joined them, wearing her signature layers of frilly clothing, today in teal and aqua colors. Jaime offered coffee, which was declined, and then left them.

"Mrs. Lopez, we have some questions for you about the man who died on the pickleball courts this morning. I understand you were watching the games yesterday during which there was an altercation between the man who died, Rudy Stephanetti, and one of the other players. Can you tell us about it?"

"Golly. So it *was* him who died," Molly said almost to herself. The Facebook gossip machine speculated he was who had been killed. "Was it a heart attack?" she asked.

"No, it was murder, but I can't say more at this point."

"Oh my! How awful!" Molly said, dragging the *aw* out dramatically, then remembered she'd been asked a question. Looking at Julia afresh, she asked, "Which altercation do you mean?"

"There were two?" Julia looked intently at the other woman.

"Yes, there was one with the club captain and the other, between father and son," Molly said.

"Okay, please tell us about what you observed."

"Well, the first one was between the man who died and Clint, um, Drayer or Brayer, I think his last name is. I couldn't hear much because they were on a court far from the bleachers. The man who died, Rudy, was yelling at Clint. That's when I noticed something was going on. Then his son and wife tried to calm him, and finally, his wife and kids split up and played with other groups.

"Rudy stood at the side of the court where his son was playing and loudly coached the boy throughout his entire next game. When his son finished his game, he more or less dragged his dad off the courts. They had their conversation directly behind the bleachers, so I could hear their argument. Not that I'm an eavesdropper, you know."

Molly stopped for a moment to take a breath, her large, turquoise-lidded eyes focused on Julia. Then she continued. "The son was angry at his dad for arguing with Clint and even madder for him being such a bully as a coach. He implied he wanted to get another coach. And his dad whispered menacingly, 'Over my dead body.' To which the son responded, angrily, 'Fine by me.' Then the son lifted his paddle as though he were going to strike his dad with it, but all he did was drop his paddle on the ground in front of his father. Then he stalked off. Rudy grabbed his son's paddle from the ground and strode back into the courts." Julia almost laughed as Molly acted out the conversation, showing Logan's movements with the paddle and altering her voice differently for the father's and son's words. Julia wondered whether perhaps Molly was into amateur dramatics.

"One of the other players mentioned Logan, the son, returned to the courts before the club players left. Did you see how Rudy and his son interacted then?" Julia asked.

"Logan came back right as the other players were preparing

to leave. It seemed almost as though Rudy was waiting for him, because as soon as Logan arrived, Rudy made this big apology speech. I didn't hear it, but Stella told me he declared he was sorry he'd embarrassed his son and been rude to Clint. The family started playing together again when everyone else was leaving. It seemed as if everything was okay by then."

"Oh! So father and son seemed to be getting along when Logan returned?" Julia asked.

"As far as I could tell, yes."

"Did you notice anything else that might be important to our investigation?"

As Molly gazed into space, considering the question, Julia was reminded of when she had previously questioned Molly in conjunction with their case last year. When Molly was thinking, her eyelids opened and closed slowly and rhythmically, giving her a toad-like expression. Julia kept her lips from twitching. Finally, when Molly indicated she didn't have anything else she thought would help them, Julia verified she hadn't been at the potluck the previous evening, and she and Ricardo thanked her and left.

In the car, Julia filled Ricardo in on a couple of parts of the conversation he hadn't fully understood. "Hmm," he said, "do you think Logan's 'fine by me' comment to his dad's 'over my dead body' statement was serious?"

"Yeah, good question. Rudy's family was pretty clear Rudy was hard to live with, so it's possible."

As they discussed the case, an unsettling realization began to gnaw at them. The family's avoidance of speaking about the heated argument between Logan and his father set off alarm bells. It was an uncomfortable detail. And raised a multitude of questions. Why had they not mentioned it during their first interview? Surely they knew someone else would. The answer remained elusive, but it undeniably thrust Logan into the unforgiving glare of suspicion.

Chapter Thirteen

San Amaro lies nestled on the tranquil shores of the Sea of Cortez on the Baja Peninsula, a charming coastal gem that seems to exist in a world of its own. Its unhurried rhythm of life, breathtaking vistas of the sea and nearby mountains, and its proximity to the United States have woven a magnetic charm drawing adventurers from across the globe. It is a refuge from the frantic pace north of the border.

But San Amaro is not just a sanctuary for international wanderers. It holds a special place in the hearts of Mexican Americans residing in California and Arizona, who return like migratory birds to its welcome shores. Events in San Amaro draw them in flocks, doubling or tripling the year-round population, which usually hovers around twenty thousand. In this town, cultures blend, creating a tapestry that adds depth to the town's vibrancy.

Driving from The Oasis, Julia noted a billboard announcing one such event. The annual Blues and Arts Festival was getting underway in a couple of days. Held at The Oasis, Julia could imagine the flurry of activity as the stage and beer-garden tents were erected on the large expanse of lawn fronting the Sea View Restaurant and golf-club pro shop.

Now in its sixteenth year, it was an event Julia had attended a few times before she became a cop. She'd enjoyed it. Now she just didn't seem to find the time. Unless she and Ricardo solved this case in record time, it seemed this year's festival would be another she'd have to miss.

Next, Ricardo and Julia spoke with Stella Monroe. They had been to her home the previous year to interview and later arrest her then husband after Stella disappeared in the desert. Julia was intrigued to see the place had been remodeled in the interim. The kitchen was redesigned and had a center island providing extra counter space and storage, something almost every house in Baja needed. New colors graced the walls and gave the home a much warmer feel. *Perhaps Stella's way of reclaiming her territory,* Julia thought.

Stella's dog Juba seemed excited to see Julia. It was as though she remembered Julia as the person who had reunited her with her beloved owner after the awful events of Stella's abduction. Julia, a dog lover herself, was delighted to see Juba again, too, and scratched the border collie's ears and long muzzle as they questioned Stella about her experience involving the Stephanettis the previous day.

Stella's account of the arguments at pickleball tallied with Molly's. Stella had briefly been at the party the previous evening but admitted she started to get a migraine just after arriving, so left shortly before eight and hadn't even met Rudy.

Next, the pair headed to Pippa Drummond's. Pippa had bought a small house in Campo Cristal upon moving to San Amaro after her husband died the previous year. It fronted the beach and had beautiful views of the Sea of Cortez from the front porch and the nearby Sierra de San Pedro Mátir from the rear of the house.

Time and the elements, the cosmic sculptors, had carved magic with those mountains. Their stark, craggy granite surfaces captured light differently each moment as the sun arced across the cerulean sky. Today, as Julia and Ricardo took seats on the back porch opposite Pippa, the mountains looked ancient, like sentinels chiseled from dark chocolate.

Julia asked Pippa to share her observations from the pickleball courts and learned nothing new from her account. However, when the questions turned to the party, Pippa provided new and revealing information.

Pippa began to relay encounters with the Stephanetti family at the party. "I was in the kitchen when they arrived, and I chatted with Gloria as she was getting settled with the kitchen ladies' group. Rudy came into the kitchen briefly to open a bottle of wine, and then he migrated to the living room. Gloria commented she liked San Amaro and was impressed with the quality of our pickleball courts. She apologized for Rudy's behavior on the courts earlier in the day and reiterated some of Rudy's apology speech. Logan needed practice on outdoor courts before he competed in Palm Springs. And since Palm Springs is four hours north of San Amaro, and the weather patterns were often similar, they had come here for Logan's last two weeks of training before the tournament."

"Yes, your explanation is comparable to what others have told us." Julia was hoping Pippa had a different perspective on the party. There was no new information in what Pippa had relayed so far.

"Sometime later, I left the kitchen, looking for a bathroom. The one on the main floor was occupied, so I went upstairs. That's where the Stephanetti kids and Suzanne's great-niece and her boyfriend were. When I was using the facilities, I heard Tiffany and Brianna talking. I gathered they had left the room in which the four of them had been having their party to have a private conversation.

"I wasn't wanting to eavesdrop, but I couldn't help hearing them. They were right outside the bathroom door. Brianna was complaining about her dad. She grumbled she was sick to death of the way he was trying to run her life. She told Tiffany, 'I like pickleball, but I have no desire to follow Dad's dream and play professionally. I have my plans, and thank God, in three weeks I'll be eighteen and leave home. Then he can't push me around anymore. He makes me so mad I'll be glad when he's out of my life. Sometimes I feel like I could kill him.' I flushed the toilet then, washed my hands, and left the bathroom, so I didn't hear any more. The girls had left the hallway by the time I came out." Pippa finished her recitation.

"Did Brianna's tone of voice give you any sense of whether she was joking or serious?" Julia asked after she relayed to Ricardo the details of Pippa's story.

"Oh, it's so hard to tell with kids these days, isn't it? I can't imagine she was serious, but I couldn't be certain."

Julia remembered Pippa had been a psychologist in her career and decided to press a little harder. "Yes, I know what you mean, but with your professional background, your insights could be valuable."

"Right. Okay, then, I'd say she was serious about being angry with her dad's plan for her future and about having clear plans of her own. And her plans didn't match her dad's. But I think the 'I could kill him' remark was to underscore those feelings rather than a statement of murderous intent. Does that help?"

"Yes. Thanks. Carry on, please."

"When I got back downstairs, I noticed a gal from pickleball I've played with a few times, Sandy McLean. She is often reserved. But last night, she was standing by herself in an alcove between the kitchen and living room. It seemed a bit antisocial, even for her. So I joined her to chat.

"I think she was watching a group of men that included Rudy, who were talking nearby. She pointed out her husband in the group, saying he doesn't play pickleball. She correctly assumed I wouldn't have met him yet, so promised to introduce me later. She's never emotionally demonstrative, but she seemed even less animated than normal.

"A few minutes later Norm—Norm Webster, that is—and Rudy moved to the couch, which was only a few feet from the alcove where Sandy and I were standing, though I don't think they even realized we were there. They had their backs to the alcove. They both drank brandy from a flask Norm had, and then it got weird.

"I didn't realize Norm and Rudy knew each other, but

suddenly, Norm exclaimed, loudly enough both Sandy and I stopped talking for a minute, 'You bastard. You're pulling me as your rep? Why? What have I done to deserve this?' Rudy answered, but I could hear only some of his reply because he was facing away from us. The parts I heard were 'not selling enough equipment' and 'brought your last commission check.'

"They talked for another few moments, then went outside. They both had cigars, so I assume they left to smoke them. Right then Sandy took me over to meet her husband. He didn't strike me as much of a party guy. He mentioned he was going for a walk on the beach, and then we rejoined the women congregated back in the kitchen."

Julia asked, "What time was that?"

"Maybe quarter to eleven?" Pippa said uncertainly. "Sorry, I don't wear a watch anymore."

"Did you see Mr. Stephanetti again?" Julia queried.

"No. But, I left about ten minutes later. I left through their side door, as it was closer to where my car was parked. So I assume Norm and Rudy were still outside the front door."

Ricardo and Julia huddled in La Chica, their expressions tense as they discussed what they'd just learned. Ricardo meticulously recapped the web of information they had uncovered so far. It was partly a way to verify he had gleaned all the pertinent facts from the interviews, but more importantly, it was an attempt to ensure they were on the right path and their pursuit of the truth remained steadfast. They felt the weight of unanswered questions.

As he finished, a heavy silence hung in the air, broken by the hum of the idling engine. Finally, he suggested what had been lingering on both their minds. "Let's go talk with Norm Webster." His voice was tinged with a sense of both anticipation and foreboding.

Chapter Fourteen

Norm Webster was medium height with a robust body that hinted at unwavering fitness. He had a full head of raven-black hair and bushy black eyebrows, which, like his hair, bore a few streaks of silver wisdom. Julia placed his age in the midsixties.

He was working in his yard loading garden waste into the bed of an older silver pickup truck sporting a logo depicting a powerful horse on the door. With resolve, Julia and Ricardo strode up the walkway. "Good afternoon, Mr. Webster," she began with a determined tone. I am Detective Sergeant Garcia, and this is Detective Sergeant Hernandez. We want to ask you a few questions about the death of Rudy Stephanetti."

"Oh my God! It was Rudy on the courts? What happened?" Norm appeared shocked, then cleared his head with a shake and continued. "Sorry, yes, please come, sit. Are you okay outside?" he asked, pointing to a grouping of chairs under a huge yard umbrella. He didn't offer them any refreshments and sat heavily in a chair he pushed back a couple of feet from the table around which they sat.

Julia drew upon the arsenal of techniques acquired during her undergraduate degree in psychology when facing witnesses and potential suspects. She firmly believed a gentle approach was key during their first interaction. With a master's degree in criminology and rigorous police training under her belt, she possessed the procedural know-how and skill set to adapt when the gentle approach no longer sufficed.

The man she was interrogating happened to be the last individual seen with the victim before the gruesome murder. This circumstance elevated him to the ominous status of their top suspect, casting an oppressive shadow over the gathering.

"Mr. Stephanetti was murdered." Then seeing Norm's face drain of color, she hurried on. "I'm sorry for your loss, Mr. Webster. Were you and Mr. Stephanetti friends?"

"Not friends, but work associates, and we were acquainted, but not close. I must say, your English is excellent," Norm said.

"Thank you, sir. Please, tell us about your work association with Mr. Stephanetti."

Norm explained he played regularly in pickleball tournaments in the amateur division, and he was a well-seeded amateur player. Several years prior, he was approached by Pickleball Pro Gear to become a rep in Baja for their paddles. He earned a commission for each sale he initiated. He also played with their paddles during tournaments and explained the benefits of them to other players. Because San Amaro didn't have a sports store that carried any kind of pickleball gear, he'd sold lots of paddles. The year after he'd started working with Pickleball Pro Gear, Rudy took over as vice president of marketing, so in effect, he became Norm's boss.

"We'd meet at tournaments in the States, and once a year, all their amateur reps were invited to New Jersey for their annual sales-force rally, and I'd see him then. We always got on fine, though he was a bit of a braggart."

"I understand Mr. Stephanetti was ending your connection with his company. Why was that?" Julia asked. As always, Julia's tone was neutral and calm.

"That's a helluva good question. He said it was because I wasn't selling enough paddles. I think it might be because I haven't been playing in as many tournaments this last year, and I've fallen in the amateur standings. Anyway, I didn't care that much. I was never doing it for the money."

"We have a witness from the party who said it sounded as though you *were* upset by it," Julia said.

"Well, I suppose I could have sounded angry. Mainly I was pissed, sorry, ah upset Rudy told me at a party with all my friends around. He was never known for his tact," Norm answered, easily.

"Tell us about your interactions with Mr. Stephanetti yesterday."

His telling of the argument with Clint at the courts tracked with everyone else's. As did the description of the early part of the party. However, when he got to the latter part of the evening, Ricardo interjected a comment on the man's body language indicating he was extremely tense. Julia had noticed it, too. *Time to dig deeper,* Julia decided.

"Several people at the party say the last time they saw Mr. Stephanetti was when the two of you stepped outside together around ten thirty or quarter to eleven. You neglected to tell us about that, so please, fill us in." Julia's tone remained friendly, but there was no mistaking she wasn't buying the man's offhandedness as innocence.

"Yes, we did go outside together, to smoke cigars. Rudy had some good Havanas. I had some good brandy. We stood outside Edie and Suzanne's for a while enjoying both. He talked about his kids. They are both excellent pickleball players, and Rudy had big plans for each of them. I don't have kids, and to be honest, never wanted them, so I wasn't paying much attention. Finally, I got bored and knocked off the end of my cigar, and headed back inside. That was the last time I saw him. My wife and I left the party about a quarter past eleven, and he wasn't outside the condo anymore," Norm said.

"And when you left Mr. Stephanetti outside finishing his cigar, did he give any indication of what he was going to do next? Was he meeting someone else?"

"No, he didn't say. Although, he had asked me whether the lights on the pickleball courts were good enough to allow night games. I told him they are. There's a group of folks who play only at night, usually between seven and nine. I told him that, too. He didn't say or ask anything else. Now, if there isn't anything else I can help with, I need to finish watering my plumeria before it gets too hot." Norm stood up, signaling he was finished, whether or not the two detective sergeants were.

It was a typical ploy with witnesses who either thought they had nothing else to offer by way of information, or by guilty people trying to avoid further interrogation. Julia refused to be deterred so easily, especially with their prime suspect. "I'm certain you can spare us a couple of minutes more of your time, Mr. Webster. We have only a few more questions." In reality, Julia didn't have any more questions but wanted to maintain control of the conversation, her instincts tingling with suspicion.

This man was the most likely suspect they had at this early point in their investigation. He had been heard having a heated conversation with Rudy and had the dubious distinction of having been the last person seen with the victim.

"To your knowledge, did Mr. Stephanetti know anyone *other than you* here in San Amaro?" Julia asked, emphasizing the uniqueness of Norm's relationship with the victim.

"I'm not aware of anyone he knew here apart from me and Fran, my wife. He'd met her once or twice at the annual reps' convention in New Jersey," Norm said.

"Did Mr. Stephanetti mention having a mistress or girlfriend to you?" Julia asked.

Norm physically reacted to her question. He sat straighter in his chair as though shocked or surprised. "Wow. Really?"

Norm's answer was simply reactive. Julia persisted. "Please answer the question, Mr. Webster."

"You don't pull any punches, do you? But, to answer your question, Rudy was known for boasting about his romantic conquests when he was with the guys. To be frank, it was repulsive to me. Gloria is a remarkable woman. Yet Rudy seemed to take pride in having her by his side despite his indiscretions. However, during the party, he didn't talk about anything along those lines."

"Do you know whether any of these conquests, as you call them, were married?" Julia asked.

"I don't think so, though I don't know for sure. He certainly never mentioned any of his girlfriends were married. I think it would have been too dangerous for him." Seeing Julia's quizzical look, he explained. "Similar to most bullies, I think he was a coward. I think he'd have been scared a husband might find out and give him a hard time. But I'm just speculating. I don't know anything specific to back it up," Norm said, picking at one of his fingers.

Julia shifted gears. "Do you use a wooden paddle when you play pickleball?"

"Oh my God, no! Wooden paddles are usually from cheap pickleball sets sold in low-cost department stores. I use a carbon-fiber paddle. I prefer the stiffness of them. Most people use carbon fiber, like mine, or graphite, now."

Julia persisted. "Do you know anyone in your club who might have or use a wooden paddle?"

"No. I know there are a couple of crappy old wooden paddles in the pickleball shed beside the courts. I think they are for new players who don't have their own equipment or if someone forgets their paddle and is desperate to play," Norm said. He kept fidgeting and picking at his hand.

"Who has access to the shed? And where is it located?"

Norm described the location of the shed as just to the right of the bleachers, by the main entrance gate to the courts. He also told her everyone in the club knew the combination of the lock, explaining that the shed was where the balls were kept. "I'd told Rudy the combination in case he needed it. It's easy to remember. Miss Universe 1958." Norm grinned, then seeing their confusion continued. "Her measurements were thirty-six twenty-four thirty-six."

Julia wrote the numbers in her notebook and then handed it

to Norm to write the instructions of how many turns in each direction between numbers. "We will need to check it," she said, ensuring she could read his directions.

"Have you hurt your hand, Mr. Webster? I notice you seem to be focused on it," Julia asked.

"Oh, I have a thorn stuck in my finger from the plant trimmings I'm taking to the dump."

"Goodness, you need gardening gloves." Julia spoke casually, not looking up from her notebook. She missed the sharp look Norm had given her, but Ricardo noticed and wondered at the man's reaction.

"Do you live here full time, Mr. Webster?" Julia asked.

Norm explained he and his wife didn't own another home anywhere, but they had a motor home in which they traveled for three or four months each summer to avoid the heat and humidity of San Amaro's hottest part of the year. To her questions about where they'd lived before San Amaro and his line of work, he revealed he'd been a lawyer in Wyoming. Julia discreetly wrote a note in her book to tread carefully when questioning him. His legal background meant he would likely discern the underlying motives behind her inquiries, where others might not.

"Thank you, Mr. Webster, please don't leave town without first contacting us. We may need to speak with you again." Julia handed him her card. "Now, is your wife at home? We want to speak with her, too."

Mrs. Webster, Fran, while friendly, was not able to provide them with any useful information. She didn't play pickleball and didn't know many of the players or their spouses. She'd spent all her time at the party in the kitchen, near the food. Apparently, the deviled eggs were some of the best she'd ever had.

To Julia's questions about her employment in Wyoming, she'd explained she had been an equine therapist, using horses to aid her in providing support and assistance to physically and emotionally damaged teens. She and Norm had owned a small ranch with several horses she used in her work.

Now she volunteered at the equestrian center at The Oasis in a therapy program she had helped start for autistic Mexican kids. Julia, not previously aware of the program, was curious about it. But now was not the time to satisfy that particular interest.

"How did your husband feel about being let go as a representative for Pickleball Pro Gear?" Julia asked.

Fran glanced toward her husband, who was busy watering some trees edging their property. "He was surprised more than anything. I think he liked being able to provide high-quality paddles to players here. He grumbled about it on the drive home, but nothing more."

"What time did you leave the pickleball party?" Julia asked.

"We got home at eleven. It takes about five minutes to get from here to the gals' condo."

"How sure are you about the time you got home?" Julia asked. Norm had said they left at quarter after eleven.

"I'm certain. My smartwatch gives my wrist a tiny buzz on the hour. We walked in the door just as it buzzed."

"Did your husband go out again that evening, after you got home?"

"I don't think he did. I was exhausted and dived straight into bed. I was out like a light," Fran said. "I don't normally drink, and I had three glasses of wine at the party. But I can't imagine he'd have gone out. I felt him get into bed. It didn't seem as though it was too long after I'd fallen asleep."

Julia didn't have any more questions, so she thanked Fran for her time.

As they settled back into the car's dimly lit interior, Julia and Ricardo couldn't escape the weight of their conversation with Norm Webster. Julia recounted the twenty-minute disparity in the timelines provided by Fran and Norm. Something to pursue.

"Norm's got means, motive, and opportunity, if he indeed returned to the courts after leaving his wife behind. It's the trifecta of a crime," Ricardo declared firmly, each word landing like a hammer blow in the confined space.

Norm had just become the prime target in their crosshairs, and the pressure to unearth evidence and meticulously trace his post-party movements surged to the forefront of their investigation.

Chapter Fifteen

According to the radar gun Corporal Luis Flores was pointing at the oncoming car, it was traveling at 130 kilometers per hour. It was a seventy-kilometer zone, though most people drove much faster. He radioed his partner, Corporal Javier Bustamente, in the squad car a few hundred meters along the road with the particulars so he could pull the driver over.

The pair had been doing speed checks all morning. It was approaching noon, and most of the vehicles they'd seen were driving close enough to the limit they had not been stopped. *Finally,* thought Javier as he jumped from his cruiser and flagged over the speeding car. It stopped just in front of his police car. California plates. Javier smiled and approached the late-model Chevy SUV.

In fast Spanish, Javier reprimanded the driver. *"Estabas acelerando. Ciento treinta kilómetros por hora en una zona de setenta."*

As he hoped, the older-woman driver looked confused and frightened. Slightly less angrily, he asked, *"¿Habla español?"*

"No," answered the driver. She looked panicked.

Perfect, he thought. Javier knew he was a good-looking man. In his boots and with his hat on, he was still well shy of six feet, but his coal-black hair was thick and slightly wavy, his dark chocolate eyes slightly hooded under trimmed black brows set in a generous oval face. He was attractive in a roguish way. But his dimples were what gave his handsome face a boyishness that charmed the women. He wasn't smiling as he stood beside the car. Not yet.

"You speed, very fast. Big fine," Javier said gruffly in his best, but still poor, English. "Hundred dolares. You pay me."

"Oh, dear. I don't think I have much money with me" came the timid reply. The flustered woman started digging through her purse and found fifty-five dollars. She showed it to Javier. "Will this do?"

"No pesos?" Javier asked.

"No, sorry," the woman whined. She looked on the verge of tears.

Javier leaned close to the window, still with a stern expression. Then he graced the woman with a full-dimpled smile and spoke softly. "Okay, is enough." He held his hand out for the fifty-five dollars. "You nice lady. I let you go. No drive so fast."

The woman handed over her money. She knew it was extortion, but she also knew she'd been speeding. She'd heard stories of Mexican cops "accepting" fines so the driver didn't have to go to the station, so she wasn't shocked. And after all, fifty-five dollars wasn't a big loss. She gave the officer a tight smile and slowly drove off.

Javier had tried to determine what Luis thought about skimming Americans for money and wasn't sure where his new partner stood on the matter. He got the impression Luis was pretty straitlaced. He decided not to mention it unless Luis asked him directly, then clambered back into his squad car.

By the end of the day, Javier had almost $250 in his pocket. *Excellent,* he thought. It was equal to a week's wages.

Luis had been intently watching the interactions between Javier and the drivers of cars with American license plates. He was pretty sure he knew what was taking place. He added a note to a document on his phone.

As he'd told Julia, he believed the idea of spying on a fellow officer wasn't right, but, and it was a big *but* in his mind, if Javier were the person who'd given police information to a thieving and murdering gringo last year, Luis could feel okay about it.

It had been the first big case Luis worked on, and Julia, his sergeant on the case, had let him do much of the investigating on his own. She'd praised his ideas and actions. And it was his work that led them to a shed that contained vital evidence in both his case, a stolen RZR, and a missing person case Julia was working. However, the garage had been set alight less than fifteen minutes before Julia, Ricardo, and Luis arrived with permission to search it. All their evidence was destroyed. If Javier were the one who sold information to the perpetrator of the crimes, then Luis figured he didn't deserve to be a policeman. Luis believed in law enforcement, not lawlessness. Police corruption needed to be stopped. This was his small part to play.

Chapter Sixteen

Julia and Ricardo locked their sights with unwavering determination on Norm Webster, starting with the pickleball shed to which he had referred them. On their drive back to the pickleball courts, Ricardo had phoned Andrés Alvarez, a nurse who worked with Dr. Serrano, their GP-cum-coroner.

Andrés had recently finished an accredited course in crime-scene forensics, offered by the US State Department in conjunction with several universities in northern Mexico's border towns. Nearby Mexicali was home to one such university. The courses were aimed at helping curb the rampant cartel violence in the US and Mexico as they vied for supremacy in trafficking drugs, arms, and people.

The US government listed the lack of high-quality, credible, and consistent forensics processes in Mexico as notably hampering their ability to prosecute Mexican traffickers in the States. So, the program was rolled out with seven accredited courses available to police, scientists, and certain health professionals.

Andrés arrived in his battered and rusting 1998 Corolla long after Ricardo and Julia called. He apologized for the time it took him to arrive, pointing out he didn't normally carry his forensics-gathering equipment. He explained he was on a house call when Ricardo phoned, and he had to go to the hospital to get his case.

Ricardo led him to a plywood shed about four feet by six feet in size and asked for fingerprints to be taken from the lock on the shed first. Next, Ricardo tested the lock to see whether it was open. It wasn't, so he opened the shed using the combination Norm provided.

Andrés inspected the inside of the shed and its contents. The latter consisted of a large wire basket of pickleballs, several personal water bottles, a couple of pieces of clothing, and a paddle. Of most interest to both Julia and Ricardo was the paddle.

Once Andrés was finished processing the contents, they inspected the paddle in detail. It was an old wooden paddle and appeared to be the mate of the one used in the murder of Rudy Stephanetti. It had the name Martha Werner written on it in felt pen. Julia left a note saying they were taking the paddle and closed the shed. She also made a note to herself. The name Martha Werner was not one she recalled from the investigation. She'd have to ask Clint whether she was part of the local league.

Back at the police station, Andrés left his collection of forensic samples with Vicente, the person responsible for the police forensics lab. The lab was on the second floor, just down the hall from the conference room Julia and Ricardo were using for their war room.

Vicente was a recent hire for the San Amaro State Police. When his grandfather, who lived in San Amaro, was diagnosed with terminal cancer, Vicente's dad had informed his dutiful son he'd have to leave college to care for his grandfather. He could return to school later. Vicente had almost finished his second year in forensic science at the University of Guadalajara. He had a year's more formal training than the previous forensics person. For San Amaro, Vicente and Andrés presented a bright new era in forensic crime fighting.

Vicente thought the San Amaro lab was woefully underequipped compared with the university lab and was disappointed to realize the station didn't have a polymerase chain reaction machine to analyze DNA. But there were enough tests he could do with the available equipment to get started.

Vicente, though used to much more sophisticated equipment at the university, had done a summer work study through the university in the wilds of a Jalisco jungle and had learned many tricks and hacks from the forensics experts leading the program. He would be able to improvise a few additional types of tests using his less formal forensics education. Still, anything requiring in-depth analysis would have to be sent to Mexicali.

Ricardo and Julia spent a few minutes updating the whiteboard in their war room and made a plan for the interviews they needed to complete in the coming days. It was suppertime when they left the room. Tomorrow would be another long day.

Before Julia departed the station, she had one thing she wanted to explore. Her biggest issue in the case was being the sole English-fluent officer on the force in San Amaro. She was grateful her grandfather, the previous station comandante, had strongly encouraged her to go to the United States to get her master's degree. As a child, she'd taken English in school, as had many of her peers, but the requirement to think, speak, and write in English every day for two years at Arizona State University forced her into fluency. It was a blessing and, at the moment, a curse.

She was a detective on this case because of her language skills. But there were nearly forty English-speaking witnesses and suspects to be interviewed, and she couldn't see how she could do it all promptly *and* monitor the other sources of information relevant to the case. So, she knocked on Inspector Martinez's door.

She updated Martinez on what she and Ricardo had learned about Norm, the altercation between Rudy and his son, and the possible threats both Logan and Brianna had made toward their father. Then, she moved on to explain the items they had given Vicente for forensic analysis. With the case update given, she came to the point of her visit.

"Sir, I have an idea I'm hoping you'll support. I suggest we bring Constable Ana Maria Verde into this murder case to do research for Ricardo and me." She paused to see whether the inspector would interject, but he simply made a hand gesture indicating she should continue. "What I plan is to help her get enrolled on all the San Amaro-specific, English-language Facebook pages. I'll give her a list of all the people involved in this case—there are almost forty—and have her scrape into a document all Facebook posts with any of the names of the people involved, use our translation software to put it all in Spanish, and then she can provide me with a report on the conversations pertaining to our investigation. I just don't have time to keep up with the Facebook chatter and conduct all the interviews." She stopped and waited. She didn't have to wait long.

"Excellent idea, Julia. I'll clear it with the comandante and get back to you, but I don't expect he'll have any problem with it."

Ana Maria and Julia sat in Julia's tiny casita in the yard behind Julia's grandparents' house. She had inherited the tiny home when her mother remarried years after her father's death and moved into her new husband's house.

Ana Maria had not needed any enticements. She was delighted she would be working with Julia and Ricardo on the murder case. Women in Mexican police departments rarely got involved in much resembling real police work. Julia was an inspiration to the other two women on the San Amaro force.

Julia had explained briefly on the phone what she was proposing Ana Maria do, suggesting they get together that evening. Now Julia was showing her the process to fulfill the task.

They were hunched over Julia's laptop at the countertop that served as her kitchen table. Ana Maria, like most people in their thirties these days, was computer savvy. She quickly grasped the method Julia suggested she use. She hadn't used the department's translation software before, but she mastered it in no time, too.

She was excited to get to work tomorrow and get started. In the short time the two had perused the posts on the local expat Facebook groups, they'd found dozens of posts relating to the death they were investigating. Between the pickleball group and the general chat groups the local expats had set up, there appeared to be a treasure trove of gossip about Rudy Stephanetti's murder.

Once Ana Maria joined all the Facebook groups on Julia's list, she would have more than enough work to keep her busy. Little did either woman know the Pandora's box teeming with secrets they were opening. Julia's relief at having help transformed into an eerie sense of foreboding at what they might uncover. For Ana Maria, the ecstatic joy of being given meaningful police work morphed into a zealot-like quest for the truth.

Chapter Seventeen

Julia and Ricardo started their day at the pickleball courts. The sun rising through light clouds cast an eerie pinkish glow over their mission. With a daunting list of nearly three dozen statements to get, they expected many of those they needed to speak with would be there. They were not disappointed. They knew within the gathered players, jovial athleticism masked brutal secrets they needed to uncover.

Seeing the courts were overcrowded, they realized they'd be able to speak with the players as they rotated off the court between games. They spoke first with Rhonda Wilburn. She had been at the party, at pickleball the day of the altercation between Rudy and Clint, and the next day when the body was discovered. From her, they learned her husband, Glenn, not a pickleball player, had spoken with Rudy at the party and thought him a self-important bore.

When asked whether anyone had been acting unusually at the party, Rhonda mentioned Sandy McLean seemed preoccupied and despondent when they spoke. "It's not as if she's usually the life of the party, you understand. She's always a bit timid, but this was more pronounced. She stood alone in an alcove just off the living room watching the group, which included Rudy. She looked sad."

Julia had heard a similar account from Pippa, but Pippa thought Sandy was watching her husband, Dean.

Many of the players had not interacted with any of the Stephanettis at the party and had nothing relevant to offer, though several reiterated the same information about the confrontation between Rudy and Clint on the courts.

One person, Gregory Fletcher, added to their knowledge, saying he'd tried to talk with Rudy after the Stephanettis split their foursome and Rudy was coaching his son from the sidelines but had been rudely told by Rudy, "Can't you see I'm trying to coach Logan. I can't talk now." Then Gregory had added, "I'm not surprised someone offed him." Julia probed more deeply, but the man strongly avowed his innocence. She let him go but placed an asterisk beside Gregory's name in her list of interviewees and made a note regarding his comment.

Denis Dumas and Gregory Fletcher both mentioned they'd seen Logan leave the party around ten forty-five. They had been on the second-floor living room balcony watching the tide come in and noticed the young man head toward the beach, then veer right and go behind another condo, in the direction of the pickleball courts. Neither man had seen Logan again that evening.

Julia and Ricardo were eager to get a few minutes with Clint Brayer and finally got their opportunity late in the league play window when he came off the courts from a game just as they finished a conversation with a gruff man named Wolfe Wagner. "Mr. Brayer," Julia called to get his attention, "my partner and I need to ask you some questions. Will you please join us on the bleachers?"

When they were seated and Clint had downed some much-needed water, Julia began. "Please tell us about the interaction you had with Mr. Stephanetti the day before yesterday." Clint's version was mostly the same as the others who had viewed the situation, though he added several details others wouldn't have been able to hear. Mainly he mentioned Rudy's wife, Gloria, placated her husband by saying, "We don't want to make enemies, dear, and I would love to play with some of the other people here."

Then Clint added, "I was a cop for thirty-seven years, and I've encountered many people like Rudy Stephanetti. I'm sure you know the type. Thought the rules didn't apply to him, and that he was more important than average people. Bigheaded and pigheaded. And manipulative. I didn't believe his apology for a second. I think he just did it to try to make people like him, to try to wipe away the reality of his tantrum because I asked them to leave the courts.

"I suspect he pissed someone off, and they took revenge. But, in case you're wondering, it wasn't me. As far as I'm concerned, he wasn't worth the trouble. I hung out with him at the potluck mainly because I was curious to see how he acted in a social setting. I've always found narcissists fascinating. He probably thought he'd fooled me into being friends.

"He enjoyed talking about himself and his family, all of whom were the 'best' at what they did, and he used his words to manipulate and impress others. I didn't like him, in case you haven't figured that out," he said with a laugh, "but I didn't kill him."

Julia chose not to respond to Clint's claim. "Can you tell me who Martha Werner is? We found a paddle with her name on it in the shed where you keep the pickleballs. It appeared to be the mate of the one used in the murder.

Clint explained she was a player a few years previously but sadly lost her battle with cancer a year or so ago. She'd donated a set of wooden paddles, which the club kept as spares. Clint headed back to the courts when Julia indicated she had no more questions for the time being.

Sandy McLean had not come to pickleball that morning. *Had she intentionally stayed away from their investigation?* Julia wondered. Her unusual behavior at the party, as described by her friends, made the detectives eager to speak with her. Her name was added to their list of people they'd have to interview at their homes. The list included a few spouses who were at the party but didn't play pickleball and a couple of players who, like Sandy, weren't in attendance. Perhaps they held missing pieces of their puzzling case.

By the time the players were packing their gear for the day and heading home, Julia and Ricardo had spoken with all the players there. They had a better sense of who their victim had been. Not a very nice guy. But they hadn't learned very much of value, though Julia was interested in finding out more about what Logan Stephanetti did when he left the party, and what was behind Sandy McLean's odd demeanor.

When they got back to the station, Ricardo had a message from Dr. Serrano. He had some initial findings from his autopsy. They headed to the hospital to talk with him.

Serrano got straight to the point. "I put the time of death between eleven p.m. and two a.m. As for the cause of death, the gash on the back of his skull was sufficient to have killed him in less than a half hour, but the stab wound to his neck ended his life before he succumbed to the head laceration.

"Both the hit to the head and the stab to the neck would have required brute force. Coupled with the terrible fist beating the man suffered, I think you're looking for an enraged and strong person, most likely a man. Someone at least five foot nine, based on the angle of the head injury. Assuming the victim was standing at the time of the attack.

"One other thing. I found dirt in several of the facial lacerations. I'd say the killer's hands were dirty, or he was wearing gloves with dirt on them. I've sent the dirt and some other trace evidence to Vicente over at your lab. Maybe he can give you some more information about it."

Ricardo asked, "Any chance you could narrow the time-of-death window any further?"

Serrano ran his fingers through his thick black hair and sighed. "Well, I haven't completed the analysis of his stomach contents, and toxicology results won't be in for a few days, but I doubt they will narrow the time-of-death window. You told me he'd been at a party, so he had probably been drinking, though I don't yet know how much. The alcohol and the overnight temperatures will both play into my calculations. After I've had time to analyze those factors, I might be able to give you a smaller window. If we're lucky. Don't hold your breath. I'll give you a call tomorrow if I find anything else," the doctor said. "Any other questions?"

Julia and Ricardo both flipped through their notebooks, but neither had anything else for the doctor. They headed back to the station and rushed directly to the forensics lab to encourage Vicente to analyze the dirt as a priority. It appeared Vicente was on his lunch break, so the two decided to do the same.

A medium-height, barrel-chested man of about sixty-five was working in the front garden as Julia and Ricardo approached. Upon introducing themselves and explaining why they were there, Julia and Ricardo were invited into a sun porch on the east side of a ranch-style house. Their host was Dean McLean, the husband of Sandy. He'd been an attendee at the pickleball party. He invited them, in a deep Texas drawl, to sit as he dusted the dirt from the knees of his sweatpants. Julia noticed he didn't remove his gloves, and they were markedly unmasculine, sporting yellow daisies and pink, grinning pigs. Dean saw her looking at them and laughed, saying, "I haven't found a place in town selling good gardening gloves. Got any suggestions?"

Neither Julia nor Ricardo answered. Julia began the questioning. "When did you first meet Rudy Stephanetti, Mr. McLean?"

"At that pickleball party at the lesbian couple's place by the beach. I'd never laid eyes on the man before that," Dean said, his Texas drawl strongly evident.

"Please tell us about your interaction with him?" Julia asked.

"Not much to tell. He came over to the group of guys I was standing with, in the living room, and pretty much took over the conversation. Seemed a bit high on himself, you ask me. Not my sort, to be honest. He talked about his work at some pickleball company and how he was a big shot there. Sounded as though he'd worked at many different places, all corporate bullshit jobs with fancy titles. Pardon my language, ma'am."

Dean seemed a bit of a rough sort to Julia, and her brief memory of meeting Sandy at the courts the day Rudy was found, she thought her to be a genteel lady. The match surprised her. "When did you last see Mr. Stephanetti, sir?"

"He and Norm wandered out to smoke cigars at some point. Maybe about ten thirty or quarter to eleven. I am not much of a party guy, so I ditched the small talk about the same time and headed for a walk on the beach. When I came back, the Stephanettis had all left. That's it. Now, let me find Sandy for you."

"Before you do, Mr. McLean, I just have a couple of more questions. What type of work did you do before moving to San Amaro?" Julia asked. She gently but firmly never let a witness control the interview.

"I was the union steward for Trinity Metro. It's the Fort Worth Transit Authority. I worked there for thirty-seven years. I started as a hostler, and worked my way up," he said with obvious pride, though neither Julia nor Ricardo knew a hostler was someone who fueled and cleaned the buses.

"So, you never crossed paths with Mr. Stephanetti in your work life?" Julia queried, remembering the Stephanettis had lived in Dallas.

"No, ma'am. I surely didn't. Shall I get Sandy now?"

Julia filled Ricardo in on Dean's remarks while he was in the house. Sandy joined them wearing blue-jean shorts and an old, white, paint-covered men's dress shirt with the sleeves rolled up. She also had a small smear of yellow paint on her chin. "Sorry, I'm kind of grubby. I'm working on a painting." She took a seat but didn't lean back into it. Instead, she perched on the front of the chair with her arms crossed and held each of her elbows cupped in the opposite hand. It was an odd posture, Julia thought, and noticed a glance from Ricardo indicating he also found the woman's body language intriguing.

Dean stood to return to his gardening. As he passed behind his wife's chair, his hand brushed her shoulder. Sandy startled, then gave her husband a small smile. It didn't reach her eyes. Julia made a note. She reiterated their purpose in being there to Sandy and began the interview. "Please tell us about your interactions with Rudy Stephanetti."

Sandy hesitated a moment, appearing to gather her thoughts, then began. "I was playing pickleball the morning he and Clint had their argument. I didn't meet any of the Stephanettis at pickleball, and frankly, I was surprised Suzanne and Edie invited them to our potluck. Rudy was unnecessarily unpleasant to Clint and his own family, I thought. But, I guess his apology ameliorated people's feelings toward him."

Julia's curiosity was stimulated by her answer. "Was your opinion of him not improved by his apology?"

"Oh, it had nothing to do with me. I don't think it affected my opinion of him one way or another," Sandy said, shaking her head, her gaze focused on the ground. Then she immediately continued to answer Julia's previous question. "I talked with Gloria at the party for a bit, and she seemed nice. I didn't interact with Rudy at all, though I was aware he was chatting with the group of men Dean was with, in the living room."

"I spoke with someone from the party who said you appeared to be watching a group of men including Rudy for some time. What was the reason for that?" Julia asked.

Sandy hesitated for a moment before answering. "Oh, it was silly. Dean and I argued, not even an argument, just a discussion before going that night. Dean doesn't enjoy parties much and asked me to go alone. I didn't relent. It's good for him to get out of the house and away from his incessant gardening." With a sad expression, Sandy looked over to where Dean was working while she said this. Julia thought it was a conversation the couple had had myriad times before. It was a classic introvert-extrovert issue with which many couples grappled.

"Anyway, I was watching Dean in the group to see whether he was having an okay time. I was glad he'd come with me, but I didn't want him to be miserable about being there, you know?" Sandy gave a small shrug, as though embarrassed by her admission.

"One of your friends said you seemed to be having an off night. You weren't your usual happy self. Why was that?"

"Perhaps I was more concerned about Dean than I realized. That's all," Sandy said and flashed Julia a bright smile, looking into her face for the first time.

"And when did you leave the party, Mrs. McLean?"

"I started packing the dishes I brought sometime after half past eleven. Then I thanked our hostesses and found Dean waiting in the car, so I guess it was around quarter to twelve when we left. I didn't see any of the Stephanettis then, so I assumed they'd already gone."

Though Dean was gardening, he was still within earshot, so Julia raised her voice slightly and asked, "Mr. McLean, why were you waiting in the car rather than back in the house?"

Dean's head jerked momentarily at the sound of his name, then he turned from his squatting position beside a pot into which he was planting some pale purple flowers. "I'd had enough of the party and was enjoying the quiet. I didn't want to ruin it by going back into the party. So I went to the car. I knew Sandy would find me. She always does." He didn't wait for a response from Julia before turning back to his gardening task.

Julia found his behavior rude but carried on with Sandy. "What type of work did you do before coming to San Amaro?" she asked.

"Oh, I was an executive assistant at a medium-sized

company in Dallas. They made compressors for the oil- and gas-pipeline industry. I left the company when Dean retired, so we could move here. I was fifty-three then, too young to retire, really. I enjoyed my job there, and I'd finally worked my way to an executive admin position. I still miss it sometimes." She stopped a moment as though reviewing what she'd told Julia, her eyes still fixed on the ground. "I don't know why I'm telling you all this, sorry. I can blather on, sometimes." Sandy looked embarrassed again.

Julia wondered why, and was curious to know more about the relationship between the McLeans.

"What did you make of those two?" Ricardo asked when they were back in the car.

"I was surprised they are together," Julia said. "They seem so different. Sandy seemed almost afraid of her husband or like she was trying to protect him. How about you?"

"I don't think they were telling us everything. Especially him," Ricardo said, his voice edged with suspicion. "And there was something about the way the woman spoke Rudy's name. Her eyes were shrouded in a veil of apprehension. Or, perhaps deceit."

Chapter Eighteen

From her casita on a hill just east of downtown, Julia's morning run took her through small side streets where vendors were just starting to prepare their food stalls for breakfast. Ubiquitous street dogs of every size and indeterminable breeds gathered near, but not too near. They hoped for morsels of food or a dollop of fat scrapings from grills as they heated up.

Julia had a soft spot for them and noted a brindle female with engorged teats among a small group sniffing around a garbage bin behind a taqueria. She'd have to alert the woman heading the San Amaro dog rescue in hopes she could find the litter. Spaying female street dogs was a major way to reduce the feral dog population, but gathering pups before they were of breeding age and finding homes for them was the next best option.

The songs of mockingbirds and phoebes greeting the morning flitted through her awareness as she ran and mingled with her usual mental preparations for the day ahead.

Today, she pored over the list of pickleball players and partygoers, revisiting what she could remember from the interviews she and Ricardo had done to date, reminding herself of points she wanted to document at the station.

Now, showered and clad in slacks and a patterned blouse, she was diligently making notes on a clean whiteboard in their war room. It was early, and most of the day-shift officers were not yet in the station. It was perfect for thinking through what she and Ricardo had learned so far in their investigation.

The first thing she did at the station, however, was to phone the woman who managed the dog rescue. She left a voice message giving her a description and location of the mother dog she'd seen on her run. Hopefully, she could find the litter.

Next, she moved on to work. She had neatly written the names of all the people at the courts on the day of the argument between Rudy and Clint Brayer. She'd put an asterisk beside each one who was also at the party. In a different color, she added names of spouses at the party but not pickleball. Finally, she'd put a check mark beside all from whom they had statements. She was grateful there were more names with check marks than without.

She gazed upon her handiwork, the tapestry of the names woven into their investigation. Getting the remaining statements was their priority. She took a picture of the board with her phone for later reference as she pondered what lies would be hidden among the truths they'd be told.

Next, she'd written some bullet points of the things they knew thus far. It was a short list.

- The victim had been hit from behind with a wooden pickleball paddle taken from a shed near the courts.
- He'd then been fist-beaten while supine, and finished off with a stab to the neck.
- He was not popular with his kids or others who met him here in San Amaro.
- The time of death was between eleven at night and two the next morning.
- The pathologist had found dirt and some other trace evidence in many of the wounds on his face.
- The dirt was with forensics for analysis.
- The killer was most probably five nine or taller and strong.
- Rudy most likely had been a philanderer.

It was a start, but they needed more information. Somewhere

among these clues lay hidden a secret yearning to be set free.

Under the heading Suspects, she had written several names. Norm Webster was top of the list because he'd been the last person anyone had seen with Rudy. Following Norm were the names of the victim's children. It was clear both had issues with their father. While Brianna didn't match the height criterion, Logan did, and she was close. Both were strong enough. Clint Brayer was on the list, too, because of the argument. Gregory Fletcher was there because his offhand remark implied he thought Rudy got what he deserved. Finally, to be thorough, she added Eduardo Escamilla. He'd found the body, and the procedure required he be considered a suspect.

She was just preparing to write motives beside her suspects when Ricardo pushed the conference-room door open with his bum, causing the door to bang against the wall and Julia to startle. His hands were full of huge cups of coffee and a bag of doughnuts. Julia laughed, shaking her head. "Really, Ricky! Doughnuts!"

"Yeah, Lucy, doughnuts. I happen to love doughnuts, even *before* I was a cop. You don't have to eat any. In fact, what makes you think I plan to share?" Ricardo asked jokingly.

They sat drinking their coffee reviewing Julia's whiteboard notes and planning the day's interviews. Among the doughnuts was a lone cinnamon bun; Ricardo placed it on a napkin and slid it across the table to Julia. It was her weakness. The smells of pungent cinnamon and sweet icing made her mouth water, and rolling her eyes and shaking her head at Ricardo, she succumbed to the temptation. He knew her so well.

As they savored their coffee and pastries, they mulled over various theories related to the case. It was still too early in the investigation to have any highly probable leads, but they both concurred the victim's cantankerous disposition and his unwavering pursuit of personal desires could serve as plausible motives for anyone who had experienced the brunt of either of these traits, or both.

As they finished their doughy breakfast, they'd mapped out the locations of the people from whom they still needed statements. The majority of them lived at The Oasis. The Oasis, however, was many thousand acres in size, more than fifty square miles. But while most of The Oasis was plotted out, just a fraction of the lots were in use. There were vast spaces with few and widely scattered homes. La Chica would be racking up the miles.

Breakfast and planning done, they headed to the lab. Vicente was busy with a set of test tubes and a jar of murky water. He was excited to see them.

"Hi, guys. I hear you were looking for me yesterday. I took a trip to Mexicali to buy this," he said, pointing to the test tubes and jar. "It's a soil-analysis kit. I couldn't find one in San Amaro, so figured I'd take a little trip for this one. Faster than waiting for one to be delivered. They're cheap but effective. I won't have any information for you until tomorrow afternoon, though. Then we'll see whether it tells us anything useful.

"Oh, but I did find something I hope will be helpful. When I analyzed the broken paddle, I found a small amount of some kind of leather stuck in a splinter. It's next on my list to figure out more about it, but I'm guessing the killer was wearing gloves. It's goldish-brown, fairly heavy, but supple. I'll see what, if anything, I can learn from it."

Ricardo responded, "Thanks, Vicente. We'll check in with you tomorrow. Of course, if you find anything else for us in the meantime, just give me a call."

When they returned to their war room, Julia asked Ricardo whether the worker, Eduardo Escamilla, had been wearing work gloves. Ricardo said he wasn't, and there hadn't been any around the shed. But he did remember the man's hands were thickly calloused, though his knuckles were not abraded. Also, Eduardo hadn't gotten to work until six in the morning, and according to the security logs, hadn't been at The Oasis between three the previous afternoon until his early-morning arrival. His alibi was solid.

Julia put a line through his name as a suspect.

Tiffany and Todd had started going to the pickleball courts about ten thirty, after most of the league players had left, and were meeting up with Logan and Brianna. Tiffany had played pickleball a couple of times back home but still considered herself a beginner. Todd had not played before this trip to San Amaro but was athletic, and he'd played some tennis.

The Stephanetti kids were enjoying sharing their favorite sport with their new friends. The T Team, as Brianna had dubbed them, were gaining skills for the game quickly under the tutelage of their friends.

It dawned on Logan he enjoyed watching the new players. He found himself analyzing their actions to determine what wasn't working well, and offering tips and suggestions. His ideas seemed to make a big difference in their play. He wondered to himself whether this might be a possible source of income when he was not playing competitively. Now his dad was no longer on the scene, he was reevaluating whether he liked playing professionally.

Today, before they started playing games, Logan led them through a warm-up exercise in which they all stood in the kitchen and tried to hit the ball back and forth without letting it bounce. Todd conveyed his concern about acquiring the bad habit of hitting the ball in the air while standing in the kitchen. Logan explained the exercise was to help them get better at the fast play just behind the kitchen. Beginners often found they couldn't keep up because the ball seemed to be coming so fast it was impossible to hit.

When the exercise was finished and they started a game, both Todd and Tiffany were shocked at how much better they were at getting those fast shots. They'd been desensitized to the speed by being so close to the net. When they stepped back a few feet to normal playing position, the balls seemed slower, and they hit them far more often.

"It's awesome of you to spend time teaching us this game. It's so much fun—I just love it—but aren't we keeping you from getting ready for the Palm Springs tournament?" Tiffany asked as they finished a game and grabbed some water.

"I'm having a blast playing with you guys. And, to be honest, I enjoy this more than getting ready for a competition. It's a good thing Dad isn't here to hear me say that," Logan said and laughed. Then he realized how it might have sounded. Quickly he explained. "I didn't mean it to sound as if I'm glad he's dead. All I meant is that I enjoy playing just for fun sometimes. I haven't been able to for a few years. Who is ready for another game? How about boys against the girls?"

Chapter Nineteen

By lunchtime, Julia and Ricardo had spoken with half the people remaining on their list and covered the north end of the ranch. Those who had been at the courts the day of the argument between Rudy and Clint all told much the same story, and nothing new was added to the detectives' knowledge.

The wife of the league president, Anne Brayer, a tall, athletic-looking woman, told them she'd seen a man walking toward the pickleball courts while she was stowing her Crock-Pot in the trunk of their car in preparation for dragging her husband home after the party. She couldn't identify the man except to say that he seemed tall and was carrying a light-colored jacket. She thought it must have been close to eleven thirty.

The description sounded like Rudy Stephanetti, as he'd been wearing a beige sports jacket at the party. The time didn't match with what they'd heard from others, though. Julia made notes of the time discrepancy and to ask the hostesses whether they remembered what time the Brayers left.

She also remembered Dean McLean saying he took a walk on the beach in their current window of death and made another note to check whether anyone living in the condos had seen him out walking, or anyone else, for that matter.

Ricardo, scanning photos of all the information they'd collected on their whiteboards, shook his head and grumbled about how hard it was to keep everyone's movements straight in his head. Julia concurred, and they decided it would help to develop a timeline of what everyone at the party was doing during their current time-of-death window.

Back at the station, Ana Maria Verde was just leaving a report in Julia's inbox as she and Ricardo entered. Upon seeing Julia, she waited by the desk to give her a verbal update. Ana Maria knew Julia was dyslexic. A verbal report would help her friend greatly when she got time to read the written version.

Julia was neither embarrassed nor apologetic about her reading disability. To her mind, it was simply important for those with whom she worked to know the best methods to communicate with her. Julia suggested Ana Maria grab her lunch and join Ricardo and her in their war room to update them on what she'd learned from her Facebook research.

Ana Maria began by explaining her process since it was news to Ricardo. First, she'd created a Facebook ID under the name of Maria Green and used it to join the various groups Julia had recommended. Because she didn't read English, there had been much use made of the station's translation software so she could correctly respond to the groups, which used questionnaires to gather information on potential new members before allowing them into the group. She was still awaiting entry into the local pickleball group, but she'd been admitted to all the others within an hour or two of submitting her requests. For Ricardo's benefit, she named the groups Julia had suggested she join.

As Julia had asked, she'd scanned the groups' posts looking for several relevant key words, mainly the victim's name, names of all the players and party attendees, the words *murder*, *death*, *pickleball*, and others Julia had provided. There were hundreds of posts meeting the criteria. All had been copied into a file and run through the translator so Ana Maria could read them in Spanish and compile her report.

Most of the posts were different versions of being awestruck at a murder being committed in their small community. At first, there was speculation about who had been killed, but fairly quickly, it was clear they heard Rudy was the victim. Some were curious and concerned about how and why such a thing had occurred.

The rumormongers put forth names of potential murderers, everyone from family members to a madman who wandered in from the beach. There was an abundance of comments about how unpleasant the victim had been to the pickleball players, his son, and Clint Brayer in particular. A few took angry sentiment further with thoughts fringing on the he-deserved-what-he-got theme.

In addition to the original posts in English and the raw translated posts, Ana Maria provided a summary list of names of all the posters categorized by the tenor of their posts: concerned, speculative, accusatory, and inflammatory. Only two names appeared under the last category. One was a name Julia had come across before and for much the same reason. Tony Ranelli.

Julia shook her head when she read his name and explained her reaction to her colleagues. "Tony Ranelli briefly dated Stella Monroe a couple of years ago. I think their split-up was acrimonious, at least as far as Ranelli was concerned. When Stella disappeared, I interviewed him as a person of interest. I found him abrasive, arrogant, and misogynistic. He didn't have any useful information at the time.

"I sense Mr. Ranelli tends to use Facebook as a platform to disparage people, relishing the anonymity it provides him. He isn't a pickleball player and he wasn't at the party the night Rudy was murdered, so I doubt he has any inside knowledge. I'll talk with him, later, and this time you're coming with me, Ricardo. I suspect he won't dare to be as nasty with a man around."

The other person in the inflammatory category was Wolfe Wagner, one of the pickleball players. He hadn't been at the party, but his comments on Facebook boldly stated he thought Rudy got what he deserved. From the brief conversation she'd had with him between pickleball games the previous morning, Julia had the impression he was a curmudgeon who found pleasure in finding the worst in people. The tone of his Facebook posts supported her conclusion. She knew they would have to speak with him again, soon.

The three discussed the contents of Ana Maria's report and developed a few questions for some of the posters. Julia and Ricardo thanked Ana Maria for her report, and Julia asked her to keep watching Facebook and compiling the posts. They planned to meet again the next day.

Julia was disturbed by one post, but she couldn't put her finger on why. It wasn't incendiary and didn't provide any new information. Still, there was something about it bothering her. She wanted to find the post in its original form. Translations occasionally used words that could have a slightly different meaning from the intended one. Reading the post in the original English might help her figure out what was troubling her. Maybe tonight at home she'd have time.

Chapter Twenty

Julia checked her voicemail and was surprised to have a message from Stella Monroe. They'd spoken the day before, and Stella didn't have any helpful information about the murder. Perhaps she'd remembered something. Julia was curious as she dialed Stella's number.

"Hi, Stella, it's Detective Sergeant Garcia. Do you have some information about the murder?"

"Oh goodness, I'm sorry, you must be so busy with the case right now. No, this is something completely unrelated and not even a police matter. I should have been clearer in my message. Pippa and I would like to chat with you, when you're not busy solving a murder, about a charity we're starting to help people—women and children primarily—who are caught in human trafficking in this area.

"My birth mother died a couple of months ago and, as you know, my inheritance is large. After my experience of being held captive, and knowing about the poor woman who died instead of me . . . ." Stella's voice faded.

Julia knew all too well the situation prompting Stella to start a charity with her inheritance, but before she could interject, Stella continued.

"This is not the time to talk with you about my charity. Sorry, I should have been more sensitive to your work situation. But, when you do have some time, would you be willing to talk with Pippa and me about this?"

Julia's reply came immediately. "I would be honored to talk with you both. As you noted, I'm busy right now, but how about I give you a call when things are a bit calmer at work?"

"Oh, yes! Wonderful! And I'm so sorry to have bothered you right now. I wasn't thinking." Stella rang off.

Julia had phoned the home of Wolfe Wagner and spoken briefly with his wife. Based on her suggestion, Julia and Ricardo had just entered the San Amaro Craft Brewery. After letting their eyes adjust for a moment from the bright sunlight outside, they spotted Wolfe on a stool at the long bar facing a row of about thirty tap handles. Above the taps on a chalkboard were written the names of all the beers available. Ricardo was curious how the Habanero Pale Ale tasted, but of course, he wouldn't be finding out today.

The inside space housed a row of shiny stainless-steel fermenting vats along one wall and several TVs, each showing a different station and currently playing funny cat videos, a soccer game, and off-road racing. There were several booths on the wall opposite the bar and a few mismatched tables in the space between. Through a swinging door on the east wall, Julia could see an outside seating area. Beyond it was a small open and currently vacant expanse of desert ending at the beach and the sea. Inside, there were about twenty patrons mostly sitting at tables, and several were playing cribbage.

Wolfe sat alone at the bar. He was a big man, with broad shoulders and carrying extra weight in a protruding stomach Julia clocked as a beer belly. She smiled to herself. Her insight was not a great act of detection, given their location.

The man they approached had thinning gray hair in a ring around his bald crown. The beer mug in front of him was a quarter full of a very dark brew. The logo on the back of his shirt showed a curled rattlesnake with "Baja Rattlers" in a font more fitting for a horror film, if the dripping paint or blood on the letters was any indicator.

"Mr. Wagner," Julia said to get his attention. "We have a couple of more questions for you. Would you care to move to a booth where we can talk more privately?"

"Nope," he replied brusquely.

"Fine, we can do it here." Julia sat on the man's right while Ricardo took the stool to his left. "You made some provocative remarks on Facebook about the murder victim, Rudy Stephanetti. Can you please explain what you meant by 'seemed like a fitting end for the bastard'?" she asked, reading the quote directly from a printed copy of one of his posts.

"Yeah, the guy was a dick. League play hours are posted with 'members only' in bold." He made air quotes with his meaty fingers, which Julia thought was an incongruous action for such a crusty fellow. "Our president was friendly when he asked the guy to leave, and the fuckhead just started yelling at him. So, I'm not surprised somebody offed him." His voice sounded as if it were a rumbling engine.

Julia couldn't help noticing the man's hands were abraded with several of his knuckles just starting to scab. Ricardo cast her a glance indicating he'd noticed the same thing. "You weren't at the pickleball potluck two days ago, were you?" Julia asked in a pleasant tone.

"Hell no. I'm not much for parties."

"Where were you between eleven p.m. and two a.m. that night?"

"I was at home in bed . . . with my wife, and since I'm sure it'll be your next question . . . you can ask her," he said and finished his remaining beer.

One of the young Mexican men serving behind the bar placed a full mug in front of Wolfe and removed the empty one. Julia hadn't noticed a signal between the two and surmised Wolfe was a regular, with specific habits, well known to the staff. "We will. How did you hurt your hands, Mr. Wagner?" Julia asked.

The man held his hands in front of his face and looked at them, back and front, as though he had no idea what she was talking about. "Shit. They're pretty beat up, aren't they? I'm a mechanic. I work on off-road rigs. They look like this all the time. Why? Was the prick beaten up?"

"Do you wear work gloves, Mr. Wagner?" Julia asked, ignoring his question.

"Nope. They just get in the way. I need to be able to feel what I'm working on. So he was beaten by someone wearing gloves. Huh!" Wolfe snorted, then returned to his previous thought. "Somebody must have been pissed at him, eh?"

Again, Julia did not respond to his questions but personally agreed, indeed, someone must have been in a rage. "Okay, that's good for now, Mr. Wagner. I recommend you keep your Facebook posts less volatile in the future. Thanks for your time."

Back in La Chica, Julia called Mrs. Wagner and asked her whether Wolfe had been out of the house at all two nights ago. She learned Wolfe had been out most of the afternoon, at the brewery, and returned home at five thirty for dinner. After dinner, he'd gone out to his garage and worked on a friend's sand rail for a couple of hours, after which they'd watched a show on TV and gone to bed.

She admitted she could hear him trying to start the engine every few minutes, so she was pretty sure he hadn't gone anywhere. She also confirmed his hands were usually scraped and rough because he didn't wear gloves when working on a vehicle.

"He didn't go out later in the evening, did he?" Julia asked.

"I don't think so. We both sleep with earplugs and take a sleeping pill at bedtime. We both snore," she explained. "Still, I think I'd be aware of him getting out of bed, dressing, and going out."

"It's a pretty weak alibi," Ricardo said when they were back in Julia's car and he'd been updated on the call.

"True," Julia said hesitantly. "But how would he have known Rudy would be at the potluck?"

Ricardo responded, "Good question. I don't know, but I still think we put him on the suspect list. Maybe we can find a neighbor who saw him driving from his home in our time-of-death window. When he talked about the victim, he cursed graphically. And his hands look as if he's been in a fight recently."

"I think he's just rough with his language all the time and free with his opinions. If he drinks here every day for a few hours and then works on engines, I can see how his hands could easily get pretty roughed up. But I don't disagree with putting him on the suspect list."

They had six more couples to speak with and only a half hour left in their workday. They headed to the forensics lab hoping to learn something new to move their case forward.

Chapter Twenty-One

As the detectives entered the lab, Luis was knocking on the door of Inspector Martinez's office. Javier had left the station immediately after they dropped the keys to the cruisers they had been using for their speed trap. Part of Luis still thought it was wrong spying on his partner but dutifully entered the office to give the inspector an update on his observations of Javier ripping off gringos caught by the radar gun.

Vicente was peering intently into a microscope when they entered the tiny lab. Ricardo cleared his throat in hopes of not startling the man. It didn't work. Vicente jerked his head away from the scope and turned to them with his brown eyes slightly widened, then laughed at himself for his reaction. "Hi, guys. I don't get many visitors here. Can you tell? Come on in."

They chatted briefly about how Vicente was settling into San Amaro and his new job and the health of his grandfather, which they learned, sadly, was deteriorating. Finally, Ricardo asked, "Have you got anything for us?"

"Maybe. The soil samples I tested contained fertilizer. It was six percent nitrogen, twenty percent phosphorus, and twenty percent potassium. I did some research on the mixture, and it seems to be a pretty common fertilizer to use in starting flowering plants and grass. The dirt itself was half high-quality potting soil and half sand. But not the ubiquitous sand here. This sand contained hardly any salt.

"For comparison, I grabbed sand samples from behind the

station and my place, which is back toward the mountains a few miles, and both of them contained large amounts of salt. From the sea, you know? Does that information help in any way?" Vicente finished his feedback and handed Ricardo the written report.

Julia answered, "Well, we can check with Adriana at her nursery and see whether she can give us any additional information about it. Hers is the best place in town to get plants and all the stuff people use on their plants. She might shed some light on that blend of fertilizer, sand, and soil."

"Yeah, it's worth a try. Her place is a couple of minutes from here. Let's see what we can learn," Ricardo said.

Vicente continued. "I haven't got anything back on the piece of leather, but I expect it will take a few more days. I don't have the equipment to properly analyze it, so I had to send it to Mexicali, and they are pretty backlogged. I asked them to rush it, but you know how it goes."

"Yep, we sure do. Thanks for getting the soil analysis done so quickly," Ricardo said.

This time, Ricardo offered to take them in his old Chevy truck. It was a beaten-up, single-cab vehicle, so did not allow any storage space in the cab. La Chica's lockable trunk was essential for keeping evidence secure and storing evidence bags, disposable nitrile gloves, and other necessities of a detective, and, therefore what they usually used. Ricardo figured for a quick trip to the nursery, the truck would suffice. Plus, he had an ulterior motive.

The nursery was on a corner lot on the main road heading south out of town. A dirt parking lot fronted the place, and Ricardo pulled his truck in between a late-model SUV and an ATV. The latter had a red milk crate duct-taped between the front fenders and stuffed with trays of flowers. He smiled to himself at the odd array of vehicles the residents of San Amaro used to get around town.

Behind the fence separating the parking area from the nursery, plants of every size and color sat in pots on the ground, in trays on tables, and toward the back of the property in a large greenhouse. Off to the left was a section dedicated to cacti of all shapes and sizes. Ricardo was relieved to see something he could identify and marveled at the myriad kinds of plants on display.

Julia knew Adriana fairly well. They had gone through school together from grade school to high school. They weren't bosom buddies but were well acquainted. She took the lead. "*Hola,* Adriana. *¿Qué tal?*" After a few minutes of general conversation, as is the Mexican way, Julia moved on to the purpose of their visit. After explaining the soil-sample results they'd received from Vicente, she asked what, if anything, Adriana could tell them about the findings.

"Your analysis guy was right, that fertilizer has a variety of general uses. So, on its own, it doesn't tell me much, but the soil and sand ratio plus the fertilizer does. It's what we recommend to anyone who buys frangipani or plumeria, as it's called in English, from us. It works the best here. Frangipani isn't hard to grow, once it's started, but the stuff you're talking about is excellent to get new plants going."

Julia's gardening knowledge was limited, to say the least. In the yard housing her casita and the home of her grandparents, they didn't have anything as exotic as frangipani. Julia was sure she couldn't identify one. She admitted as much to Adriana, and Ricardo echoed her confession. Adriana walked them to the back of the nursery and showed them a tree about eight feet tall with a sturdy trunk and a rounded canopy. Ricardo admitted it just looked like an ordinary tree.

Adriana took them into a greenhouse at the back of the property and showed them a smaller frangipani tree that was just beginning to bloom. Clusters of delicately colored yellow with pink-edged petals in a pinwheel formation popped from the little tree. As Julia stepped closer, she caught a fruity aroma from the flowers. The fragrance was pleasant, and the flowers were beautiful. She could see the appeal. Andriana explained that soon all the frangipani trees would start blossoming and stay in bloom for about seven or eight months.

"How many do you sell?" Julia asked.

"They are fairly expensive. So, we don't sell many. Maybe ten to twenty a year. The thing is, when treated properly, they grow well from cuttings. So most people in this area get cuttings from someone else's tree and start their own rather than buying them from us. We mostly sell plumeria to landscape companies." Seeing Julia and Ricardo's crestfallen faces, she provided some hope.

"There is a group of expats in town focused entirely on frangipani. They have regular meetings, share cuttings, and they even do tours of one another's yards to admire their plants. You see, it comes in a wide variety of colors from solid white to ones like this with multiple colors. I can give you the schedule of their meetings and the leader's name if it would be of any use to you."

Julia took the proffered information, and they thanked Adriana. Back in the pickup truck, Ricardo suggested they grab some dinner at his favorite food stand so they could talk about what they'd just learned.

Julia was torn. She liked Ricardo, but she loved her job. Since female police officers in Mexico were mostly considered a joke by their male counterparts, often the closest they got to serious policing was searching female arrestees or accompanying male officers to domestic disputes to assist women victims. Julia knew she was uncommonly fortunate to be doing real police work, to have become a detective. Dating another cop held the real possibility of undoing her hard-earned credibility.

Ricardo knew the score. They had talked about it before. He was respectful of her ambition, her abilities, and her fears. As with most men, though, he heard "no" and interpreted it as "not right now," so tested the waters from time to time. Julia considered all these things before agreeing to have a taco and a beer with him. *We are off duty and in plain clothes,* she considered, *and it is just a taco.*

Over dinner, Julia read aloud the Plumeria Club newsletter Adriana had given them, which was in English, and learned the next meeting was in two days. Reading aloud was not something Julia enjoyed. Being dyslexic caused her to stumble over words occasionally, more so when mentally translating from English to Spanish. If Ricardo noticed, he was gentlemanly enough not to show it.

They decided they would make an appearance at the plumeria meeting and see what they could learn. "Perhaps one of the suspects on our current list will be there," Ricardo said.

"Oh!" Julia exclaimed, and she began to flip rapidly through her notebook a couple of times. When she couldn't find any notes about the slight memory haunting her, she asked Ricardo. "Do you remember one of the men we've interviewed mentioned something about plumeria?" she asked.

Ricardo scrunched his eyes closed and scratched his head, thinking. "No. It's not a word I remember hearing before today at the nursery. Do you?"

"I can't remember who it was, but I think it might have been Norm Webster. If he's at the meeting, it will give us one more piece of evidence against him."

Chapter Twenty-Two

Over the phone, Jeremy Kronberg told Julia he and his wife had been at the party, but not at pickleball the day Clint and Rudy argued. Still, he replied, he and his wife, Lily, were happy to speak with Julia and Ricardo. So, the detectives drove to The Oasis to start their day.

Baja Highway Five bisects The Oasis with the majority of the thirty-five thousand acres on the mountain, or west, side of the highway. The portion on the east side is home to the golf course, pickleball courts, restaurants, homes, and several small swimming pools, one for each group of condos.

The Kronbergs' home was on the south fence of the east side of The Oasis. It was a rare two-story home and was elegant in its design. A beautiful ironwork staircase wound from the doors of the main floor up and around the side of the home to a second-level balcony and from there to a rooftop deck.

The landscaping was simple with groups of date palms clustered strategically around the property. The driveway and sidewalk were paved with locally made, multicolored brick, giving an inviting warmth to the front entrance.

Jeremy, a tall, lean, Scandinavian-looking man in his mid-sixties, invited them in, taking them through a formal foyer with marble floors and another wrought iron staircase leading to the second level and into a well-lived-in, comfortable living room. While the entrance and foyer were formal and somewhat austere, this room was the heart of their living space. Overstuffed armchairs in a bright floral pattern and a large L-shaped couch in soft browns promised comfort and made good on its pledge.

Lily entered from the kitchen as Ricardo and Julia were led in by her husband. She, too, had the high cheekbones and aquiline nose of a northern European. Both were blond, though Jeremy's hair was transitioning to white while Lily's was not. Julia couldn't say whether her color was natural, but if it wasn't, the dye job was a good one. Both were tall. Lily looked about five ten, and Jeremy was a few inches taller.

Once seated, with coffee and homemade cookies, Julia checked the photo she'd taken of the whiteboard on which she'd made all their notes the previous day. She remembered neither of the Kronbergs had been at pickleball either the day Rudy's body was discovered or the next day, when she and Ricardo questioned many of the players. She'd start there.

It turned out that neither Jeremy nor Lily was as avid a player as most of the people with whom the detectives had spoken. The Kronbergs fit pickleball in around their other activities of golf, volunteering, playing Mexican Train, and poker. They attended the pickleball party with a group of pickleballers with whom they also regularly played Mexican Train. They and their friends stayed in an upstairs seating area with an outside balcony with a group of their closest friends. The two officers were previously unaware of the group upstairs.

"Did you see Rudy Stephanetti at the party?" Julia asked.

"We never met him officially, but I saw him standing with a group of guys when I got Lily and me some snacks and refilled our wineglasses. And, I met his wife then and his kids upstairs. The young people were having their party across the hall from the upstairs sitting area and balcony," Jeremy answered redundantly.

"I didn't meet him, either," Lily said, "or his wife. The kids, well, they just said a generic hi to us all when they headed downstairs to get food. Oh, and we saw the son when he left."

"Did you happen to notice what time that was?" Julia asked.

"It was about fifteen minutes before Jeremy and I headed home, so maybe about quarter to eleven or eleven."

"So, neither of you interacted with Mr. Stephanetti at the party at all?"

Lily shook her head, but Jeremy surprised Julia and Ricardo by saying, "No, but we saw him from the balcony when he was smoking with another guy."

"His name is Norm Webster, honey." Lily supplied the name.

"Okay. Well, Norm smoked for a few minutes with the guy who got killed before going back inside," Jeremy said.

"And did you see what Mr. Stephanetti did?" Julia asked, hopefully.

"He finished his cigar and stood looking at the sea for a few minutes and then left. I figured he was going home. He walked to the end of the block and turned to go toward the condos farther from the beach, behind Edie and Suzanne's," Jeremy said.

"Do you know what time that was?"

"Well, it was just before we left. So, likely within the time frame Lily just mentioned."

Julia continued. "Seems as if you had an excellent view of what was going on. Did you see anyone else leaving the party?"

Jeremy answered. "There were a bunch of people who left in the fifteen minutes before we did. They all got in their cars and drove away. I don't know all their names, though. Oh, and there was a guy who left on foot about the time Rudy and Norm were on the front steps. I don't know him. Do you remember the guy in the Hawaiian shirt and jeans, Lil? Do you know his name?"

"I remember the person you mean, but I don't know him, either. He headed toward the beach, but there's a bit of a drop-off there, and I didn't see him once he trotted down the slope," Lily said. "Right after, I headed downstairs to get the platter I brought for my deviled eggs and say goodbye to Suzanne and Edie."

After a quick burst of Spanish from Ricardo, Julia asked, "When you drove away from the party, did you leave the condos by the road going past the courts?"

"No," Jeremy said. "Because we live here, on the south side of the golf course, we're on the opposite edge of The Oasis from the courts and the condos, so we drove the other way."

"Did you see any of the cars head toward the road that goes past the courts?" Julia asked.

"Yes, but I couldn't tell you whose cars, I'm afraid. You're better with that sort of thing than me, honey. Do you remember?" Lily asked.

"Honestly, I wasn't paying much attention. But, now you ask, I remember seeing Jeep Wrangler brake lights come on at the turn to that road. But I couldn't see anything else. It's so dark here at night I couldn't tell you what color it was," Jeremy said.

"And you could identify the vehicle as a Wrangler solely by the taillights?"

"Yes, they are unique, square," Jeremy said.

"How many Wranglers were there the night of the party?"

"Probably two or three, just guessing. So many people here drive them. But I couldn't tell you whose."

"Well, thank you. Is there anything else you think would help our investigation?" Ricardo, familiar with Julia's interview-closing phrase, gathered himself up.

"Can't think of anything," Jeremy said. Lily shook her head and stood to show them out.

Their next stop was Suzanne and Edie's. Tiffany and Todd agreed to wait at the condo to talk with Julia and Ricardo before heading off on an adventure to see the giant cacti, the *cardóns*, a few miles south of San Amaro. Julia and Ricardo knew *los Gigantes,* the

Giants, well. Growing over five stories high, they are the largest cacti in the world and grow in Baja only.

Ricardo jumped at Tiffany's offer of coffee, remembering how delicious the last cup he'd had there had been. Julia declined. They had convened in the upper seating area with Todd and Tiffany. Julia realized this was the area where the Kronbergs and their group had spent the party and paid particular attention to the excellent view from the upper deck.

Todd took the lead in telling Julia and Ricardo about their party-in-a-party with Brianna and Logan. They had chatted and gotten to know one another and then started playing *Call of Duty* on Todd's Xbox. Limited by having just two controllers, they alternated players. Tiffany and Brianna spent more time talking than playing. They had all gone to get food at one point. Later in the evening, neither of them could remember when exactly, Logan had opened a fresh beer and spilled it all over himself. He admitted he couldn't stand wet clothes and had gone home to change.

"How long was he gone?"

Neither of them could remember, but Tiffany commented it seemed longer than she'd expected.

Julia queried Tiffany about the conversation Pippa had overheard while using the upstairs bathroom. According to the young woman, Brianna was fiercely opposed to her dad's vision of her future and had gone on and on about what a tyrant he was. She also mentioned Logan had chimed in with his agreement to his dad's iron rule of their household and ended by saying there was no way she'd let him control her life the way he did Logan's.

"Did Brianna leave the party at any time?" Julia asked.

"Not until their mom came and got them both to leave," Todd replied.

After a couple of more perfunctory questions, Julia and Ricardo thanked the pair and returned downstairs. Edie and Suzanne were just returning from pickleball, so Julia asked whether they remembered anyone other than Rudy wearing a light-colored jacket at the party.

Edie laughed and answered. "No one other than Rudy was wearing a jacket. All we retired folks dress far more casually."

Julia next asked whether they remembered anyone wearing a Hawaiian shirt and Edie was able to list several people who had, saying they were the dressed-up version of T-shirts and shorts many people wore for socializing. The list included Dean McLean, Andy Stevens, Logan, and one of the women. While not a button-up shirt, Norm had been wearing a T-shirt silk-screened to look like a Hawaiian shirt.

"With regard to Logan, was the Hawaiian shirt what he was wearing when he arrived, or after he went home to change," Julia asked.

"He left?" Both Edie and Suzanne asked simultaneously.

Julia explained about Logan spilling beer on himself and going home to change.

"It's what he was wearing when the kids came to get their snacks. I have no idea whether he changed before or after getting his food," Edie said.

"That's fine. Thanks. One other question," Julia said. "Does either of you remember when the Brayers left?"

"It was sometime between eleven and eleven thirty," Edie said. "As close as I can remember."

Julia and Ricardo thanked them and left.

Leaving The Oasis, Julia noticed the tents for the blues festival were erected and the stage was nearing completion. She wondered wistfully whether she'd get a chance to see any of the bands listed on the billboard. She recognized a couple of the names and would've loved to be able to catch even one of them for an hour.

On the drive back to the office, Julia brought her mind back to the case. Her voice carried a hint of frustration and determination. "There are so damned many people tangled in this case. Keeping track of everyone's movements is like trying to catch smoke. Once we're back at the office, we need to dive into the timeline and piece together the sequence of events. There's bound to be something hiding in the details."

Ricardo's response was laced with urgency. "You're right. Let's scrutinize our notes. Maybe we can find cracks in someone's story. This case is turning into a spider's web, and we need to find the spider lurking at its center."

Julia was grateful she had been partnered with Ricardo. He treated her as an equal. She couldn't imagine having to work day-to-day with any of the other handful of detectives in the station. She got enough sexist and derogatory comments just from walking to her desk. At first, it had eroded her confidence, but her grandfather, the ex-comandante, had explained to her early in her career that to be accepted, she must do exceptional work.

She realized she wasn't going to change opinions forged from centuries of cultural sex bias. Most Mexican men showed animosity upon seeing women employed in professions or trades they deemed men's work. Those mores would not be easily changed. She had never gotten used to the bigoted, misogynistic jokes and comments. They still hurt. She had, however, realized if she were to succeed in her chosen career, she had to figure out a way to ignore them. The verbal assaults continued, but she gradually learned to let them slide by without letting them undermine her confidence.

Chapter Twenty-Three

Julia stopped into Inspector Detective Martinez's office over her lunch break and thanked him for arranging to have Ana Marie Verde help her with the Facebook analysis. "She's helping," she'd told her boss.

This afternoon, she had a new request. She asked Martinez whether it would be possible to get a small team of constables to do a house-to-house canvass of the condos at The Oasis. When faced with his concern about the language issue for the English-only speakers they would encounter, she was ready with a solution.

She showed him some five-by-seven-inch cards she'd prepared the previous evening at home. In large print on each card, she'd written the same message: "Did you see anyone walking in the vicinity of your condo between ten thirty and two in the morning on the night of February 24?" At the bottom of the card in the left corner was the word *YES* and in the right, *NO*.

Julia explained her idea was to have the constables do the canvass and gather the names and phone numbers of any condo residents who pointed to *YES*. On the back of each card was written: "An English-speaking officer will be in contact with you soon."

Martinez promised he'd see what he could do. Once again he was impressed by her ingenuity.

Next, she headed to the forensics lab to see whether Vicente had anything new information on their case. She also wanted to tell him his soil analysis had provided a possible lead she and Ricardo would be checking out in a couple of days.

Vicente wasn't in the lab, but she noticed the pickleball paddle handle used to dispatch their victim hanging in a tent made from a sheet of clear plastic and some PVC pipe. Also inside the tent was a candle with a small tray suspended over it. Beside the tent was a partial tube of Super Glue.

Julia had read about cyanoacrylate, aka Super Glue, fuming as a method of finding latent fingerprints on certain surfaces and was curious to know whether Vicente would find anything more of value on the handle. She'd check in with him later to learn the results.

Ricardo, who had taken off in his rusty pickup truck a bit before their lunch break, was climbing the stairs to the war room as she returned there herself. He wasn't his usual happy-go-lucky self. "What's up, Ricky? You look miserable," she said.

"Dentisth, root canal," he said with a slur, lifting a hand to his jaw.

"Oh, poor baby!" Julia said in her most sarcastic voice. "Want to work on our timeline, then? Probably best not to inflict your grumpy puss on the remaining party attendees we have to interview.

Ricardo nodded his head, which caused him to cradle his jaw again.

Julia wasn't sure how this was going to work with Ricardo reading his notes and giving her the details for the timeline with his current state of numb-face slurring, but she was willing to try it. His handwriting was almost illegible, so no point in having him scribble on the board. Plus it appeared movement exacerbated his discomfort. Despite her sarcasm, she was not unmoved by this apparent pain.

By midafternoon, they had a timeline drawn across the bottom of several whiteboards, extending from one to the next. It included the coming and going times of all the people for whom they had the information. Also shown were the time-of-death window as a red line beneath the main black timeline, and events such as

Pippa's overhearing Brianna's conversation with Tiffany and Norm and Rudy's migration to first the couch and then outside.

They both sat for a few minutes in silence, seeing what new information they might be able to infer from the drawing. Ricardo's jaw had finally gone from a mix of numb and painful to just plain painful. Julia wanted to compare her notes on the timing of things with Ricardo's. After reading through her notes, she was able to add a couple of additional times, but Ricardo had captured the important points.

Ricardo's voice broke the silence, carrying a sense of gravity. "What the hell was Logan doing for so long? It's a five-minute walk from the party venue to their condo. And it damned well didn't take him close to an hour to change his clothes. Also, why did he even come back? His mom gathered him and Brianna to leave less than ten minutes after he got back to the party. Seems weird to me. There's some kind of deception going on."

Julia couldn't disagree.

"And why do you suppose Dean McLean didn't go back into the party when he returned from his walk? If that's actually where he was. I think it's odd he'd just go to the car and not at least tell Sandy where he was. More deception, don't you think?" She paused for a minute to flip through her notes, finally finding what she sought. "The people on the upstairs balcony did see him heading in the direction of the beach, though, so maybe his story is true. But it makes me wonder."

Dean McLean was added to their expanding list of suspects.

Realizing she hadn't had a chance to tell her partner about her plan to have a canvass of condo dwellers done by some constables Inspector Martinez selected to help them, she told him of her plan. "It should happen tomorrow and, hopefully, will give us some new insights," she said.

Looking at the list Julia had written of names of party attendees and pickleball players with all her asterisks and check marks, Ricardo noticed she'd updated it while he was gone. "Looks as if we have three remaining initial interviews to get. We can probably get them all done in what's left of the afternoon. Do you want to go do them now? I promise I'll try to leave my *grumpy-puss* temperament in the car," Ricardo said. "Or, I could stay here and try to call everyone to find out whether they drove a Jeep Wrangler to the party." Both of them laughed at the impossibility.

Just then Martinez knocked on the conference-room door and stuck his head in. "Do you have time to give me an update?"

Ricardo suggested he could do the update and Julia could do the calls about what vehicles people drove to the party. Hector agreed. Julia decided to make the calls from her desk downstairs.

Ricardo walked his boss through the new information they had just amassed on the whiteboards and their ever-lengthening list of suspects. Hector expressed encouragement for their work so far and their planned path forward.

"Have you formed any theories about what happened or how or why the killer committed the murder?" Hector asked.

"Well, no one but people who were at the party knew the Stephanettis were there. So, we are pretty sure the killer had to have been at the women's condo for the party. However, there is one man, Wolfe Wagner, who has made several angry and inflammatory remarks on Facebook about the victim. He wasn't at the party, though, so that seems to rule him out.

"There were two people from the party known to be out of the condo during the time-of-death window: Logan and Dean McLean," Ricardo said, pointing to the timeline. "The problem is, everyone at the party left during our current time-of-death window and potentially could have stopped at the courts to commit the crime.

"The difficulty is—how would anyone have known Rudy was at the courts unless someone followed him or drove past the courts when leaving and saw him there? We are hoping the canvass of the condos will give us some new information to go on. At this point, our main suspects continue to be Logan, Dean McLean, and Norm Webster."

Chapter Twenty-Four

Most of the officers of the San Amaro State Police had some English. Most Mexican schools teach it for at least a few years. None of them except Julia, however, was fluent. But the three constables selected to do the canvass of the condos all spoke enough English to introduce themselves to the condo occupants they would be querying with Julia's prepared five-by-seven cards and a clipboard on which to gather contact details.

They were dropped off at the condos at ten in the morning. Each carried a map of the condo campus with their area marked off with a red felt pen. Each also carried a couple of the five-by-seven cards matching the one Julia had shown Inspector Martinez and a stack of photocopied notes to be left at condos where the occupants were not home.

The notes asked the same question as the five-by-seven cards but indicated that if they had seen something, to call Julia. They provided her office number, at which they could leave a voicemail. With almost three hundred condos, the canvass was expected to take several hours, even though not all of the condos would be occupied. The squad car was scheduled to return to the drop-off spot at three that afternoon to retrieve the constables.

The layout of the condos was a rabbit warren, with many cul-de-sacs. The two-story buildings, each housing two to four condos, were arranged in pods or groups with most clusters having small pools for their residents. The exteriors were all painted in muted brown and beige tones with each cluster having a slightly different hue from those next to it. Fortunately, the numbering system, boldly emblazoned on each building, made it easy to differentiate the pods and helped the canvassers to stay in their assigned areas.

Julia and Ricardo were eager to see how many people the house-to-house interviews would uncover who had seen something the evening Rudy Stephanetti had been killed. Since they had hours to wait, they planned to finish their interviews in the interim.

First on their list was Glenn Wilburn. They had spoken with his wife, Rhonda, the previous morning at the courts. Not a pickleball player himself, Glenn had attended the party with his wife. Their home was on the mountain side of The Oasis.

Rather than a house, as the officers were expecting, they found at the Wilburns' address a huge motor home, parked under a ramada built of cinder-block pillars supporting corrugated metal roofing. Attached to the ramada was a small building, which they soon learned contained a kitchen, small sitting room, and bathroom; and nearby was an expansive brick patio and a three-car garage. Uncertain whether to knock on the door of the motor home or the building, Ricardo started toward the motor home.

Before he could knock, however, Glenn came from the garage and across the patio, saying he'd heard their car drive up. His T-shirt and shorts were covered in grease and oil smears. He was pulling off a pair of blackened rubber gloves as he rounded the corner of the ramada and shoved them into a rear pocket to shake hands with the police officers.

Both officers noticed the rough and broken skin on the man's knuckles. A brief look passed between them. Julia had spoken with his wife, earlier that morning, before they headed here, out to the back end of The Oasis, near the first low mountains in the chain separating San Amaro from the Pacific side of Baja. She had assured them he would be home and had alerted him to expect Julia and Ricardo's visit.

"Buenos dias, oficiales," he said in perfect Spanish, *"bienvenidos."*

Ricardo was hopeful and asked whether Mr. Wilburn would prefer to have the interview in Spanish. *Sí* was the reply, causing Ricardo to give a happy smile to Julia as they followed the man toward the motor home.

Glenn led them into the small building beside the ramada and pulled a ragged towel from a chest beside a large, well-used leather recliner. He spread it over the seat before he sat in his greasy clothes.

"Where did you learn Spanish?" Julia asked as they were getting situated.

"I was raised in Venezuela. My mom and dad both worked for Citgo in the States and had the chance to transfer to Maracaibo when I was three. They stayed there for ten years. So, when we moved back to the US, my Spanish was better than my English for a while."

"Well, we appreciate you taking the time to speak with us. It looks as if you are in the midst of a project of some sort," Ricardo said, glancing at the man's clothing.

"Oh, yeah. I'm rebuilding the carburetor in my sand rail. The engine is from a 1985 Mustang, and it's been getting harder and harder to start. I figured it was time. And, there's a poker run this weekend, so I want it running well for that. I usually do my car repairs when Rhonda is at pickleball. We head to the pool when she gets back so we can make the lunchtime water-volleyball games. We play every day."

No wonder he has a deep tan on his face and arms, but not on his legs, Julia thought.

"Is it the Holley four-barrel carb?" Ricardo asked, showing off his knowledge of Mustang engines. Getting a nod from the other man, he continued knowingly. "Ah, a project to keep you busy for a day or two."

Julia watched her partner and was reminded how good he was with people. He always found a personal level on which to reach them, and people warmed to him quickly.

As she observed him, she was aware of how well their interview styles complemented each other. She had an arsenal gathered from her degree in psychology. Ricardo's well-developed observation skills were allowing him to get a baseline on the man's nonverbal cues and speech patterns in a general conversation. He'd use the information to notice small changes and shifts in those patterns when he began the questioning.

She was impressed.

"Well, as you know, we're here about the murder of Rudy Stephanetti three nights ago. And, we wanted to ask you a few questions about your experience the night of the party." Glenn nodded his head again. "Did you meet him at the party?"

"I did. I spent more time with the upstairs group than with the guys in the living room, but I did stop by and chat with Clint for a few minutes when I was heading to the kitchen for more libations. I met Rudy then. He seemed okay to me. A career man, for sure. He was talking about his work while I was with that group. You know, we retired folks here don't talk much about our working life. It's behind us and not relevant here.

"No one cares whether you were an executive or a janitor, so it was weird to hear him boasting about his work prowess. To me, he seemed a bit of a misogynist, too, and I didn't care to be around him, so I headed back upstairs."

"Did you have any other interactions with him?" Ricardo asked.

"Yes. I popped out for a cigarette a couple of times through the night, and the second time I did, he was smoking a cigar, so I joined him for a minute while I lit up. I walked toward the beach while I smoked, so I didn't talk with him for long then. When I was coming back, Rudy was still alone on the steps. So, he and I chatted for a minute or two before I returned inside."

"What did you talk about? Did he give you any idea what he was planning to do when he finished his cigar?" Julia interjected a question. Ricardo just smiled at her. They were both interested in his answer.

"He talked about pickleball. He probably thought I played, which I don't. So, I wasn't listening closely, but he did say he thought he might check out the courts under the lights. He thought it might be good for his son to practice some night games while they were here," Glenn said.

"Did you see anyone else while you were outside? Or when you walked toward the beach?" Ricardo asked.

"Yeah, his son left the party and so did another guy, at almost the same time. Dean, I believe. I don't know him well, though his face is familiar. I probably met him at a previous potluck. Forgetting names seems to happen more these days," Glenn said with a shrug of his shoulders. "I didn't see anyone walking on the beach, though."

"Do you know what time it was when the two men left the party?" Ricardo and Julia asked almost simultaneously, causing both to smile.

"I don't wear a watch, so I don't, sorry. It was later in the evening, if it helps."

"Do you suppose Logan and Dean could have heard Mr. Stephanetti say he wanted to go to the pickleball courts?" Julia asked.

"Hmm. It's possible. I don't remember. Rudy might have already left by then, but I'm not sure," Glenn said, looking apologetic.

"When you left the party, did you drive out past the courts?" Ricardo asked.

"No, we didn't. We drove home the other way," Glenn said.

"How did your hands get roughed up?" Ricardo asked.

"Have you ever removed a carburetor from a sand rail? Whoever built mine managed to make it difficult to reach. I finally put on a pair of gloves in the hope they would save my knuckles, but the damage was already done. Would you like to have a look for yourself?" Glenn asked.

"Sure, I'd be interested in seeing it."

The two men left the room and were gone for a few minutes. Julia used the time to glance at the photos on a table behind the couch and to read over her notes from their interview to see whether she had anything she wanted to explore further. Nothing jumped out at her, from either her notes or the pictures.

When they came back into the room, Ricardo looked over at Julia and raised a querying eyebrow to ask whether she had any more questions. She took the cue. "Thank you for your time, Mr. Wilburn. You've been helpful. Is there anything else you think we should know for our investigation?"

"Yes, there was one thing. It may be nothing, or not. You've met my wife, Rhonda, right?" Glenn asked. Both officers nodded. Both officers retook their seats, and Julia pulled her notebook back out. "Well, then you know she is still an attractive woman. Plus she's younger than many of us old fogies here.

"Well, anyway, she told me on the drive home it seemed as if Rudy were coming on to her when they were both waiting for the bathroom partway through the evening. She mentioned he touched her shoulder and arm a couple of times and told her what a beautiful woman she was. Even asked her whether she'd care to join him for a cocktail the next day."

"And what did your wife do?" Ricardo asked.

"She told him to get stuffed and batted his hand away when he tried to escort her back to the kitchen. We are happily married, plus she doesn't tolerate chauvinism. She said he looked pretty miffed when he walked away from her. I don't think many people tell him no. We laughed about it on the way home."

"Did either of you leave your house after you got home after the party?" Julia asked.

"No. We didn't."

"Is your wife home now?" Ricardo asked. "We need to speak with her, too."

"No, she and a friend drove to Mexicali this morning to do some shopping. She should be home about four thirty."

"All right, then," Ricardo said, standing. "Thanks again for your time."

Glenn accompanied them as they headed toward their car. Julia noticed trees lining one side of their yard and, thinking they looked like frangipani, asked, "What type of trees are those? They're lovely."

"Honestly, I have no idea. They are green all year and give the yard a bit of shade. I don't know anything else about them," Glenn said.

Back in La Chica, Julia posited the Wilburns could easily have driven out past the courts and dispatched Rudy on their way home. "Perhaps Rhonda is a Plumeria Club member. If so, we've got two more people to add to the list of suspects. This is getting crazy. How are we going to reduce the list when each new bit of information seems to give someone else a motive?" she asked, almost to herself. "And why didn't Rhonda Wilburn tell us any of this when we talked with her at pickleball yesterday?"

Chapter Twenty-Five

The midafternoon sun shone brightly as Javier and Luis clambered down the rear, outside stairs of the police station, reflecting their mood. They'd been scheduled for patrol duty again today, but Inspector Detective Martinez had left word with the duty sergeant he wished to temporarily move the two to a different assignment. As they left the inspector's office, they each experienced a thrum of excitement. They had a case!

The wind was up, causing the Mexican flag on the police station to snap and creak to the rhythm of the breeze. It carried the surprisingly sweet scent of creosote bushes. Neither man noticed the wind, the wafting aroma, or the distant cawing of a crow. They had a case, and they were excited.

It was true Luis had worked the missing RZR case with Julia last year and Javier had worked the stolen restaurant equipment investigation a few months back, but as with all the cases they'd worked, both had been assigned to a sergeant who directly oversaw their work. This case was their responsibility alone. The detective inspector would be requesting regular reports, but they had the opportunity to show what they could do. Two constables, on their own.

It was an interesting case, too. Over the past three days, eight locals had come to the police station to report the theft of their comal, a large thick clay, plate-like disk used over a wood fire for heating tortillas and roasting chiles. In each case, the family had an outdoor cooking area from which the comal had been stolen. All the thefts had occurred overnight, and none of the people in their homes had heard anything. There didn't appear to be any pattern to the targeted homes. They were scattered all around the town.

There was not much to go on, but the two men had a file containing the police reports on each robbery, and they decided their best starting point would be to visit each location and speak directly with the owner about the family's stolen comal. They also decided to visit each location in the order in which the robbery reports had been filed. It might give them some insights into the person or people perpetrating the crimes.

Their first stop, therefore, was a small farm two or three miles south and west of downtown. The area comprised small holdings, two to five acres each, all facing the dirt road Luis and Javier explored. Most had a mix of vegetables and small livestock. Chickens wandered the ditches in front of most places. A few had a couple of goats or a cow or two. Horse manure was evident along the road, though they didn't see any horses in any of the fields. Finally, they reached their destination.

The property they entered was fenced entirely with aging forklift pallets nailed together and attached to regularly spaced fence posts. The pattern they created appeared random. Some pallets had their slats horizontal to the ground, some were vertical with no apparent plan, and many had broken or missing slats. It made Luis think of a person with crooked teeth.

The house was of unpainted cinder-block construction, small, but with a large veranda around two sides of the house. An outdoor cooking area had been constructed at one end of the overhanging eaves. A girl of about fifteen and her mother were just building a fire under the outdoor grate. They stopped upon seeing the police car enter their yard.

Luis explained why they were there, and the woman spoke with passion. She told them her comal was a wedding gift from her grandmother. She didn't want to have to buy a new one. Apart from having sentimental value, there was the cost, almost as much as her husband earned in two weeks. And, after years of use, it was perfectly seasoned.

When asked to describe it, she held her hands about twenty inches apart to indicate its diameter. She explained it had a small rim of green painted an inch from the edge and was deeply blackened on its slightly convex bottom. The top was a rosy color from the use of oil and heat on the natural clay.

While Luis was speaking with the woman, Javier took pictures of the yard, the location of the road, the outdoor cooker, and the doors and windows of the house. He noted the outdoor cooking area was visible from the road. The road, however, was not well traveled, most likely used solely by the people living on it. Luis asked whether the family had any regular deliveries or perhaps sold eggs, anything to cause outsiders to be in their yard, but the woman couldn't think of anyone or anything fitting those criteria.

While they drove to the next victim's location, they speculated on this type of theft. Virtually all Mexican families had a comal in their home or outside cooking area. Though the clay ones were still the most popular, metal ones and even electric comals were available. Why would anyone steal one, let alone eight? Yes, they were expensive, but if someone needed one, they would steal one, they theorized, not eight.

"Maybe it will become clearer after we've spoken with a few more people," Luis said as Javier maneuvered the car back over the bumpy, dusty road.

Karen Platz, the wife of Willie, had been at the pickleball potluck because, as she put it, she never missed a chance to party with friends. She struck Julia as vibrant and joyful. Unlike so many of the shorts-and-T-shirts American women Julia was used to dealing with in San Amaro, Karen was in full makeup. Her hair was perfectly coiffed, and she was elegantly attired in impeccable, neutral-colored linen slacks. Her deep purple raw silk blouse added a touch of regal flare. She practically bounced when she led them through to the well-appointed kitchen of their home.

A jug of homemade lemonade and a plate of cookies, freshly baked ginger snaps announced by a tantalizing aroma, awaited the detectives' arrival.

"I thought you might enjoy a little snack in the middle of your day. Please take more than one each, or I'll be offended," she said, in a bubbly soprano voice.

Once they were all settled with ice-cold glasses of lemonade and mouth-watering cookies, Julia began. "We want to ask you some questions about the pickleball party four nights ago, about the murder of Rudy Stephanetti."

"Sure, go ahead. What a terrible thing! I don't think I know anything helpful, but I'll certainly answer your questions. And I just have to say, your English is impressive. I wish I could learn Spanish, but my mind just doesn't seem to work in Spanish. It's kind of embarrassing to live here and not speak your beautiful language," Karen said, giggling. Julia wasn't sure whether her comment was meant to be humorous or whether this woman was just a bit spacey.

Ricardo wasn't catching what the woman said, but everything about her made him think she was what he'd heard called a trophy wife. She was not particularly young—he put her age in the early sixties—but she was beautifully presented. She had a blond helmet of perfectly coiffed hair, full makeup, a slim, yet curvaceous body, and might not be particularly bright.

"Do you play pickleball, Mrs. Platz?"

"Oh, no. And, you have to call me Karen. Everyone does. Mrs. Platz was Willie's first wife. And, mmm, no, I don't play pickleball. I do water aerobics, yoga, and Zumba. I don't care much for sports. I just want to keep fit. Actually, the main reason is I love my wardrobe and I don't want to outgrow it, if you know what I mean." There was a twinkle in her eye as if she were bringing Julia into a little secret. For a moment, Julia thought she was going to wink, too. And was relieved when she didn't.

"Did you meet Rudy Stephanetti at the party?"

"Oh, you bet. I made a point of talking with everyone there. I enjoy learning about people and hearing their stories. People seem to open up to me. Maybe I should have been an interviewer, like Barbara Walters, you know. I also talked with his wife and kids, but the kids didn't want any of us dinosaurs interrupting their private party. Though all they were doing was playing video games. Not much fun, if you ask me."

"Please tell me about your conversations with Rudy and his wife," Julia asked, trying to get the woman back on track.

"I talked with Gloria more. She's a lovely woman. A nurse. It's a hard job, you know. Anyway, she told me Rudy can be a handful sometimes, since he's often abrupt when he talks with people and he upsets them. I heard he had an argument at the pickleball games that morning. Gloria was embarrassed by it. She admitted she was afraid he was going to punch Clint Brayer for not letting them play together as they wanted. That wouldn't have been smart. Clint used to be a policeman, and he would certainly have made short work of Rudy. But it never came to that, thank goodness."

"Did Mrs. Stephanetti tell you anything else about her husband?" Julia asked quickly to stem the flow of this woman's chatter, then made a note of the fact Gloria seemed to believe Rudy could get physical when upset.

"Let me see," Karen said, cocking her head to one side and thinking for a few moments. Her perfect blond hair didn't move a millimeter. "Yes, she said the strangest thing. She said I might not want to find myself alone with him. What an odd thing to say, don't you think?"

"Did she say why? Or add anything more to the remark?" There was an eagerness in Julia's voice.

"Um, no. He came into the kitchen right then. I don't think he heard her, but she didn't say anything more to me about him," Karen said. "She went back to the other women in the kitchen.

"I started talking with Rudy then. He got some food and another glass of wine and started to head back into the living room. But I followed him, and we started chatting. He bragged about his kids. He seemed proud of them. I guess they're both accomplished pickleball players.

"He seemed nice enough to me at first, maybe a little bit flirtatious, which doesn't bother me like it does some women. I flirted back a bit with him. Willie knows I'm not seriously flirting, but then Rudy seemed to lose interest. And I sort of understood what Gloria meant about him being abrupt. As soon as he'd answered a couple of my questions about their stay in San Amaro, he told me he wanted to get back to the group of men. It kind of reminded me of an uncle of mine who had Asperger's. He, my uncle, I mean, got so frustrated when things didn't go the way he wanted, and sometimes he'd be downright rude."

Julia knew about Asperger's from her undergraduate studies. Rudy might have been on the spectrum. But was it in any way relevant to their case?

"What did Mr. Stephanetti say about their visit here?" Julia asked.

"Not much. He mentioned the pickleball courts were in good condition and the weather was nice."

"What else did you talk about with him?"

"Nothing. As I said, he wanted to get back to the men's group in the living room. It was kind of weird. At first, he seemed interested in talking with me, but then he appeared to lose interest. He just left me standing by a little alcove between the kitchen and living room. I didn't mind. He's one of those people who never asked you a question back. It's kind of hard to have a conversation that way."

"Did you see him or anyone else on the pickleball courts when you and your husband left the party?" Julia asked after a brief conversation with Ricardo.

"No, sorry, we left the other way."

"Thanks for your help, Karen. Is there anything else you think we should know that might help our investigation?"

"I don't know whether this is anything, but my friend Sandy was having an off night. She's kind of shy, but she and I usually have fun together at parties. She seemed sad or preoccupied. Maybe she and Dean were having trouble. All married couples do from time to time, don't they? But she didn't say anything to me about what was bothering her. Which seemed a bit unusual.

"Oh, but there was one other thing I noticed when I was getting ready to head upstairs to chat with the group up there. Gloria got a message on her phone. I heard the notification sound. It's the same one I use. She immediately skulked off to the bathroom, holding her phone as though she was going to make a call and wanted privacy. It was probably nothing," Karen said and cocked her head, and looked to the ceiling. "I can't think of anything else."

"The thing with Gloria and her phone is bugging me." Julia told Ricardo about how Gloria had received a message the day of Rudy's murder and had appeared to immediately hide the phone without looking to see who sent the message. "It was as though she knew who it was from and didn't want anyone else to see. Very secretive."

"Hmm. What if she hired someone to murder her husband?" Ricardo asked. "It sounds was as if he were a challenging person to live with. Maybe she'd had enough and figured taking care of the situation when in a foreign country would be a safe way to get rid of him."

Julia considered Ricardo's theory for some moments. "It is possible. But how would she connect with a killer-for-hire? She doesn't seem that resourceful. I'm not discounting the idea, though."

"Unless she found someone back in the States who followed them here to do the deal. It would explain how the killer knew Rudy was at the pickleball courts," Ricardo said, not willing to let his theory go yet.

"It's true. The killer would have had to know Rudy was going to the courts." Julia recounted the possibilities she was considering on her fingers. "Either by hearing him say he was going there, following him, or being told by someone else who knew or followed him. Let's keep the theory under consideration."

Chapter Twenty-Six

Ana Maria Verde impatiently awaited the return to the station of Julia and Ricardo. At forty-five, she was already a grandmother twice over. Her jet-black hair was starting to get a few streaks of gray. She normally wore it in a bun at her nape for work, but as was her habit when nervous or excited, she had undone and reformed the bun three times before Ricardo and Julia returned.

The Facebook posts about the murder were exploding across several of the local expat groups and in some interesting directions. She'd spent yesterday and all of this morning scraping and analyzing the recent relevant posts. Now that she had completed her report, she was sure the detectives would find some leads in her results. It was the end of her shift and she would have to get home to feed her family soon, but she decided to wait a few minutes more.

Family responsibilities were the number one reason women in policing in Mexico did not get more opportunities for advancement. The vast majority of Mexican men still maintain cooking, cleaning, and raising the kids is a woman's work, even when she has a job outside the home as well. It is a twofold problem. Husbands and boyfriends have those expectations, and male police officers also hold the same misogynistic idea. Therefore, they don't want to give women officers much responsibility because, they contend, the women will always choose their family responsibilities before those of their job as police. Unmarried and childless women officers, such as Julia, are a small minority.

Fortunately, Ricardo and Julia did not keep Ana Maria waiting too long.

The three convened in the war room to hear Ana Maria's findings from the last two days. As she expected, the two detectives were intrigued by what they learned. They both agreed it was time to make interviewing Tony Ranelli a priority the following day. And, in case there was any truth to the many theories being generated by Facebook posters, they would need to speak again with many of the people they'd already interviewed, starting with Gloria Stephanetti.

One person, using the name Che Guevara, posted a drone video of the crime scene shortly after the body had been removed. The post suggested the murder had been a decapitation. Finding the true identity of their videographer would be an important next step.

Given they had the Plumeria Club meeting to attend tomorrow, it was turning into a hectic day.

Almost as soon as Ana Maria had exited the war room, the team of canvassers from the condos entered, wanting to share the results of their questioning of everyone who had been home during their time knocking on doors. It gave Julia a sense their investigation was finally gaining traction. She was eager to hear what they'd learned.

Both Ricardo and Julia were delighted to learn some of the condos were owned or rented by Mexicans. San Amaro was a popular vacation spot for people from nearby Mexicali, two hours away, and for the large Mexican population living just across the border from Mexicali in Calexico and El Centro in the States. This meant the canvassers were able to interview about ten percent of the in-residence condo dwellers directly during the canvass.

Julia quickly realized she needed to add the information they were receiving directly to the timeline on the whiteboard, rather than wasting time taking notes first and later updating the board with people's movements. They also had the names and addresses of a few expats who indicated they had information, but no Spanish-language skills.

She asked the three canvassers whether they'd spoken with anyone who had mentioned having or displaying a drone in their condo. A constable who looked too young to shave informed them one of the condos he canvassed was being rented by a family from Mexicali. They'd told the constable they weren't there on February 24, but two teenage boys from the family were flying a drone. The constable had not noted the condo number nor taken the name of the person with whom he'd spoken because, as he said, they hadn't been in San Amaro at the time of the murder. Julia sent the young man back to The Oasis to see whether he could remember which condo number and name of the family.

As Julia and Ricardo prepared to depart from the station, their heads were filled with a wealth of newfound information begging for validation from both the party hostesses and the revelers. An elusive lead had emerged, intertwined with the mysterious drone flyer. The horizon held two or three days of relentless activity for the duo, days packed with tension, brimming with secrets, and pregnant with the unknown.

Chapter Twenty-Seven

Shortly after ten, La Chica rolled into the parking lot across from the building used for small group meetings at The Oasis. Julia and Ricardo had spent their first couple of hours planning a strategy for their next round of interviews before heading to the Plumeria Club meeting. About a dozen other cars were in the lot. One of them Julia recognized because of a horse logo on the door.

Norm Webster *was* here.

As they entered the small meeting room, it appeared the meeting was just coming to order. The room was occupied by fifteen people with a good mix of men and women. Looking around the room, the detectives recognized five people they had previously met.

One of them was Rick Whorton, a good friend of Stella Monroe's and Molly Lopez's. He had been involved with the prime suspect from their missing person/murder case the previous year. Julia remembered Rick's yard had been beautifully landscaped but hadn't realized he was the gardener. So many of the local expats hired local landscapers to tend their plants. The other familiar faces the pair knew from their current investigation. Perhaps now they could finally narrow their suspect pool.

On their drive to The Oasis, they'd discussed how to approach this meeting. They didn't want to tip their hand to the group to the fact dirt in the victim's wound potentially implicated someone who grew plumeria. But, their plan was flimsy, so when she first spotted Rick among the attendees, Julia quickly formed a new plan and rapidly and quietly told Ricardo as they approached the group.

"I'm so sorry to interrupt your meeting, folks. My partner and I just need a quick word with Mr. Whorton, then we'll be out of your hair," Julia said, using her breeziest tone.

The three stepped outside, with Rick wearing a bewildered expression.

As soon as the trio was a few feet from the clubhouse door, Julia spoke. "Hi, Mr. Whorton. I'm sorry to put you on the spot, but your being here is a godsend for Ricardo and me. We are investigating a death that occurred here at The Oasis a few days ago. For reasons I can't yet share with you, we needed to see whether any of our suspects were at this meeting today."

"Okay," Rick said, tentatively. "What does it have to do with me?"

"Do you know a man named Rudy Stephanetti?"

"Oh, I've seen posts on Facebook about him. The guy who was killed on the pickleball courts. No, I'd never heard of him before. Stephanetti is an unusual name. I'd have remembered if I'd met him."

"I figured. Then this has nothing at all to do with you. I hope I haven't put you in a difficult position by pulling you out of the meeting. Just by viewing the attendees, Ricardo and I have the information we need. You've provided us with the perfect reason for being here if . . . Would you be okay with just saying we needed a word about an incident involving a friend of yours we needed help locating?" Julia asked.

"Okay, sure. Should I say anything about what it pertains to, or have a friend's name ready?" Rick looked a little hesitant.

"No need to say anything other than we asked you not to share our inquiry with anyone. People know we police don't want to divulge information on an ongoing inquiry. Will you be comfortable with that?" Julia asked.

"Of course. It makes it easy for me. Thanks. I'm glad I can help."

"Before you go, would you please write down the names of the people in the meeting for me?" Julia asked, handing him her notebook and pen.

When he had finished, he handed back her notebook. "Good luck finding your murderer. And call me Rick." Then he headed back into the meeting.

While Julia was talking with Rick, Ricardo had documented the names of the people in the meeting they already had on their radar as either pickleball players or people at the potluck or both. Anne Brayer, Norm and Fran Webster, Rhonda Wilburn, and Dean McLean now topped the list of suspects. One name from Rick's list, Gretchen Wagner, was a surprise. Having a connection to the plumeria club might also implicate her or her husband.

Julia hadn't gotten the woman's name when she'd phoned the Wagner home previously looking for Wolfe's location and to verify he'd been home the night of the party. From her answer to the latter inquiry, Julia and Ricardo had decided Wolfe didn't have a strong alibi. Since his wife was his alibi, it seemed, she didn't have one, either.

Chapter Twenty-Eight

When they got back to the station, Ricardo updated Inspector Martinez on their progress while Julia made a dozen calls in hopes of setting times to meet with the people flagged by the Plumeria Club meeting, condo canvass, and Facebook posts.

There were three English-speaking people flagged by the door-to-door canvass of the condos who indicated they had information pertaining to the case. Julia and Ricardo wanted to speak with all of them. And since the young constable had provided them with the name and location of the drone flyers, they wanted to speak with them as well. The detectives started there.

The Padilla family turned out to be three family units: two brothers with wives and kids, plus the men's parents. In total, eleven people were staying in the three-bedroom condo. Neither Julia nor Ricardo was the least bit surprised by this. Vacationing with extended family and cramped sleeping arrangements were normal.

Once the pair of detectives had entered the condo, they were offered Coke with chips and salsa. They declined, and Ricardo began the interview after a few moments of general conversation. He started with the timing of their arrival. The first brother, Ivan, repeated what he'd told the constable the previous day. He and his family arrived late in the day on the twenty-fifth.

After ascertaining the families had not traveled together, Ricardo turned his attention to the other brother, David. Upon learning his portion of the Padilla family arrived the previous day, they turned their attention to David's family.

Julia pulled out a photo of Rudy Stephanetti and asked whether David knew him. Getting a negative reply, Ricardo asked to speak with the other members of David's family. David introduced his daughter, Luna, who appeared to be about eight. He also told the police his elder kids were newly turned sixteen-year-olds, twin boys.

After a few more questions, the police learned the twins had received a drone for their birthday gift and were spending all their time flying it. Eloy and Basilio were produced after their younger sister had been dispatched to find them and bring them home.

"Were you flying your drone the morning of February twenty-five, between seven and eleven?" Ricardo asked the boys.

They looked at each other conspiratorially before Eloy spoke. "Yes" was all he said.

"Did you fly it over the pickleball courts?" Ricardo asked, and then had to explain he was referring to the area across the street and about a hundred meters west of their condo.

Again, the solo word came from Eloy. "Yes."

"Did you take any video from your drone?" Ricardo asked.

This time it was Basilio who answered. "Yes."

"Okay, no more one-word answers, boys. I need you to tell me what you saw from your drone," Ricardo said sternly.

After admonishment from their dad, the boys finally told their story. They had seen all the cars and people gathered outside the courts shortly after they'd arisen that morning and were curious about what was going on. So, they decided to see whether they could use their new drone to figure it out.

They saw the crime-scene tape and became curious. Then, they'd done a flyover and seen the body and the blood. Before Eloy could set his phone to record video, they saw the body being loaded into an ambulance in a body bag and figured someone had died. So, the video they took showed the crime scene after the body had been removed, but still revealed a large blood pool.

"Did you post any of your videos on Facebook?" Ricardo asked.

"Yes. I posted it," Basilio said, looking sheepish and getting a shocked and angry look from his father. "I joined a local Facebook group I found when researching San Amaro. I wanted to see whether there was anything fun to do here other than lie on the beach. So, I lurked in the group to see whether I could find anything going on we might enjoy. But once we saw the video from the drone, we figured it wouldn't be good to post it under our real names. So, I created a fake account and posted it under that name."

"And the name was Che Guevara, right?" Ricardo asked.

"Yeah, that's right," Basilio said, garnering another unhappy look from his dad. "I just finished reading *The Motorcycle Diaries* and thought he was cool. His name just popped into my head when we were thinking of one to use on Facebook."

"Do you know who the person in the body bag was?" Ricardo asked and dipped his head toward Julia, who again showed the photo of Rudy when alive.

"No. I've never seen him before. Was he the man on our video? His head was so beat up, I couldn't say it was him. I almost puked when we first watched it," Basilio said.

"You need to remove your post with the video and refrain from making any more wild speculations. The man had not been decapitated. I need to confiscate your phone until we can analyze the video and any other photos you may have taken of the crime scene," Ricardo said, holding out his hand for the phone.

Basilio looked horrified at having his phone taken and looked pleadingly at his dad.

"Don't look at me for help. I'm thinking of taking the drone, too. It's one thing to fly it around and see something awful by chance and something else entirely to post what you saw online. What were you thinking? I hope I didn't raise a paparazzo or a ghoul."

While Ricardo was speaking with Basilio, Julia had been searching police databases from her phone. She leaned over and whispered into his ear, "None of the members of these families has a record, outstanding warrants, or even unpaid parking tickets." Ricardo nodded.

"Does any of your family here play pickleball, Mr. Padilla?" Ricardo asked, changing directions.

Eloy piped up. "It looks pretty interesting. We've watched bits of games from the drone, and Basilio and I even talked about seeing whether we could try it while we're here. There are a couple of people who aren't too old who said they could show us. We were thinking of doing it in a couple of days after all the old people are finished for the day."

"And who were these people?" Ricardo asked.

"Their names were Toad and Tiffancy," Eloy said.

"Are they perhaps Todd and Tiffany?" Ricardo asked with a straight-faced. Julia coughed to cover her smile. Both boys nodded seriously. Perhaps they didn't notice the difference. Curious, he asked whether the boys spoke much English.

"Enough to talk with our new friends," Eloy said.

The detectives continued talking with the Padilla families for twenty more minutes. Other than the inappropriate posting of the crime scene, it appeared they had no involvement with the Stephanetti family. Julia left Basilio with a receipt for his phone, and she and Ricardo took their leave.

As they walked to the car, Julia faintly heard a familiar bass lick, the beginning of her favorite blues song, wafting from the stage. She was hoping to hear more, but all she got were a few bars of the intro. *They must be starting sound checks,* she thought.

The next person flagged by the canvass lived in a condo in the pod adjacent to the Padilla families and almost directly across from the pickleball courts. Merriam Proust opened the door to Ricardo's knock with a thundering hello in no way matching her skeletally frail and stooped body.

She had thinning gray, wiry hair sticking out in all directions and was clad in a floral muumuu several sizes too large. But what struck Julia most about her appearance were all the tattoos the woman had. Most were faded, as was the lily poking out the top of her dress and winding from her back over her shoulder to end by her right ear, but a couple looked fairly recent. She thought again, as she had many times throughout her career as a police officer, how the expats drawn to Mexico were an interesting bunch. She was sure they all had fascinating stories to tell.

"Well, you must be the detectives," Merriam yelled, leading them into her living room and pointing them toward a pair of Queen Anne chairs, which Julia discovered were far more comfortable than they looked. "All I can offer you is Coke. It's all I drink. You want one?"

Ricardo and Julia declined. After her usual preamble about why they were there and having been admonished to call their host by her first name, Julia began the interview to learn what this woman could tell them. "So, Merriam, please tell us what information you have about the night of February twenty-four."

"Sorry, what'd ya say?" Merriam asked loudly.

Julia, realizing the woman was hard of hearing and thus the booming voice, repeated her request, with more volume.

"Right, well I don't sleep much anymore, so I was up watchin' TV." Merriam gestured toward the TV, which was flanked by two tall narrow windows looking toward the courts. "I'm too busy durin' the day to watch, so I catch up on my shows once it's dark. Anyway, that night, I saw a man go into the courts. I suppose it was sometime after eleven.

"I'd caught sight of him because he walked under the streetlight there to the right of the main entrance to the courts, and the movement made me look up. Unfortunately, as you can see, there is sailcloth attached to the chain-link fencin' on this side of the courts. It's because of the wind. I guess it makes the game hard to play. So, I couldn't see him once he entered. He was tall, probably six feet, and had on a blue shirt. He turned on the lights. I hate those lights. They shine right in my windows," Merriam yelled, pausing a beat between each sentence.

Julia gave Ricardo the gist of the woman's story. They agreed, her description matched Rudy's and tallied with other statements about Rudy's movements.

"Great. Did you see anything else?" Julia asked.

"Oh, yeah. A couple of minutes later, he came back out and visited the storage locker. It's around the side, so I can't see it from here, but I know it's where he went, because he came back with a ball and a paddle and returned to the courts."

Julia was going to interject another question when the woman continued. "A few minutes later, I went to get some more Coke, and I came back just as the court lights flickered off. I watched for a couple of minutes, but I didn't see him leave. He didn't leave through the main gate. I figured he must have gone out the back one. I thought it was weird, because there's not much back there except a bunch of dumpsters where we throw our garbage.

"I continued watching my show, but a few minutes later I saw a car go by. I guess I shouldn't say I *saw* it. It was more as though I was aware of a car going past my window. I get pretty desensitized to the sound and the lights, so I didn't see what kind of car it was, sorry."

"When you say car, do you mean a vehicle like a sedan, or could it have been a truck or an SUV or a Jeep, for example?" Julia asked.

"No. I have no idea what the heck it was. It just made noise."

"Were there any vehicles in the pickleball parking lot?" Julia asked.

"There was a truck in the lot. Light colored. Had some kind of logo on the door. It could have been one of The Oasis maintenance trucks. They all have The Oasis logo on the doors. I couldn't see it clearly from my angle of vision, though."

"Okay, great. Was there anything else you wanted to tell us, Merriam?" Julia asked.

"That's everything. Hope it helps."

"Of course. You've been most helpful. Thank you."

Julia and Ricardo sat in La Chica for a couple of minutes dissecting what the woman had told them. If nothing else, it confirmed what they had heard from other witnesses and what they'd surmised about Rudy's movements after leaving Suzanne and Edie's front steps. And the new information helped them form a more complete theory.

They speculated no one except the murderer would have left by the back gate, especially since dumpsters were there. Assuming the killer knew of them, she or he may have thrown something away. And if the murderer didn't, she or he left the back way to avoid being seen.

So, Ricardo and Julia had just collapsed their time-of-death window to the hour between eleven and midnight.

Hoping their killer had thrown something away into the dumpsters, they drove around to the back side of the courts to verify the garbage had not been picked up. All the dumpsters were overflowing with trash. They reeked of rotting garbage, which could have alerted the murderer to dumpsters being present. Ricardo phoned Inspector Martinez with an update including the possibility of evidence in the trash. He asked whether there was any way Martinez could spare a constable or two to go through the garbage looking for clues.

Martinez called them back five minutes later. The officer available was Lucia Juarez, a constable about ten years older than Julia. Julia and Lucia were friendly, though not close friends. They had, however, bonded in the way outcasts do, over the poor treatment women in the police in Mexico received.

Luis and Javier had finished interviewing all eight families from whom a comal had been stolen and were now trying to figure out what to do next. At Javier's suggestion, they had started checking with street vendors and small open-air restaurants in neighborhoods all over town. They wanted to see whether anyone had been around trying to sell comals. So far, no one they'd spoken with had been approached to buy anything in the way of cooking implements.

There were still many places the constables needed to check. They continued, undaunted by the lack of success. They wanted to prove their ability and, so far, Inspector Martinez seemed satisfied with their actions.

Lucia had on a set of dark blue coveralls with the legs rolled up to fit her five-foot, slightly pudgy frame. She was ready for Julia to pick her up by the time La Chica drove into the back parking area of the station. Ricardo had stayed to ensure the dumpsters were not emptied before the women returned.

Fifteen minutes later, Lucia looked at the three dumpsters and sighed. Even from twenty feet away, the smell was strong. It was going to be a long, smelly afternoon. Pulling her shoulders back and putting on a smile, she headed toward her task, trying to convince herself it was better than filing.

Chapter Twenty-Nine

"While I've been hanging out here, I keep hearing bits of music every couple of minutes. The musicians for the blues festival must be here. I think they're doing sound checks or maybe just getting the soundboard set up. You like blues, don't you? Are you going?" Ricardo asked when he climbed back into La Chica.

Julia smiled and responded. "Yeah, I do, but solving this murder comes first. I doubt I'll make it to see any of the acts this year. You?"

"Nah, I'm more of a cumbia and Latin pop fan. You know, Shakira, Selena, Julio Iglesias. Much better for dancing."

Ricardo tried to show off his dance moves while constrained by a seat belt. As Julia pulled her car to a stop in front of a condo, she spoke with mock scorn and a chuckle. "I'm surprised the ladies can stay away from that."

Their next interview was with a young couple renting a condo for a month just around the corner from Suzanne and Edie's. Lorenzo and Tina Vela, and a medium-sized yellow Lab, named Charlie, came to the door to greet the detectives and led them through to the living room. Julia noted the layout of their condo appeared to be the mirror image of Suzanne and Edie's. It was not, however, furnished anywhere nearly as nice. *Perhaps it's the difference between owners who lived in and owners who rented to visitors,* Julia thought.

Lorenzo was of Mexican descent, but he quickly disabused Ricardo of the idea he spoke Spanish. Julia would be the lead again. As they took their seats, Charlie plonked himself at Julia's side. As she scratched his ears, she led the pair through the purpose of the interview and kicked off the questioning in her usual gentle way.

The Velas had determined there must be a party the night in question by the increased traffic past their condo, mostly between seven and seven thirty and then again after ten thirty. Tina also mentioned seeing a family of four walking with wine and some hors d'oeuvres when she'd taken Charlie for a walk at about seven thirty.

At hearing his name and the word *walk* in the same sentence, Charlie looked expectantly at Tina. There was no leash at the ready, and his owner wasn't getting up. Dejectedly, he realized he wasn't getting one now and replaced his head on Julia's knee.

"Did you see any walkers later in the evening?" Julia asked.

"Oh, yeah. I did, anyway," Lorenzo said. "I was awake reading until about midnight." He pointed to a recliner with a reading lamp set near the large picture window with a view of the road. "As I said, we rarely see much going on here in the evening, so the movement on the road caught my attention. It was around eleven when the man who had been toting the wine earlier walked past. He didn't seem to be in a hurry. It looked as if it were a stroll. He was heading that way." Lorenzo pointed in the direction of the pickleball courts.

"And did you see anyone else around the same time?" Julia asked.

"Well, I went to make a sleep-aiding tea in the kitchen. I was gone for about five minutes. But, maybe ten minutes after getting my drink, the young man who was part of the foursome we saw earlier came past. He was going in the same direction as the first guy, but he was jogging. Then he came back a few minutes later, but this time he was running fast," Lorenzo said.

"Do you recall what he was wearing?" Julia tried to keep her voice calm. Her pulse had quickened with this new information.

"No. I don't think so. I know it was the same guy only because of his red hair. It's all I noticed."

"Did you notice anything else about the younger man on his return?" Julia asked after having a burst of Spanish cast at her from Ricardo.

"Like what? Lorenzo asked.

"Oh, perhaps changes to his clothing. Anything you might have noticed," Julia said.

"Ah, no, I don't think so. I just glanced up to see what the movement was and realized it was the same guy. I didn't pay much attention at all. Then another dude came past going that way." Lorenzo pointed away from the courts. "He wasn't walking down the middle of the road as everyone else had been, though. He was walking in the shadows. Away from the lights. I could hardly see him. I thought it was weird, so I looked for a few seconds trying to figure out what he was doing. I remember he had on dark pants and a light-colored coat, in the style of a bomber jacket, you know."

"Are you sure the two sightings were not the same person?" Julia asked.

"I . . ." Lorenzo began and then paused. He looked as if he were trying to recall. "I don't know. At the time I thought they were different people, but I may have assumed it because one was in the middle of the road, you know, and the other looked as if he were hiding in the shadows. But I can't be sure whether it was the same guy or two different ones. Oh, hang on," he said, scrunching his eyes closed. "I think the second guy I saw was a bit stockier, though it could have been because of the jacket, I guess. Sorry."

"Would you have any idea what time all this happened?" Julia asked.

"Well, it was before midnight, when I climbed into bed, but I'm not sure when exactly," Lorenzo said, looking apologetic.

Tina chimed in. "I headed to bed just before eleven."

"Okay, I think it was closer to when I went to bed than when Tina did," Lorenzo said. "Sorry, I can't be more specific. I hope it helps."

"Yes, thanks. Was there anything else you happened to see?" Julia asked.

"It might be nothing, but there was this rugged-looking Jeep, with a lift and tricked out for the desert. It came past going toward the party, and then it did a U-turn at the corner and came back past our place again. Seems a weird time to be out driving around looking for something, 'cause that's what it looked as if he were doing. He drove slowly and then after the U-turn retraced his route driving faster," Lorenzo said.

"Could you describe the man driving or anything more about the Jeep?"

"Well, I couldn't actually see who was driving. But the Jeep was dark colored. Maybe dark green or blue. I'm not sure. I don't think it was black, though. There were lots of lights on a bar across the top and an orange light above the spare tire on the back. Oh, and a winch in the front," Lorenzo said. "It zoomed by before I saw the people walking around. Not too long after Tina went to bed."

Once Julia had given Ricardo the gist of Lorenzo's information, Ricardo interjected in rapid-fire Spanish. He reminded Julia when they talked with Wolfe Wagner at the brewery that there had been a dark green Jeep matching the description Lorenzo provided parked out front. Julia nodded.

"This has been helpful. Is there anything else you think we need to know for our investigation?" Julia asked.

Tina shook her head, and Lorenzo said he didn't have anything else to add. Ricardo and Julia left, with Charlie escorting them to the door.

In the car, Ricardo shared his thoughts. "So, we have confirmation on the Jeep lights at the corner there and what sounds as if it were a sighting of Wolfe Wagner's Jeep in our time-of-death window. It appears he was here and not in his bed as he told us. I wonder who it was in the dark pants and bomber jacket? I suppose it's possible it was Logan, though no one mentioned he wore a jacket. Anyway, it feels as though we might be getting somewhere."

"I still don't see how Wolfe would have known Rudy was at the party or had left the party and was walking around on that street. I suppose he did know where the party was being held from Suzanne's announcement at pickleball. It was clear he didn't like Rudy, but why would he kill him? I agree we are getting somewhere, I'm just not sure where," Julia said. "But which of our suspects would you describe as stocky?"

Ricardo considered her question. "Not Wolfe. He's just fat. But both Norm Webster and Dean McLean fit the stocky description."

"I was thinking the same," Julia said and started the car.

Their final stop at the condos was to interview a woman named Lillian Wong. She met them at the door wearing a tight-fitting sundress. The woman's thick white hair was attractively coiffed in a shoulder-length bob. When she turned to lead them into a small sitting area, however, the hair on the back of her head was mashed flat, with a matted swirl that looked as if she'd been sleeping on it.

It quickly became apparent Lillian was lonely, looking for company, and probably didn't have much to tell them. Julia tried several different approaches and questions to encourage her to divulge anything she might know related to their investigation. Finally, she got the woman to admit she hadn't seen any walkers or vehicles the night of the party, apart from her neighbors across the road. After ten minutes of probing, Julia gave up. She thanked the woman for the tea and cookies with which she had plied them. She and Ricardo headed to the car.

"Wow, her loneliness was sad," Julia said as they walked to her car. "Pretty bad when you have to fill your need for company with a police visit."

"Good cookies, though," Ricardo said brightly, obviously not being affected the same way Julia had been by the aged widow.

"Oh, yoo-hoo, officers," Lillian called to them just before they got into La Chica. "I remembered something."

The pair returned to the stoop in front of the condo door. "What did you remember, Mrs. Wong?" Julia asked patiently.

"When I got to my bedroom that night, those darned bright lights were on over there." Lillian pointed behind her condo in the direction of the pickleball courts. "Then the next second they were turned off. I was relieved. I don't like closing my blinds. I prefer to wake up to the rising sun. It's so beautiful, you know. Well, of course you do. Those lights are too bright for falling asleep."

"And do you have any idea of the time when the lights turned off, Mrs. Wong?" Julia asked, trying to keep the excitement from her voice.

"It was eleven twenty-three. I have a digital clock beside my bed."

"Can you see the pickleball parking lot from your bedroom window? And if so, did you notice any vehicles parked there?" Julia asked.

"I can see it, yes. Now was anything parked there?" the woman asked herself and then looked off into space. "Yep, there was. Some kind of pickup truck. White, maybe, with a logo on the door. I think. The maintenance trucks here are white. They sometimes leave one there. They do have The Oasis logo on the door. Could have been one of them. I'm not sure."

"Thank you so much, Mrs. Wong. And thanks again for the cookies."

"At last, we might have uncovered the time of death," Ricardo said as they returned to La Chica. "So, do you think someone stopped here and killed Rudy on their way home from the party?"

"Or came back and did."

Julia had meant to stop by the condo dumpsters before leaving The Oasis. Lucia may have finished going through all the garbage. But she remembered only when they were almost back at the station. Once there, the desk sergeant informed Julia that Constable Juarez had not yet called for a pickup. *It'll be dark soon,* Julia thought and rang Lucia's cell phone to check how she was doing.

"I was just going to call you and let you know I'm finished with this horrid job." She paused dramatically. "And, something I found might interest you. If you're coming to pick me up, we can talk about it on the drive back to the station."

Leaving Ricardo at the station, Julia excitedly hopped back in La Chica and headed back to The Oasis.

Lucia was not at the dumpsters when Julia drove up. Julia's heart rate quickened momentarily wondering whether something had happened to her friend. Then she caught a glimpse of someone sitting on the bleachers and blew out the breath she hadn't realized she was holding.

Beside her on the bleacher were two evidence bags, one much larger than the other. She brought them along to Julia's car. The larger one contained the overalls she'd worn for her filthy job. She explained she was trying to reduce the smelliness of them by carrying them in a sealed bag. *Perhaps Lucia was inured to the stench on her,* Julia thought and vainly hoped she'd be able to get the smell out of her car. But regardless, she thanked Lucia for being so thoughtful.

The other evidence bag was what held Julia's attention, and she could hardly wait for her friend to get belted in before asking what she'd found.

As they drove back to the station, Julia had Lucia phone the desk sergeant to see whether their forensics guy, Vicente, was still at work. He was. Less than ten minutes later, the evidence bag had been logged and placed in a locking cabinet for analysis the following day. Before Julia left the lab, he handed her a manila folder and a cell phone.

"I printed all the pictures and put the video from the drone kid's phone on a memory stick. I didn't see anything worrying. Have a look and see what you think. Then I guess, the kid can get his phone back, right?"

"Thanks, Vicente. But, I think whether or not he gets his phone back will depend on his dad. He was none too happy about what his kids had done."

Julia drove Lucia home. Otherwise, she would have to call a relative to come and collect her. Her husband was long since at work, with the family's only vehicle.

Julia hoped they had running water so Lucia could have a proper shower. However, as she dropped Lucia at her home, she realized all they had was a water tank on their roof that would provide nothing stronger than gravity-based water pressure. *I hope it's recently been filled,* Julia thought.

Chapter Thirty

The next morning, the third annual Baja Rattlers Poker Run began at eight o'clock with registration. The off-road vehicles present included RZRs and Can-Ams, Jeeps, chopped VW Beetles, and sand rails. In all, there were twenty-seven vehicles and over sixty people registered by ten. Not all those registered planned to gather poker hands; many were along for the ride and the fun. By ten everyone was in a vehicle and awaiting his or her starting flag. Vehicles left at one-minute intervals.

The off-road group started hosting the fun event as a way to raise money for the local dog rescue organization while enjoying a day in the desert. With an entry fee of seventy-five dollars for those wanting to play poker and less for the riders only, the group was hoping to provide the rescue with something in the range of $4,000. It would help feed, house, and provide health care for the rescued dogs until they were adoptable. At the time, the rescue housed well over a hundred dogs.

There were no prizes for speed, but the best costume awards were highly prized. Most of the participants had gone all out with their costumes. Clowns and hoboes vied for attention with goths and what appeared to be dogs. Or, at least people in dog costumes. Spectators at the starting gates were snapping photos sure to grace Facebook pages over the coming days. This year's participants included not just the Baja Rattlers, but also members from other organized off-road groups in the area, and many were just people who used the event to get some desert time and help a good cause.

While the poker run participants were congregating for their day in the desert, Julia and Ricardo were sitting, frustrated, in an all-hands meeting at the station. They'd hoped their case would give them a pass, but Inspector Martinez mandated their attendance. It was a boring update on procedures. A few had changed.

Surely they could just have done this in a memo, Julia thought. And sure enough, halfway through the meeting, they handed out a printed copy of the changes. Julia used the rest of the meeting to think about the next steps in their case.

When the meeting finally ended, Julia and Ricardo headed to Suzanne and Edie's. They started their interviews with Tiffany in the upstairs den. "Do you remember what Logan was wearing when he returned after going home to change his clothes?" Julia asked.

"Yeah. He was wearing a black long-sleeved T-shirt and black jeans. I remember because I asked him whether he was moonlighting as a cat burglar. He said he was just running out of clean clothes."

"Did he act any differently when he came back? Preoccupied, anxious, anything you noticed?"

"Well, now you mention it, he appeared a little uneasy. He was fidgety, tapping his foot, that kind of thing. I hadn't noticed anything similar earlier in the evening," Tiffany said.

"Did you notice whether he'd changed his shoes?" asked Julia, after a quick exchange with Ricardo.

"Yeah, he was wearing hiking sandals when they arrived and kicks, you know, sneakers, when he came back after changing. You don't think he did anything to his dad, do you?"

Julia ignored the question and carried on. "Did he say anything out of the ordinary after he returned?"

"No, but he might have been a bit quieter than earlier. Nothing pronounced, though. I certainly didn't think anything was out of the ordinary, anyway. It was ten minutes or so after he got back when his mom came to get him."

"Okay, thanks. Is Todd around?"

"No. He took my great-aunt's RZR out to do the poker run. Brianna and Logan joined him. It's not my thing. I'm heading to the beach in a bit. It's more my style."

The detectives thanked the young woman and headed back to the main floor to talk with Suzanne and Edie. Julia called their names a couple of times but got no response. Tiffany stuck her head over the railing of the stairs and said her great-aunt had gone to the pickleball courts to see whether anyone wanted a few more games. They'd had an appointment in town first thing in the morning, so missed most of league play.

There were not many players on the courts. Julia figured it was because the others were participating in the poker run or had already left. Edie was just coming off a court at the end of her game and joined Julia and Ricardo on the bleachers. "Were you hoping to talk with Suzanne and me again? We didn't mean to run out on you. I just figured you wanted to talk only with Tiffany. I can grab Suzanne out of her game if you like."

"You may be able to answer our questions, but I would appreciate hearing from both of you."

When Edie and Suzanne joined them, Julia began. "Do you recall anyone at the party wearing a red short-sleeved shirt and jeans? We have canvassed the condos and have reports of several people out walking between ten and midnight the night of your party. We're trying to eliminate descriptions of people not matching any of the folks at your place."

"The one person I remember wearing a red shirt was Glenn, but I don't recall whether he had on jeans," Edie said. "He might have because it was a party, but most of the time he wears shorts. Even in winter."

"No, not jeans or shorts. He was wearing blue sweatpants. Remember I was joking with him when they arrived because of them," Suzanne said. "Asked him whether he was planning on doing a run on the beach after the party. But, they *were* dark blue."

Julia continued. "Okay, how about someone other than Rudy wearing tan khakis?"

It was Edie who spoke first. "Yes. Now, who was it?" She closed her eyes and lowered her head as she thought for a few moments before going on. "It was one of the guys who mainly hung out upstairs." Another pause. "Ah, right. It was Jeremy Kronberg."

"That's right," Suzanne said. "And Todd was, too."

"Did Todd go out at all during or after the party?" Julia asked.

"Not during the party. Or after it. He and Tiffany were helpful. They cleaned the upstairs den and the sitting area where one group spent most of the evening. Then, Todd helped dry the dishes. After, they retired to their room. Suzanne and I stayed up for another hour having a nightcap and unwinding after the party, and neither of the kids came downstairs. It was around two when we finally hit the sheets."

"I understand Todd and the younger Stephanettis are doing the poker run," Julia said.

"Yes, he took our RZR. Our rig is a four-seater, so he invited Logan and Brianna to join him. None of them has ever done anything similar to it before, though Todd's dad has a Can-Am two-seater back in Oregon, so he has experience driving one. RZRs and Can-Ams are similar," Suzanne said and then put her hand to her mouth. "Sorry, you probably already know that."

"So, Gloria is alone? I'm surprised the kids would leave her."

"We invited her to come over and have lunch with us. She should be there in a few minutes. We better be going," Edie said. "She told me she was looking forward to a bit of alone time after the kids left for the poker run. Said she hasn't had a moment to herself since Rudy's death. But we persuaded her to come for a light lunch, since it doesn't sound as if she's been eating much. If you have more questions, would you mind walking back to the condo with us and we can talk on the way?"

The detectives agreed. Ricardo asked Julia something, and they spoke for a couple of moments. Then Julia asked the women, "Would you have any idea who among your guests drove Jeep Wranglers the night of your party?"

Edie answered. "I'm a bit of a car nut, so I do take notice of what people drive. I'm not sure who came in their Jeeps, but there are a bunch of the pickleball people who have them. I suspect Glenn and Rhonda were here in theirs. Glenn drives it all the time, though they have a newer car, too. It's Rhonda's. And Wolfe Wagner also drives one all the time. Oh, but he wasn't at the party. Clint and Anne have an older Wrangler, but I doubt they drove it to the party. It's mostly for off-roading. I doubt Anne would agree to go out socially in it. I can't think of anyone else who has that model. If I remember anyone else, I'll let you know."

As they approached their condo, Tiffany was leaving carrying a beach towel and wearing a wide-brimmed hat. Julia called to her and asked her about whether she or Todd had left the condo the night of the party. She said they'd gone for ice about six before any of the pickleball people arrived and then had stayed in the rest of the night.

As the four walkers entered Suzanne and Edie's condo, Edie continued what she'd been saying. "I think all of the people I just mentioned are doing the Poker Run today, so you could hang out at the brewery at about three this afternoon. The participants should all be finishing about then. The brewery is the last stop. The poker players get their final card there, and then the awards are presented. We were thinking of going there for a beer and to watch the finale. It can be pretty fun."

Just then, there was a knock at the door. Suzanne came back with Gloria on her arm. Julia and Ricardo started to leave and let the three have their lunch, but Julia couldn't resist the opportunity to see whether Gloria would be okay with answering one question before they took their leave.

Getting an affirmative nod of the head, Julia proceeded. "Did you know Logan was planning on getting a new coach?"

Gloria sighed deeply before answering. "Yes. I overheard him talking with someone a few days before we left to come here. When I asked him about it, he told me he had already arranged to start working with a coach whom he met at his last indoor tournament. Apparently, they had made a deal, and Logan had already signed a contract with him.

"The coach's name is Will Pritchard. He's pretty well known in professional pickleball. He works out of New York City but was planning on meeting with Logan in Palm Springs. Rudy didn't know, and Logan was trying to figure out how to tell him. I think he was afraid of Rudy's reaction. You've already heard he had a quick temper. Still, I'm sure he would never hurt Logan."

"Well, thank you all. Have a nice lunch." Julia wanted to ask Gloria about her mysterious phone calls and texts but thought she'd have more luck getting the truth from her when she was alone.

When they were back in La Chica and Ricardo had been updated on the details, they speculated about whether Will Pritchard might actually have been in San Amaro for a few days to get Rudy out of the way permanently. It didn't seem probable. But still, something Julia would have to check.

When Julia told him Gloria said Rudy wouldn't hurt Logan, Ricardo reacted strongly. "In my experience, when someone says they're sure a person wouldn't do a certain thing, it's because they think it's highly possible the person might do the thing."

Julia couldn't disagree. A shiver had coursed through her when Gloria said Rudy wouldn't hurt Logan. Also, Gloria had confided in Karen Platz she feared Rudy might have been on the brink of striking Clint when they argued.

Could Logan have shared the same concerns she and Ricardo were contemplating? Was he afraid his father might resort to violence, perhaps to the point at which he felt compelled to take action and remove the threat? The chilling possibility gnawed at her like an unsolved riddle, adding an unsettling layer of tension to the case.

Chapter Thirty-One

Back in their war room, Ricardo promised to use his best printing to update the whiteboards with the information they'd been gathering. Julia, meanwhile, was on the phone checking in with several folk with whom she and Ricardo had already spoken. The new information they'd gathered recently spawned additional questions. Her first call was to Rhonda Wilburn.

"Mrs. Wilburn, I've recently spoken with your husband, and he mentioned Rudy Stephanetti was making unwanted advances toward you at the party. I was curious why you hadn't mentioned it the previous time we spoke. Can you fill me in, please?" Julia asked.

"Oh heavens, Glenn is making too much out of it. It wasn't a big deal, but it made me realize Rudy was not a pleasant man. I'm sorry I didn't say anything about it. It was nothing!"

"Still, I want to hear about the encounter, please. In your words."

"Okay. Well, Rudy and I were waiting for the main-floor bathroom at the same time. Or at least, I thought that's what happened. I was waiting for the bathroom, and he came and stood with me. I *assumed* he was waiting in line. He started chatting to me and he was a bit handsy, if you know what I mean?"

"Actually, I need you to describe it to me, so I do understand."

"Well, when he arrived behind me, he placed his hand on my shoulder. I was wearing a sleeveless top, so he was touching my skin. It startled me, and I turned to see who was there and realized it was him. I'd met him briefly earlier in the day, at pickleball, so I knew who he was.

"We talked about pickleball. He even suggested we could play some singles games while he was visiting San Amaro and then grab a drink afterward. The bathroom came open right then, so I didn't have to reply.

"Then when I left the bathroom, he put his hand on the small of my back as though to escort me somewhere. I realized he hadn't been waiting in line, he'd come over specifically to chat me up. I twisted away from his hand and said I wouldn't be playing singles with him or having a drink, either.

"He was persistent. He laid a hand on my arm and gave me a dazzling smile and, I think, he was going to say something else, but I simply pushed his hand away and left him standing there," Rhonda said.

"Sounds frustrating," Julia said, hoping Rhonda would say more. She did.

"You're a pretty woman. I'm sure you get hit on by men all the time. When it's someone you're not interested in, it's just an annoyance. Rudy was just annoying. Fortunately, he got the hint when I pushed his hand away from my arm. He just sauntered back to his group, and I hurried back to mine."

"Did you interact with him later in the evening?"

"No. I didn't see him again." Rhonda shook her head to emphasize her assertion.

Julia also ascertained Rhonda and Glenn had not driven past the courts on their way home, nor seen anyone walking in the condo area. When Julia shifted her questions to Rhonda's presence at the Plumeria Club meeting the previous day, Rhonda admitted she wasn't as passionate about the plants as most of the members. She mainly attended because she and Gretchen were friends, and it was something they did together before going out to coffee once a month.

Julia believed she'd gotten the information she needed. She thanked Rhonda and ended the call.

She scanned the updates Ricardo was making to their whiteboards. Satisfied she could read his printing, she returned to her phone calls.

Next on her list was Gloria Stephanetti. It hadn't been appropriate to ask her any more questions at Edie and Suzanne's, but looking at her watch, Julia figured Gloria should be back home after her lunch.

Julia dialed the woman's cell phone, and Gloria answered on the third ring. After getting confirmation she wasn't interrupting her lunch with Suzanne and Edie, she tackled the challenging questions about Rudy's potential abuse of his family.

"From a comment you made in a previous conversation with me and a comment from a person at the pickleball party, I have the impression your husband's temper bordered on violence. Was he ever physically abusive to you or your kids?" Julia asked.

"No, no. He was never physical. Sometimes, he got so angry it seemed as if he might, but he never did," Gloria said firmly. "I would never allow violence in my house. Ever!"

"I have to ask these questions. I hope you understand." Julia felt apologetic but kept the emotion from her voice. "Do you think Logan feared his father might become violent?"

"He never admitted it to me. I think he would have if he were concerned." Gloria was quiet for a moment, before continuing. "But, I think we were all a bit on pins and needles whenever Rudy exploded. I was concerned once or twice when he got furious that he might lash out. But, he never did. Thank goodness."

"Gloria, I appreciate your honesty. It's a hard subject. I know." Julia moved on to her final question. "Do you happen to have Will Pritchard's phone number? I want to check something with him."

Gloria took a minute to find it but was able to give Julia the new coach's number. Julia thanked her again and rang off.

Julia called several more people who had been at the party, but no one had noticed anyone out walking when she or he left the party. Julia was grateful the residents of the condos were more observant. She mentioned this to Ricardo, and he surprised her with his response.

"Do you notice people when you're out driving? I have to admit, I hardly register them. But if they are walking around my house, I pay attention. I think it's just human nature to be more observant or protective of your own personal space and home. What do you think?" he asked—his way of inviting conversation.

"Yeah, I think you're probably right," Julia said absently. Her attention was on her current task. She grabbed the handset of the conference-room phone again. "I have one more call I want to make."

She got an answering service and left a message explaining the purpose of her call and requesting a callback.

"Okay, nothing more for now. So, show me what you've added to our whiteboards."

They spent the last few minutes in the station refreshing themselves on all the facts they'd amassed so far.

They had gathered initial statements from party attendees and everyone who had witnessed Rudy's altercations at pickleball. There was still follow-up to do from the Facebook analysis. The character of their victim was becoming clearer. Most probably he was unfaithful. He was a self-centered bully. He was volatile, but he'd never been physically abusive to his family.

Their time-of-death window from the coroner was between eleven and two. But new witness statements narrowed it to sometime between eleven and eleven-thirty, most probably just before eleven twenty-three. There were several things they knew had occurred within the ominously short time frame.

They had eyewitness accounts of Rudy and Logan and possibly another person lurking in the shadows at the courts. A tricked-out Jeep, possibly driven by another as-yet-unknown suspect, had been seen driving in the vicinity. Logan and Dean

McLean were both absent from the party. Several of the potluck guests also left the party around the same time; among them was Norm Webster, whose truck may have been seen in the pickleball parking lot.

Because of the dirt in the wounds, they believed their murderer grew plumeria, which gave them a list of suspects comprising Norm Webster, Dean McLean, Anne Brayer, and Gretchen Wagner.

Logan did not appear to have any plumeria connection. Still, he was on the list, as he'd been away from the party for a long time during their window and had a precarious relationship with his dad. And because of a sighting of a Jeep similar to Wolfe Wagner's. He was on the list, too. Either of the latter two could have found gloves already sporting a dusting of the dirt found in the wounds.

As Ricardo lamented the list was too damned long, Julia glanced at the clock. They had hoped to have time, while they were in town, to have a word with Tony Ranelli. Julia wanted to see whether he actually had any useful information or whether he was just blowing smoke with all his Facebook tirades. But, if they wanted to get to the brewery in time to see the Poker Run participants arrive, they wouldn't have time for Tony today.

The brewery was a few minutes away, and there was always a food truck or two there. Since they hadn't eaten lunch, they decided to see whether anything on offer would satisfy their hunger.

En route to the brewery, Ricardo's cell phone played a few bars of "Bidi Bidi Bom Bom" by Selena, a Mexican-American and one of Mexico's beloved, now deceased singers. He quickly answered, giving Julia a sheepish grin for his new ringtone. It was Vicente. Ricardo put the phone on speaker.

". . . figured you'd want this information immediately. I haven't even finished reading it myself. I thought I heard you in the conference room here recently, but I must have just missed you."

When Julia gave Ricardo a questioning look, he mouthed *toxicology report*.

Vicente was speaking again. "He had alcohol in his bloodstream, which we already knew. What I hadn't expected to see was diazepam, Valium, in his system. Not a lethal amount or anything, but more than I'd expect from a prescribed dose, even if he had extreme anxiety."

"Was it enough to impair his normal functioning?" Julia asked.

"Well, it depends on why he was taking it and how recently he'd taken it. If he did have extreme anxiety, I'd expect a blood level of about five to ten milligrams. The lower if he'd taken it earlier in the day, the upper end if he had recently taken it. His was twenty-five, which as a regular user wouldn't be enough to incapacitate him. If he wasn't used to taking it as part of a daily regimen, it would have affected him more. Not enough to debilitate him, but he was probably feeling pretty mellow. He hadn't had an excessive amount of alcohol, thank goodness, or he would have been dozing off in a corner somewhere," Vicente answered.

"I don't suppose you can tell how he ingested it?" Ricardo asked.

"No way to tell, I'm afraid. It would have been orally. There were no injection marks on his body, but I can't tell whether it was in something he ate or drank, or whether it was taken directly. The Valium was the only unexpected thing in the report. I hope it helps."

Ricardo looked at Julia and said, "What the hell, eh? From what people have told us about Rudy, I didn't get the impression he was the anxious type. Do you suppose on top of everything else, he'd been drugged on purpose?"

"Yes. And, I'm pretty sure it was one of his family," Julia said. *But who? And why?*

Chapter Thirty-Two

Fortified with Coke and wood-fire-cooked, mouth-watering shrimp tacos, the pair of detectives was among a small crowd at the brewery in the outside seating area awaiting the return of the Poker Run participants. A band was readying its equipment on the outside stage, behind which the expansive sea provided a beautiful backdrop.

While they were eating, Pippa Drummond and Stella Monroe came out of the brewery, each carrying a glass of beer. Seeing Julia and Ricardo, they joined them at one of the long tables.

As they sat, Stella asked, "Are you two here on business or pleasure?" She was wearing a T-shirt from a previous poker run with blue-jean cutoffs.

After Julia swallowed the last delicious bite of her taco, she responded, "It's business for us today, Mrs. Monroe."

"You must stop calling me that. I'm Stella and this is Pippa, all right?"

"Yes. Okay. Anyway, we have a few questions we were hoping to ask several of the people in today's race. I'm not sure this will be the best venue for it, but we thought we'd come and see. And besides, though Ricardo has, I haven't been to one of these before. So, maybe there is an element of fun, too."

"I did the one last year, with"—Stella hesitated before saying the name of her ex-husband, who was now in prison for accessory to murder—"Simon. It was fun. Do you know how they work?"

"Not really," Julia confessed. "I know people dress in costumes and drive through the desert to different stops where they get cards, but that's about it for my knowledge."

"You've got the gist of it. They are fundraisers supporting a specified charity. The point is to get the best poker hand from the five cards you collect at the various stops. In this run, players got a card at the start, and they'll get one here, at the end. There were three stops on the route where they'd have collected the other cards. The desire is to get the best five-card-stud hand. Vehicles have to finish the race within a specified time, but speed isn't the measure of success. It's all about the poker hand. And the fun, of course. There will be prizes for the individual best costume and the best team's costumes in addition to the poker aspect. Prizes are usually tokens rather than something worth the value of the entry fee because everyone knows it's for charity."

"Thanks for the explanation, Stella. It does sound fun. Do any Mexicans ever participate?"

"Oh yes. There are a few groups in most of the poker runs held around San Amaro. And I heard there's a volunteer at the dog rescue with a four-seater Can-Am who has three of the local kids who work at the dog shelter along with him. San Amaro is great for getting everyone involved in local events. If you want to try it, you could join me in my Jeep for the next one."

"Sounds fun. Let me know, and I'll see how things are at work."

Just then the first racers vroomed to the finish line, and three of the four passengers were handed a playing card. This prompted a question from Julia to Stella.

"Why didn't everyone get a card?"

"There are three categories of participation: people who are playing poker, those who are along for the ride and the fun, and one for folks along for the ride who also want the T-shirt. The entry fee is different for each, though they all include a beer at the finish line and a light meal. Every person in the vehicle gets a wristband denoting his or her level of participation. So, that group has one person who isn't playing poker," Stella said.

"Okay, thanks."

Two more vehicles had arrived, and one of them contained Clint and Anne Brayer. Julia and Ricardo excused themselves from the group and headed over to where the Brayers were climbing from their Jeep. They wore identical black T-shirts with skeleton ribs and a sternum in the front and a spine and ribs on the back, and each sported Day of the Dead–like face makeup. Each clutched a poker hand.

Clint was the first to spot the officers. "Detective Sergeant Hernandez and Detective Sergeant Garcia. I'm guessing this isn't a social visit. What's up?" he asked.

"A couple of simple questions is all," Julia said. "Did you drive your Jeep to the pickleball potluck?"

It was Anne who answered, emphatically. "Absolutely not. Look at this thing, would you go to a party in it?"

Looking at the dusty white vehicle, Julia took in the high lift, the light bar mounted on a roll bar over the passenger seats, no doors or roof, and quickly agreed she would not. "Mr. Brayer, for which police force did you work?"

"I spent my entire career in Saint Paul. We moved here when we both retired."

"Thank you both. Enjoy the festivities."

Nancy and Helen were at the finish line gathering the last cards for their poker hands as Ricardo and Julia left the Brayers. Both women were costumed simply in blue shirts with rolled-up sleeves and the tails tied at their midriffs, with red bandannas tied over their hair. Julia recognized the Rosie the Riveter look immediately. She and Ricardo approached their two-seater RZR. Helen smiled at the police officers. Nancy's face maintained a mask of indifference.

"I won't take but a minute of your time, ladies," Julia said. "I wanted to ask what time you left the party and whether either of you had seen anyone on or near the pickleball courts when you left the potluck. Or even out walking."

"We left earlier than most people. Probably about ten fifteen or ten thirty. Our path home from the party took us the opposite way from the courts," Helen said. Nancy nodded in agreement. "And the one person we saw walking was a man with a large, husky-type dog."

"Okay, thanks." They hadn't heard about someone walking a husky before. As they walked away from the women's rig, Ricardo pointed out neither of the pair was tall enough nor strong enough to have killed Rudy Stephanetti with either the blow to the back of his head or the stabbing coup de grâce.

Julia reminded him that if Rudy were feeling the effects of the Valium, he may have been more easily subdued. Then both spoke at once—"Neither woman was part of the Plumeria Club"—and smiled at each other.

The final participants they awaited were Wolfe and Gretchen Wagner. Wolfe's Jeep was one of the later vehicles to arrive at the finish line. With him was a woman they assumed was his wife, and Julia remembered her from the plumeria meeting. She was almost the same height as Wolfe. As Julia and Ricardo approached and introduced themselves, the woman confirmed her suspicion by saying, "Hi, Detective, I'm Gretchen. We spoke on the phone a few days ago."

Neither was wearing a costume per se, but both sported horned Viking helmets. Julia chuckled inwardly, thinking they reminded her of Hagar the Horrible and his wife, Helga, from the newspaper comics. "We have a witness who described your Jeep as having passed by his home the night of the pickleball party. As he described to us, it drove slowly down his street, did a U-turn, and drove past again going faster. Can either of you explain that to us?"

Julia's voice carried no note of accusation or bias. It was calm and friendly as usual.

Wolfe replied on the offensive. "We didn't go to the party, and neither of us drove around in the condos that night. I already told you several times."

"The description the witness gave of your vehicle was specific." Julia shifted her gaze toward Gretchen as she spoke.

"I never drive Wolfe's Jeep. My car is a little Mini Cooper. People call it my clown car, I guess because I'm tall and it's small."

"Is there a chance someone else was driving your Jeep, Mr. Wagner?"

"No. You've got the wrong Jeep. Have a look around. There are a bunch that look similar to mine. It wasn't me." Wolfe's face was starting to get red, and his temper was showing. But Julia noticed his language was not colored with expletives. *Gretchen must disapprove,* she thought, wryly.

"Good suggestion. We will. Thanks for your time." Julia and Ricardo walked toward the parking area, ostensibly to check out other similar vehicles to the Wagners'.

Ricardo admitted when they were out of earshot of the two, "I don't believe him. I think he's lying."

"I think you're right, but this isn't the place for that conversation. Let's take a picture of his Jeep and any others we find matching Mr. Vela's description. We can give him a photo lineup of all the Jeeps and see whether he can identify the Wagners'."

They found three other Jeeps dark in color and similar to Wolfe's and took pictures of each and one of the Brayers' as well. It was white, but otherwise matched Mr. Vela's description of the one he'd seen on the road in front of their condo.

As Julia left Ricardo beside his battered truck at the shabby police station, a sense of productivity buoyed her. She couldn't help believing they were making headway in unmasking the murderer. Yet, an unsettling notion gnawed at her thoughts—the nagging question of motive. None of their suspects appeared to possess a reason potent enough to unleash the ferocity and brutality witnessed in Rudy's assault. As she started her journey home, the enigma deepened. How and why did Valium find its way into Rudy's system? The puzzle remained as elusive as ever, adding an ominous layer of tension to their ongoing investigation.

Chapter Thirty-Three

Julia's pre-case introspection on hold, she reverted to using her daily morning run to review her current case. The preceding day had given Ricardo and her several leads, and she was hopeful the evidence Lucia found in the dumpster was, in fact, related to their case. Vicente had promised to make it his priority. It might take him awhile, so she contemplated what needed to be done in the interim and developed a mental list of activities for the day. She hoped Ricardo would concur.

"All Lucia found out of the ordinary was a pair of tan-colored, leather work gloves. They appear to be covered in blood. Also, a small piece of missing leather appears to match the fragment Vicente found lodged in the killer pickleball paddle handle," Julia told Ricardo when he joined her in the war room when he arrived for work. "He'll be analyzing the blood on the gloves to confirm it belongs to Rudy Stephanetti and promised to call as soon as he runs the requisite tests. Plus he'll verify whether the piece of leather in the paddle handle matches the gloves."

While she'd been waiting for her partner to get to work, she'd spent about an hour making a new chart on a vacant expanse of a whiteboard. On the horizontal upper edge of the chart were the following attributes: *tall enough*, *strong enough*, *owns a Jeep Wrangler*, *wore a Hawaiian shirt*, *Plumeria Club member*, and *wore khakis*. She'd thought about adding *takes Valium*, too, but decided anyone could get it from a pharmacy in town without a prescription, so it might not be helpful to include. The left-hand edge contained the names of suspects and their spouses. Then she'd placed an X indicating which of the attributes applied to which suspects. It was illuminating and grabbed Ricardo's attention immediately after he entered the room.

According to the chart, and without a convincing motive to limit it, the list of suspects had expanded to twelve people. A few were probably not strong or tall enough, and a couple were unlikely based on their statements. But, the detectives knew people lied to the police all the time. Both agreed the Plumeria Club members and Logan were their strongest suspects, but it was imperative they established a clear motive for the murder so they could begin to shorten the list.

"Wow, Lucy. This is good. It should help as we move forward. Can you please add a column headed 'seen near courts'?"

"I can. Though at this point, I think the only person we know for sure who was seen near the courts apart from the victim was his son, right?" Julia asked.

"True. At this point." Ricardo cupped his ubiquitous coffee in his large hands, evidently thinking. Julia waited. Eventually, he asked, "So, what other things have been bumping around your big brain since yesterday?"

She told him about her suspicion Logan may take Valium. "We know he was bullied by his dad. Which could cause a person to experience depression and anxiety. Interestingly, Brianna doesn't seem to have had the same reaction to her dad. From what she's said, I don't think he was any less bullying toward her than Logan. Regardless, it sounds as if she held her ground against him more than Logan did. I wonder whether Logan had just had enough of his dad's bullying and snapped."

Changing back to Julia's initial topic, Ricardo spoke. "I hope it doesn't take Vicente too long to analyze the gloves. They might be our biggest lead so far." Then changing direction again, he said, "Do you want to talk to Logan next?"

"Well, since Tony Ranelli lives here in town, I was going to suggest we talk with him first. Then we can head out to The Oasis and talk with Logan. Sound okay to you?"

"Yes. Perfect." Ricardo retrieved his coffee.

"Ricardo, would you grab that folder and the cell phone, too? Let me know what you think of the photos the Padilla twins took. I didn't see anything worrying, so if you agree, we can give it back to Basilio, or more accurately, to his dad."

Tony Ranelli's home was much as Julia remembered it from her last visit to interview the man regarding inflammatory Facebook posts related to the missing person case eleven months prior. She still remembered Molly's admonishment to talk with Mr. Ranelli before noon, as after, he was usually intoxicated and even more surly than usual. He lived in the sole mobile home park in San Amaro, in an aging, though well-maintained, single-wide trailer. He opened the door moments after Ricardo's knock.

Ricardo knew the man had dated Stella Monroe a couple of years ago and was surprised at the person standing before him. Stella was a fit and active woman. The man before him was slovenly, grossly overweight, and had attitude leaching from his pores.

"I remember you," Ranelli said upon seeing Julia behind Ricardo. "What the hell do you want? I see you had to bring reinforcement this time. Typical woman."

This last comment was directed to Ricardo, though he understood only the word *woman*. Ranelli's intonation and accompanying sneer, however, gave Ricardo all the information he needed. He stepped back and let Julia enter the man's home first.

"Mr. Ranelli, I'm here for much the same reason as my last visit. You have been making some malicious Facebook posts about the murder of Rudy Stephanetti. My partner and I need to know whether you have any valid information about the man or the case."

Julia wanted to add *other than the bile you've been spewing* but didn't. Despite her dislike of the man, her voice remained neutral.

"There's no need for you to sit," said the unpleasant man. "I just want to know whether you've checked into why he changed jobs so often. It wasn't for career advancement, even though I suspect that's what his mousy little wife told you."

"Sorry, sir, we aren't leaving. Unless you'd prefer to continue this conversation at the station." Julia spoke more firmly but without rancor.

"Yeah, all right. Don't get your panties in a wad. What do you want to know?" Ranelli rolled his eyes as he took a seat in a battered, old leather recliner. He acquiesced by waving a hand toward the other two chairs in the room. They sat.

"Did you know Rudy Stephanetti in the past?"

"Yeah, not well, mind you, but enough."

Julia was surprised. "Please tell us about it."

"I was a line supervisor at a manufacturing company back in Seattle when he worked there. He used to come onto the manufacturing floor and try throwing his weight around. Never had anything useful to say, so we mostly just ignored him. What does anyone from marketing know about manufacturing, right?"

"And do you know why Mr. Stephanetti left that job?"

"Not all the details, but it had something to do with a secretary. Rumor was he was *inappropriate* with her," Tony said, stressing the word as though it was distasteful to him. "Why can't they just say what it is, instead of using weasel words? He tried to rape her is how I'd say it."

"Do you have proof?" Julia asked, trying hard to keep her voice and tone even. "Was Mr. Stephanetti charged with attempted rape?"

"Well, what do *you* think inappropriate means?" Tony asked in a mocking tone.

"It could mean any number of things other than rape, Mr. Ranelli. So, if you have any verifiable information, please share it with us."

"Okay, okay. Rudy Stephanetti left the company with no warning. The only time I've seen that happen is when someone's fired. So, do your job and talk with the companies where he's worked. They will probably continue whitewashing his actions, but still, it should paint a picture even you two can understand." Tony paused for a beat, then added. "Got any other questions for me?"

"What was the name of the company where you worked together?"

"Romany Manufacturing. In the Industrial District of Seattle. In the late 1990s."

"Mr. Ranelli, where were you the evening of February twenty-four?" There was more of an edge in Julia's voice than she usually used during a first interview. Ricardo glanced over but kept his lips from twitching. *She doesn't like this guy*, he thought.

"I was in Ensenada for a few days with my new girlfriend. We got there on the twenty-second and returned on the twenty-sixth. I didn't kill the bastard," Tony said with satisfaction and a sneer.

Julia gathered the girlfriend's name and number, pledging to contact her to verify his alibi. "Thank you for your cooperation, Mr. Ranelli," Julia said with a cool smile. "We'll let you get back to your day. However, I must ask you to refrain from any further inflammatory Facebook posts about Mr. Stephanetti."

"Wow, what a jerk," Ricardo proclaimed before Julia had had a chance to update him on the details of the conversation. "I'm glad I was there. Was he even worse the last time you interviewed him?"

"No, about the same. His information certainly was useful, though. We need to find out whether the wives of any of our suspects worked with Rudy. We might finally have a motive strong enough to match the horror of the crime."

Chapter Thirty-Four

At about the same time Ricardo and Julia were leaving Tony Ranelli's, Rick Whorton was walking into La Casita Restaurant for breakfast. His friends were already there, just getting settled at a table for four in the front corner to the left of the door. Stella saw Rick first and yoo-hooed to him, opening her arms for a hug as he walked over to their table. Molly, though already seated, stood for a hug of her own.

The three had been close friends for almost ten years, ever since both Molly and Stella chose to move to San Amaro upon retiring from their teaching careers in Montana. Stella, fairly recently widowed at the time, wanted to live somewhere warm and discovered the little fishing village on the Sea of Cortez met all her needs. Molly, also single and wanting a change, chose to join her longtime friend in her new adventure.

Molly had met and married a local restaurateur within a year of moving to San Amaro. Jaime, Molly's husband, would normally have accompanied his wife to this monthly breakfast, but, as Molly explained to her friends, he wasn't there because he had to attend to some family business.

As the friends settled, Rick was jittery with excitement. As they made their beverage and food orders, he started the conversation. "You'll never guess who came to the Plumeria Club meeting yesterday."

"You're right, because I don't know why *anyone* in his or her right mind would go to a meeting about a tree," Stella said, quipping with a twinkle in her eye.

"Ha ha!" Rick mocked a scornful tone.

"Okay. Who was it?" Molly asked.

"Sergeant Julia Garcia and her partner, Sergeant Hernandez," Rick said with a flourish.

"What on earth were they doing at your plumeria meeting?" Stella asked with a hint of incredulity in her voice. "And they are both detective sergeants now, by the way."

"Oh, good for them! They're on a case and . . ." Rick started to say, then paused, remembering Julia's admonishment. "Actually, they asked me not to say anything about it." His initial excitement at having something interesting to tell the women diminished.

"Well, actually, we've talked to her a couple of times this week, too. She's investigating the murder of Rudy Stephanetti, the man at the pickleball courts. So, not a big secret," Stella said.

"Oh. Okay then, but promise you won't share this part with anybody." Rick leaned toward his friends in a conspiratorial way. Molly and Stella also leaned in. "They told me they wanted to see whether they knew anybody who was at the plumeria meeting. They didn't have a plan other than to just walk into the meeting, but upon seeing me, Sergeant Garcia used my presence as an excuse to be there. She used the ruse of saying they needed my help on a fictitious case.

"I don't know who they were looking for at the meeting or why, but it was kind of fun to be an unwitting part of their little cloak-and-dagger stunt for a couple of minutes. Did they speak with you about this murder thing?" Rick asked.

"Yes. We were both there at pickleball the day before the man's murder, when he argued with the club president. Then Stella was at the party that night with all the pickleball people, and so was the victim. They just wanted our statements. It was informal. We didn't have to go to the station. But it was still exciting," Molly said in her flamboyant way.

Their food was being served, and they were silent for a few moments while they all sampled the beautifully presented plates of food in front of them. Stella had opted for divorced eggs, a Mexican favorite mimicking their flag. A fried egg on a tortilla with a mild green sauce, and a fried egg on a tortilla with spicy red sauce, separated by bits of fried tortillas covered in white Mexican cotija cheese. Rick chose his favorite, chilaquiles. Basically, tortilla chips cooked and served in a spicy sauce with onions, cream, cheese, and chicken. Molly had her usual, machaca: shredded beef, cooked with peppers and onions and mixed with scrambled eggs to produce a delicately flavored delight of tastes and textures.

La Casita, as its name implied, was a small, house-like building and home to one of the best Mexican restaurants in town. A couple of blocks off the main drag of Calle Guadalajara and far from the Malecon, the out-of-the-way location didn't limit its success. Molly, Rick, and Stella were the only expats in the crowded little dining area. It was as popular for its ambience and service as for its delicious food. Truly a hidden gem.

As they finished their meals, the three shared their ideas and theories about what had happened to Rudy on the pickleball court, rehashing what they'd read on Facebook and their personal involvement, small as it was for each of them. In the end, they got reasonably close to the truth when Stella surmised there must have been some evidence on the body, leading the police to suspect someone involved with plumeria. It made for a more rousing conversation than usual at their regular breakfast get-together.

Molly was just about to move the conversation in a different direction when Rick seemed to have an epiphany. "At the end of the plumeria meeting, three people asked me what the police wanted. Gretchen Wolfe, Norm Webster, and Dean McLean. I guess I should let Julia know. It might be important."

"Absolutely, you should tell her. I have her phone number. Let me give it to you," Stella said emphatically. "It could make a difference to their case!"

Chapter Thirty-Five

Before she drove away from Tony Ranelli's, Julia made some phone calls. The first had been to his new girlfriend. When asked about her whereabouts on February 24, she said in Ensenada with Tony and confirmed his alibi.

Next, Julia phoned Rhonda Wilburn.

"This is a bit of an odd question, but what type of gardening gloves do you wear?"

"That *is* an odd question," Rhonda said. "But, if you must know, I wear rubber gloves. You know, the kind some people wear to wash dishes. I get them at a little store on Calle Guadalajara. My main hobby is doing mosaics, and I often have small cuts on my hands from the broken tiles I use. When I first started gardening, I got a bad infection in one of my little cuts, so I stopped wearing cloth gloves and started using rubber ones." Rhonda's tone carried the unspoken question *Why do you need to know that?*

Julia noticed it but didn't respond, instead simply thanked the woman, and said goodbye.

Her last phone call, to Gloria Stephanetti, informed the detectives Logan had just returned from playing pickleball and was showering. By the time the two made it to The Oasis, they expected he'd be ready to talk with them.

As they approached the condo door, Ricardo noticed a plumeria tree near the front of the condo the Stephanettis were renting and pointed it out to Julia. There was fresh sandy loam filling the top of the ring of stones rimming the tree. The hairs on her neck tingled.

"Logan, we have a witness who saw someone matching your description, after your *unfortunate* beer-spilling incident." Julia's intonation made it clear she didn't believe it was an accident. She wanted to see whether Logan would admit to having done it on purpose. "A person matching your description was seen going to and from the pickleball courts. Can you please explain that to us?" Julia asked.

Logan's shoulders sank, and he looked toward the kitchen, where they could hear Gloria rustling about. He blew out a long breath before beginning, and when he spoke, it was in a subdued and hushed voice. "I decided the night of the party was a good time to tell Dad I had signed on a new coach. He's usually in a better-than-normal mood after he's had a few drinks.

"I left the party and walked to our condo. Since he wasn't there, I figured he might have gone to the beach. When he wasn't there, either, I knew he must have gone to the courts, because he'd mentioned he was interested in seeing how bright the lights were, for potential night training. I'd already been away from the party longer than I'd expected, so I was jogging."

Julia and Ricardo were silent waiting for him to continue.

"When I got there, he was already dead. It was awful, well, you saw. He was lying in a pool of blood. His face was beaten to a pulp, and that thing sticking out of his neck almost made me throw up. I was so scared, I wasn't thinking. I just took off.

"I knew Todd and Tiffany were waiting for me, so I just rushed back to their condo. Thank God Mom wanted to leave just a few minutes after I got back. I could barely keep it together." When he finished, his body sagged back into the couch. He had the appearance of a deflated balloon. His face was ashen, and he looked as if the telling had made him want to vomit.

"Why didn't you tell us this immediately?" Julia asked after quickly sharing Logan's statement.

"I think I was in shock, mostly. But after I thought it through, I worried there isn't anyone here who even knew Dad. Everyone had seen us arguing at pickleball that morning. I was convinced you'd charge me without a second thought. I . . ." Logan sputtered to a stop and began to quietly cry.

"We need to take you to the station and get your story recorded officially."

"I didn't do it. I would never. He was a bastard sometimes, but he was my dad. I loved him. Please . . ." Again, sobs took over.

By this time, Gloria must have sensed something going on. She rushed to her son's side and held him. Looking at Julia, she demanded to know what was going on.

"Your son lied to us in his previous statements, Mrs. Stephanetti. We are taking him to the station to get an official statement. At this point, that's all we're doing. You can come to the station if you wish, but you may not be in the interview with him."

"Oh, my God. Logan, what's going on?" Gloria asked.

The young man said nothing, so Julia responded. "We have a witness who places Logan at the pickleball courts within the window of time in which your husband was killed. And your son has confirmed he was there.

"We need to get a full statement. Once that's done, we'll see what happens next. I need to take the clothes he was wearing that night. A black long-sleeved T-shirt, black pants, and sneakers, plus the clothes he was wearing before he changed. Please show me where I'll find them."

Ricardo stayed with Logan while Julia popped out to her car to grab some evidence bags, and then she and Gloria climbed the stairs to the bedrooms. Julia returned moments later with three sealed plastic bags. Gloria slowly followed her down the stairs.

"Logan, where are the rest of the clothes you were wearing when we arrived at the party? I can't find them," Gloria said, tensely.

"They should all be in the drawers in my room. If they aren't there, I don't know where they are," Logan said quietly.

Ricardo spoke quickly to Julia. She nodded.

"What did you do with them, Logan?" There was now an edge in Julia's voice.

"I don't know where they are. Mom, you should have washed them the first time you went to the laundromat. Don't you remember?"

"They aren't in your drawers, and I don't remember one way or the other whether they were in the laundry."

"Maybe you left them in one of the machines by mistake," Logan said.

Gloria and Julia returned upstairs and combed through both Brianna's and Rudy's clothing. They desperately hunted for any sign of the Hawaiian shirt and shorts Logan had worn to the party. The tension in the room grew with each fruitless search, and Julia's displeasure was palpable.

Julia's mind raced, forming a sinister idea of what may have happened. She knew this theory would need to be unveiled during the formal interview, but a creeping dread had already begun to consume her thoughts.

Logan was escorted to the old brown Honda in the driveway, and Ricardo joined him in the back seat. As she watched the car drive away, Gloria collapsed on the couch and began to weep.

Chapter Thirty-Six

Javier and Luis had now spoken with all the families from whom a comal had recently had been stolen. Eight in total. The stories were all similar. Their comal was kept on an outside cooker, all were wood fired, and all were taken during the night. The locations from which they had been taken were also similar. Except for one on the edge of town, all were somewhat rural, and the occupants had an acre or more of land.

Luis had observed as they were leaving the last of their interviews whoever had done it must know the rural areas around San Amaro well. Perhaps their thief was a rural dweller himself. He mentioned his idea to Javier.

"Could just as easily be a woman. Cooking is a woman thing, right? And comals are used for cooking. They're not overly heavy, either, so a woman could easily carry one," Javier said.

As they drove back to the station, they speculated on what type of person might visit the rural areas and have knowledge of people who had large comals in easily accessible places outside their homes. They zeroed in on delivery people but hadn't checked with every family about deliveries. They'd have to talk with some of them again. First, however, they wanted to update Detective Inspector Martinez. As usual, Javier suggested Luis go alone to their boss's office.

Julia meticulously fingerprinted Logan, her hands steady but her mind racing with anticipation. Afterward, Ricardo secured their crucial evidence and hurriedly delivered it to Vicente, the forensics expert. He emphasized the importance of making the examination of the clothes a priority, especially focusing on any potential traces of blood. The clothes seemed to have undergone a thorough washing, but Vicente assured them with the right tests, he could likely unveil whether there had been any prior presence of blood on the items.

While in the lab, Julia seized the opportunity to inquire about the other pieces of evidence he had been carefully analyzing, the air thick with suspense.

"I struck out with the cyanoacrylate test, the Super Glue test, on the handle of the pickleball paddle," Vicente said, adding the retail name of the glue upon seeing Ricardo's uncertainty at the chemical name. "There were a bunch of prints on the paddle handle—a couple were Stephanetti's—but the rest were all smudged. I have, however, been able to determine the blood on the gloves found in the dumpster behind the courts is a match to the murder victim, and the small bit of leather from the pickleball paddle was torn from the gloves. They were definitely worn by the murderer.

"I tried to get fingerprints from inside the gloves, but the surface is too irregular. There were none. But there was some blood on the inside that didn't belong to the victim. If you can get me samples from your suspects, I can see whether any of them match the blood I gathered from inside the gloves."

Not yet, Ricardo thought, *unless Logan's blood type matched.* They didn't have enough evidence on anyone yet for a warrant to compel a DNA sample, though he hoped Julia would ask whether Logan would give blood voluntarily.

As Ricardo was coming out of the forensics lab, he saw Inspector Martinez exiting his office. He began updating his boss about having Logan in an interview downstairs. "Yes," the detective inspector said. "Julia just called me to let me know. I'm heading there now to see whether she wants any assistance. Were you planning on sitting in with Julia?"

"No, sir, I was thinking I'd listen in using the translation software we got last year. It works pretty well and then I can hear in near real time how it's going. Did you want me to sit in?"

"No, Ricardo, you do what you were planning. I'll sit in so she isn't alone with him. Text me if there's anything you want us to ask the suspect during the interview." As Martinez and Ricardo descended the stairs, Ricardo mentioned that the gloves found in the dumpster contained a small sample of blood from the person wearing them. Martinez said he'd see whether they could get Logan to provide them with a sample.

Before delving into the questioning, Julia secured Logan's agreement to provide a blood sample. The stress level in the room increased as Vicente was summoned and arrived quickly to take the sample. While his blood was undergoing analysis, Julia had Logan recount the story he'd told Ricardo and her at the condo. This time it was being recorded—an essential step in building a case against him should any evidence contradict his assertion his father was already dead when he got there. This time, however, Julia pressed on with the questions, and Logan was more composed, at least initially.

"On the day of the party, you were heard arguing with your father just beside the pickleball courts. You said"—Julia found her notes and read from them—"'Fine by me' to your father's comment of 'over my dead body.' Those are threatening words, Logan."

"Oh, come on. It's just one of those things people say but don't mean literally. I would never hurt my dad. Never, no matter how much of a jerk he was."

"Did you really spill your beer by accident, Logan? Your mom told us she knew of your plan to tell your father about your new coach. Was the spilled beer your way of having an excuse to leave the party?"

"Yes, that's right. I did it on purpose. I wanted to talk with Dad when he was relaxed. When he was in a good mood, you know. I've never been able to deal with him when he's angry. It always ended in a huge fight."

"Yes, when we first spoke, you implied arguments between you and your father were normal. Why did you change into all-black clothing before you headed to speak with your dad? You can see how your actions look suspicious—as though it was premeditated."

"No, no, you've got it all wrong. I never had any intention of doing anything other than talking with him. When I got home, they were the only clean clothes I had left. You can ask Mom. She hadn't found a laundromat yet. The washing machine in our condo doesn't work. Check it. I'm not lying." Logan's statements were staccato, like verbal bullets he shot at her.

He was panting.

Julia needed to keep him calm, so changed the line of questioning. She wanted him off-balance, not panicking.

"When you left the party, was there anyone on or around the front steps of the condo?"

Logan took a breath and thought for a minute. "I didn't see anyone, but I wasn't paying attention, either. I just wanted to get a chance to talk with my dad."

"Okay, good. Did you see or hear anything near the courts when you were there or on your route there and back?"

"When I got there and saw Dad's grotesque body, the shock was paralyzing. I stood there for a minute or so before I bolted. During that time, I heard rustling behind the courts. It sounded as if someone or something was lurking back there. It sounded like plastic bags, garbage bags maybe."

"And what time was that, Logan?" Julia asked.

"I don't know." Logan's voice trembled. He took a ragged breath, his gaze fixed on the stark ceiling of the boxlike interview room. Gathering his thoughts, Julia surmised. But when the young man began talking, his words rushed out in a frenzied torrent. Julia could barely absorb what he was saying.

"I left our condo just after eleven, I think. Then I jogged to the beach but didn't see Dad, so I ran to the courts and after finding his body, I ran back to the party. So, um, it was probably sometime around eleven thirty," Logan stammered, looking back and forth between Julia and Martinez.

He's terrified. I can't let him freak out or he's liable to start fabricating things to try to appease us, Julia thought, watching his wild eyes.

"Logan, I want you to take a deep breath for me before we go on. And have a drink of water." When he seemed a bit more composed, she continued. "Did you see anyone else while you were at the beach or en route to your condo or back to the party?"

This time before answering, Logan appeared to consider the question and give it some thought. "On my way to the condo to change, I saw a man walking a big, fluffy dog, a husky, I think. He nodded to me as we passed. At the beach, there was no one I could see. And other than the rustling sound behind the courts when I was there, I didn't see or hear anyone. I suppose it could have been a coyote back there going through garbage. I don't know. I didn't kill my dad. I didn't."

There was a knock at the door of their interview room. The detective inspector answered it. He stepped outside for a moment and then returned. He spoke quickly to Julia in Spanish, and at his desk, Ricardo's shoulders sank.

Vicente had sprayed luminol on all Logan's clothes. If a human bodily fluid had been on the clothes, it would fluoresce under ultraviolet black light. There were no traces of blood anywhere. The shoes, however, did have telltale blood on the soles. *It was possible he'd stepped into the blood pool as he checked on his dad,* Julia thought. Finally, he revealed that the blood on the inside of the gloves used in the murder was not a match to Logan's.

Julia knew from the brutality of the attack and the voids in the blood pool that the perpetrator's clothes would have gotten bloody. She turned back to Logan. "Logan, do you take Valium?"

Logan looked bewildered by the change in direction. "What? No. My mom does, though. What does that have to do with Dad's murder? Was he drugged?"

Just then, Martinez's phone dinged with a message from Ricardo. The inspector read it, responded with the message *Good idea* and then handed the phone to Julia. The two officers stepped out of the interrogation room and spoke for a couple of minutes, then retreated to the war room, where Ricardo joined them. Time to let their suspect sweat for a bit.

Chapter Thirty-Seven

When Julia and Hector returned to the interrogation room, a couple of hours later, Julia's demeanor had changed markedly. Logan complained at being left so long, but the pair ignored his protestations.

"Logan, you were gone from the party for almost an hour. Here's what I think happened. You left the party and went directly to the courts, still wearing your shorts and a Hawaiian shirt. On your way, you found a pair of gloves and took them. When you got there, your dad was still alive and in no mood to hear about a new coach. You argued. You hit him with a paddle. He fell, and you beat and stabbed him. You tossed the bloody gloves into the dumpster behind the court and turned off the light. Then you ran home in the shadows, changed, and made a show, for anyone who might be watching, of jogging in the middle of the road to the courts, then running back to the party. I suspect you threw away the clothes you were wearing when you murdered your father."

It was time to get tough.

"Oh my God, this is exactly what I was afraid would happen. You're fabricating a story so you can charge me. You don't even care that I didn't kill my dad. I'm the easy solution to your case. I need a lawyer. You're trying to railroad me. You've fabricated everything. It's all a lie. I didn't kill my dad. I didn't!" Logan exclaimed, his voice wavering between fear and anger.

"You may retain a lawyer if you wish, Logan. There are a couple in town who speak English. I will give you their numbers." She then spoke with the inspector for a moment. She wanted his input as to whether they had enough to hold Logan in their cells. Martinez didn't think they did. Julia's thoughts were just speculation at this point. She agreed.

"Logan, I will be keeping your passport, and I will notify the military checkpoint north of town not to allow your rental vehicle to leave the area until we inform them otherwise. You're not under arrest, but don't leave San Amaro. Understood?" Julia asked.

The young man must have expected the worst. He must have thought he was going to be charged with his father's murder. At Julia's words, his eyes widened in disbelief. At the same time, his body seemed to crumple inward, as if he had been bracing himself for the worst, only to suddenly relax, like a marionette whose strings had been cut.

Gloria and Brianna were huddled together in the entry area of the station, where several mismatched chairs provided seating. They had been waiting for hours. Perhaps they also feared the worst, because upon seeing Logan, both gasped, and Gloria began to weep. Julia spoke to the women. "You are welcome to take Logan home to the condo, though he is still a suspect. Logan may not leave San Amaro unless I tell you differently. You can take him home now, but before you leave, Gloria, I need something from you.

"Would you please make a list of the companies and cities where your husband worked and the time frames of his employment with each?" Julia asked, handing her a yellow pad of lined paper and a pen. Brianna and Logan started to leave the station to wait for their mom outside.

"Brianna, I want a word with you, too, please," Julia said to stop them from leaving the station. She dismissed Logan. "Your sister will join you in a minute."

With Gloria and Brianna together in the otherwise deserted waiting area, she asked the question. "Which of you gave Rudy the Valium the night he died?"

Gloria's head whipped toward her daughter before she was consciously aware of her action. Brianna glanced at her mom with an apologetic look. "I did. I knew Logan was hoping to tell Dad about his new coach that night, and I thought it might make Dad less volatile, less likely to . . ." She didn't finish the thought. "I put it in the glass of wine he had at dinner before we left for the party. That's not what killed him though, right?" There was a pleading tone in her voice, and her eyes were beseeching.

"No, it didn't kill him, but it may have made him less able to ward off his attacker." Brianna looked as if she were going to head out to the car, but Julia stopped her and led her out of earshot of her mother. "You were overheard at the pickleball potluck saying your dad made you so mad you could kill him. Did you find a paddle ideal for the job?"

"Oh my God, no!" Brianna said emphatically, causing Gloria to look over at the pair. "I could never hit anyone, let alone my dad. It was just an expression of frustration, nothing more."

Julia kept at the girl for a minute, but she'd figured as much. Still, it was a question she needed to ask so she could cross the lead off the list. "You can go join your brother."

Julia returned and sat beside Gloria as she continued writing her list. "When did you discover the washing machine in your condo was broken?" Julia asked. She needed to verify Logan's assertion about it.

"It was a couple of days after Rudy was . . ." Gloria trailed off, not able to say the words. "We were all running out of clean clothes."

Julia moved on.

"Gloria, at the pickleball courts, you were heard telling your husband he shouldn't make enemies. Was he in the habit of alienating people?"

"Oh dear. No, not intentionally, I don't think. He could just be abrupt and hardheaded when things didn't go as he wanted them. His manner was off-putting to some people. I was just trying to get him to take a breath and be more aware of other people's needs, too. It worked."

"Gloria, do you have any friends or relatives who are able to support you through this ordeal, even from afar?" Julia had been trying to figure out a gentle way to initiate a conversation about the woman's surreptitious phone habits and decided this might work.

Gloria stopped writing and looked intently at Julia. She was silent for several seconds before answering. "I've been in regular contact with my best friend at home. She is a great comfort to me, even though she's thousands of miles away. She's trying to work out a way to come here to help me deal with everything. I hope she can . . ." Gloria's eyes brimmed with tears. She used the back of her hand to dab at them.

"Is she a family friend? Do Logan and Brianna know her?" Julia didn't think now was the time to probe into other calls Gloria may have been making, but her intuition told her not to leave the subject completely.

"No. I didn't want my family to know her," Gloria said cryptically as she was completing the list of Rudy's employers. Julia saw the action for what it was. Gloria was putting an end to that conversation. Julia let her, for now, but knew there was something more to be uncovered, later.

Gloria finished the list and handed the pad and pen back to Julia, saying, "He was working in Kansas City, Missouri when we met, but I don't remember the company name. These are all the other places he worked." The list contained the names of six cities and nine companies spanning a twenty-five-year period. *Less than three years at each company,* Julia thought and pondered the implications.

Chapter Thirty-Eight

Julia desperately wanted to ask Norm Webster whether he wore leather gloves for his gardening. She'd racked her brain to try to remember whether he'd had any on when they'd first interviewed him. She just couldn't remember. If he were their killer, with his law background, she feared he'd know immediately they'd found the bloody gloves and lie. She'd just have to be patient.

Rick had gotten off the phone with Stella earlier in the day. They had arranged another pickleball session for that afternoon. Troy was in town for three more days and was eager to play again at least once before he had to head home. Stella assured him she'd find a fourth player. She figured Pippa would be interested.

While chatting with his friend, Rick was reminded he hadn't yet phoned Julia. He left a voicemail for her after ending his chat with Stella.

When Julia returned to her desk, she had the message from Rick Whorton. She had a prickle of excitement as she dialed him back.

"Hi, Mr. Whorton, this is Detective Sergeant Garcia returning your call. I hope we didn't get you into any difficulty by pulling you out of your Plumeria Club meeting."

"Hi, Detective. No, no trouble at all. But I am calling about the meeting. I probably should have phoned sooner, but it didn't strike me as important at the time. And, I don't know whether this is important or not, but I thought I should tell you. After the Plumeria

Club meeting was over, three people came to me individually to ask me what you wanted."

Julia's excitement increased. She grabbed her notebook and said, "Okay, who?"

"Gretchen Wagner, Dean McLean, and Norm Webster. I told each of them what you suggested, you were looking for a friend of mine concerning an incident you're investigating. They seemed fine with that answer. As I said, I don't know whether it's important, but there you go."

"It is useful information, Mr. Whorton. Thank you for taking the time to call me. And, don't hesitate to call again if anything else comes to mind."

Julia walked over to the whiteboard containing their list of suspects, and with a red colored marker drew circles around all three names, plus Logan's.

Moments later Vicente, looking shamefaced, joined her in the conference room. He'd been doing some additional research. "If bloody clothes are washed in a detergent called Vanish, it could remove all traces of blood from them. I'm sorry I didn't know this before. So, I can no longer say with complete certainty the clothes I just tested never had blood on them. And I haven't found any other test able to give us that assurance."

Had Rudy Stephanetti's killer just walked out of their station?

Chapter Thirty-Nine

Responding to Inspector Martinez's request, Julia and Ricardo spent their entire morning in a relentless pursuit of more evidence against Logan, each moment carrying the weight of building a damning case. Julia was consumed by a series of phone calls, engaging first with Will Pritchard and then with a slew of individuals within the American pickleball community who could shed light on Logan's abilities, Rudy's coaching prowess, and the intricate father-son dynamic.

Meanwhile, Ricardo, occasionally guided by Martinez's insights, meticulously cross-referenced and analyzed the ever-increasing treasure trove of information Julia had uncovered, a process marked by escalating tension and mounting pressure.

The three met for a crucial midday rendezvous, the weight of their case against Logan heavy in the air. Martinez phoned a district judge who could provide a verdict on their evidence against the young man. Was it strong enough to prosecute? The trio systematically presented their evidence against Logan.

As the conversation reached its culmination, the judge made his pronouncement. Their case lacked sufficient strength to prosecute. Martinez requested they continue to look at other suspects while keeping Logan firmly in their sights.

Ricardo gathered the eight-by-ten-inch photographs taken at the poker run of five tricked-out, off-road Jeep Wranglers and Rubicons, the upscale version of the Wrangler, and placed them in a manila folder, a photo lineup to present to their witness. Lorenzo Vela was awaiting their visit.

At the dining room table of their rented condo, Lorenzo carefully looked at the pictures. He ruled two out right away because he was adamant the Jeep he'd seen the night of the party had a winch on the front bumper.

Julia watched as Lorenzo looked at each of the three remaining photos. He was being thorough, holding each picture for a long time. Occasionally he'd nod his head and eventually, he pushed one photo toward the two officers, stating he was sure it was the one he'd seen. It was Wolfe Wagner's dark green Jeep. Time to pay the man another visit.

Given it was well after lunchtime, they decided to check the brewery first to see whether Wolfe was following his usual pattern. As they arrived at the building, Ricardo nodded at Wolfe's Jeep, parked near the door. Inside, the man they sought was sitting on the same stool he'd inhabited the last time they found him there. This time, Julia didn't give him the option of staying on his stool, insisting he join Ricardo and her in a booth in the corner.

"Mr. Wagner, we have a witness who saw your Jeep driving past the condos around the corner from Suzanne and Edie's condo the night of the pickleball potluck right in the time frame when Rudy Stephanetti was murdered. What were you doing there? And why did you lie to us the last time we spoke?" Julia asked in a conversational tone.

"Well, that's just bullshit. I was at home asleep, with my wife that night. I keep telling you. It had to have been someone else's Jeep your witness saw. Gimme a break, this town is full of them. You might have noticed," Wolfe said with a sneer.

Ricardo pulled out the five pictures of similar Jeeps and set them on the table. Julia continued. "We showed our witness these pictures, and he was certain it was yours he'd seen that night." Wolfe shuffled through the photos and then tossed them back on the table.

"I don't know what to tell you. It wasn't me. I was sleeping in my bed with my wife. Nobody else ever drives my Jeep, so your witness is wrong."

Julia noticed his language had cleaned up. He wasn't cursing, and he appeared earnest in his denial. She thought perhaps he could sense the gravity of the current questions. "Perhaps it was your wife driving it, then."

"We were in bed together. How many times do I have to say it? It wasn't her, either."

"Your wife told us you both sleep with earplugs and take sleeping pills. Isn't it possible she left while you were sleeping?" Julia asked.

"But she didn't know the guy from Adam. Why would she?" Wolfe asked.

"Did your wife work outside the home, Mr. Wagner?" Julia asked.

"Yeah, she did. We didn't have any kids. She was a career woman. Worked in accounting for a couple of engineering companies."

"And where were these companies located?"

"Kansas City, Missouri," Wolfe said.

"Do you remember the names of the companies?"

"No" came the belligerent reply.

The detectives headed next to the home of Wolfe and Gretchen Wagner. If Wolfe wasn't driving the Jeep, they were left with one alternative.

Ricardo was quiet on the drive. Julia glanced his way a couple of times but could see he was lost in thought. Finally, he spoke.

"We've got to unearth a clear, strong motive!" he exclaimed. "I feel as if we're running around in circles chasing maybes and theories. And yes, I know. It's how cases go sometimes. But, aren't you getting frustrated?"

Julia admitted she was. The case had so many players; at least one, Logan had means and opportunity, but the judge decreed his motive was weak. He was an adult and was bound to his father/coach because he had chosen to be. Surely, being concerned his dad would get mad at him for signing with a new coach wasn't sufficient cause to murder the man. Frustrating was an understatement.

The shadow of suspicion stretched over another potential suspect who seemed to align with all the criteria—Norm Webster. Apart from the victim's family, he was the solitary figure in San Amaro who shared a long-standing connection with Rudy. However, they couldn't escape the gnawing concern: if Logan's motive appeared feeble, Norm's was even more fragile.

Yet, amid the swirl of speculation, Julia offered a tantalizing theory. "What if," she suggested, "despite his claim that money wasn't his primary motivator, it was, in fact, a driving force? Financial desperation can drive even the most steadfast individuals to commit shocking deeds. Perhaps, Norm's financial situation deserves deeper exploration, as we can't rule out the possibility money played a role in this dark puzzle. Norm's potential involvement merits a closer examination." The room hung heavy with the realization their focus had now shifted toward Norm. Before tackling Norm, however, they still had another lead to investigate.

Chapter Forty

The Wagners' house was on the mountain side of The Oasis, a mile or two from the highway. The area contained a mixture of simple cinder-block homes standing naked on the bare sand, RVs under ramadas, compounds with several buildings and full landscaping, and everything in between.

Gretchen and Wolfe's property had a bit of everything. On the west side of their lot stood a large, bus-like RV under a ramada built to match the architecture of their home. A building beside the ramada contained three bays each with its own garage door. The center bay door was open, showing a sand rail on blocks with the wheels off. The garage also matched the design of the hacienda-style house.

The yard was fully enclosed by a five-foot concrete wall with a sliding metal gate that stood open. Several palm trees graced the south side of the property, the shadows from which created evenly spaced lines of shade on the brick patio. Along the north side of the property, both Julia and Ricardo could now recognize three plumeria trees, all sporting new buds. It was a beautiful compound.

As soon as they were all settled at the kitchen nook in a surprisingly messy, but well-appointed, home, Julia started the questioning with almost the same lead-in as she'd used with the woman's husband. "Mrs. Wagner, we have a witness who identified Wolfe's Jeep driving on the road just around the corner from the location of the pickleball potluck around the time Rudy Stephanetti was murdered. We've spoken with your husband, and he is adamant it wasn't him. Can you explain that?"

"Oh, my goodness. How do you know it's our Jeep?" Gretchen asked. Her face was flaming.

Ricardo again pulled out the five photos and laid them on the table.

Julia explained that a witness had identified with certainty Wolfe's Jeep as the one he'd seen.

"I see. Well, this is embarrassing." Gretchen looked back and forth between the two detectives, then lowered her head.

Julia recognized shame when she saw it. "Mrs. Wagner, why don't you tell us what you were doing there?"

"There is a man from pickleball whom I've been seeing. Denis Dumas." Julia remembered his name from the players gathered at the courts the day Rudy's body was found.

Gretchen explained the man was fairly new in San Amaro, and he lived close by the Wagners' home. Wanting to be a good neighbor, she had taken him a lemon meringue pie shortly after he moved into the area.

"He's a lovely man. A widower. We started meeting for coffee in the afternoons while Wolfe was at the brewery and . . . well, one thing led to another. Isn't that what they say?" Gretchen looked miserable.

"Tell us about the late-night Jeep trip to the condos the night of the potluck." Julia prompted the woman to get to the part of the story relevant to her and Ricardo.

The story came out slowly with Gretchen looking more and more unhappy through the telling. A few days before the party, Denis told her he wanted to stop the affair. At first, Gretchen agreed. She was feeling guilty for cheating on Wolfe.

"But I quickly found my feelings for Denis were deeper than I'd realized. I missed him terribly. Not the sex so much as the closeness we had. Wolfe isn't one to talk about his emotions, but Denis is different. I felt a deep connection to him." Gretchen stopped and took a drink of her coffee.

When it appeared Gretchen wasn't going to continue, Julia prompted her. "The night of the party . . ."

"Right. Well . . ." Gretchen paused as she sought the courage to tell the police her story. "The night of the potluck, I got the idea in my head Denis had found someone else. I believed he was at the party that night with another woman. So, I didn't take my sleeping pill, and once Wolfe was asleep, I slipped out of bed, dressed, and drove to the condos. I wasn't sure what street Suzanne and Edie lived on, so I was driving around looking for a bunch of parked cars. I found it after a couple of tries and parked at a vacant driveway a few condos away from theirs. I was hoping to see Denis. Of course, by the time I got there, people were leaving. I sat there for about ten minutes but was feeling more and more pathetic, so I left and came home."

"You told us you have a car you normally drive, your clown car. Why did you take the Jeep and not your own car?"

"Wolfe had drained the oil from my car in preparation for changing it the next day. The Jeep was the only drivable vehicle."

"Mrs. Wagner, did you and Rudy Stephanetti ever work at the same company?" Julia showed her a picture of Rudy that Gloria had emailed her.

"Oh, God. That's why I thought I recognized the name. Yes, he was a junior marketing coordinator for a company I worked with in the mid-1990s. I didn't know him, but I saw him around a few times. Stephanetti is an unusual name. He was single back then and thought he was every woman's dream, from what I heard. Wolfe and I were happily married and I didn't give him any notice, though the gossip at the time was he spent more of his time hitting on the secretarial staff than doing his job. He joined the company just as I was leaving. We overlapped for a few weeks."

"What company was that?" Julia asked.

"GE and C, sorry, Grosvenor Engineering and Construction," Gretchen said.

Julia made some notes. The company wasn't on the list she'd received from Gloria. It was, however in Kansas City. "Was Mr. Stephanetti ever inappropriate with you at work?"

"No. I never got that close to him. Our jobs didn't give us any cause to interact with each other. Even in the short time we overlapped, I did hear comments he was always pestering the young female admin staff. Unfortunately, that behavior is not all that unusual in engineering companies. They are usually over eighty percent male, and the testosterone can get a bit overwhelming."

"Okay, thank you. I think that's all for right now, Mrs. Wagner, though we may need to speak with you again." She and Ricardo rose to leave.

"Do you need to tell Wolfe about any of this?" Gretchen asked, a sad expression marring her otherwise attractive face.

"At this point, we don't, but since we've already spoken with him today about his Jeep being at the condos, he may be asking questions of his own when he gets home." Julia spoke as gently as she could. It was not her job to judge people's behavior except as it pertained to her investigations. And making moral assessments was neither her responsibility nor her desire.

As soon as they got back to the car, Julia phoned Denis Dumas to verify Gretchen's story. Denis confirmed he had been seeing Gretchen and had broken off the relationship a few days before the party. Her story alone didn't get Gretchen off the hook. Her reason for being in the vicinity when Rudy was murdered may or may not have had anything to do with the excuse she'd given Julia. Claiming she'd been trying to see whether Denis had a new girlfriend may have been a lie. She admitted to having been in the area at the time of Rudy's murder.

She was still a suspect.

Julia and Ricardo sat in La Chica for several minutes before they left the Wagners' driveway. They discussed the recurring comments they were getting about Rudy pestering the women with whom he worked. Given Tony Ranelli's assertion that Rudy was sexually inappropriate with female staff, their motive was becoming clearer. Julia posited that while a few of the women may have found the attention flattering, in her experience, more often it was not appreciated.

Ricardo knew that his experience as a cop in San Amaro bore as much similarity to Julia's as a seagull to a bull. Women in Mexican police departments were a minority and, for the most part, highly undervalued. He accepted Julia's comments as true and hoped he wasn't as bad as the majority of male officers. It was a conversation they came back to occasionally and was the underlying reason, Ricardo suspected, Julia would not move their relationship beyond friendship.

"I hope you'll tell me if my antics ever become creepy. You know when I call you Lucy, it's because I enjoy having a closer relationship with you than the other guys at the station. If I ever thought it was offensive to you, I'd never forgive myself," Ricardo said with more seriousness than Julia usually saw in him.

"Don't worry, Ricky, I'll keep you on the right side of that line. What I'm talking about is not something friendly, like we have. It's a pattern of interaction that's about power and control. Men who use language, belittling jokes, and innuendos to diminish women, keep them in subservient roles, and in an attempt to show other men around them how vastly superior they are to mere women.

"Believe me, it isn't just in the police, and it isn't just in Mexico. But, if I ever do catch you doing any of that, you'll know. In no uncertain terms.

"It's becoming clear to me Rudy had the *creepy* factor. I think it's our best line of inquiry."

Chapter Forty-One

Detective Inspector Martinez, sensing the young constables were at a loss about what to do next on their case, had provided them with a couple of suggestions. So, Javier and Luis had been scouring online auctions and independent seller sites on the internet looking for someone selling secondhand, or more frequently described by sellers as *properly cured*, comals, but so far had not found any they considered viable.

His other suggestion to the two constables was to go to the Saturday swap meet at The Oasis, where local vendors and expats alike sold a wide variety of items to one another. It was a few days until Saturday. And, they'd get to go to work in street clothes for their *undercover operation*, as they had dubbed it. They were excited.

Through this investigation, Luis was reminded of how much he'd liked Javier when they were in the same station in Mexicali as newly minted police officers. He had a good sense of humor, which made being his partner more enjoyable than some of the sad sacks he'd worked with previously. And, Javier's quick mind often led him to appropriate next steps before Luis got there himself. Because of that, he was starting to have a pang of conscience about spying on him.

Saturday morning had finally arrived. Luis was thinking about the report he'd given to Martinez after witnessing Javier ripping off gringos during traffic stops. Today, as they wandered into the swap meet hoping to appear as just a couple of regular joes, he was contemplating his next report. It needed to balance out such concerns with the good work Javier had done so far on this investigation.

Those thoughts, however, were soon to vanish.

Since Julia had planned to be busy making phone calls during morning, Ricardo had been asked by Inspector Detective Martinez to assist a pair of young constables under his purview, Ramos and Medina, with their interview of a suspect in a case they were working. He told Ricardo he didn't have time to participate in the interview himself and didn't feel either constable was ready yet to take the lead in the interrogation. Ricardo agreed and headed to Interview Room Two, where the constables waited to fill him in on their case.

Julia's first call was to Pickleball Pro Gear. She wasn't sure who would be the right person to talk with about amateur reps, as she thought it would be under Rudy's work umbrella. She'd decided to start with Rudy's boss, but the receptionist told her the company CEO, Rudy's boss, was overseas at the moment. She was forwarded to Rudy's second-in-command instead.

Having identified herself and her purpose as an investigator delving into Rudy's mysterious death, Julia plunged into the conversation, pressing for the information she sought. The man on the other end acknowledged he could assist her.

Julia discovered Norm Webster had served as an amateur representative for a substantial five-year stretch, silently weaving himself into the tapestry of the company. His amiable nature had endeared him to the marketing team and his fellow amateur representatives. Yet, beneath the surface, she glimpsed the enigma. Norm's paddle sales might not have set records, but he managed to rake in a few thousand dollars each year. That detail lured her deeper into the theory of money having been a motivator for Norm.

Her final question remained unspoken. This man would not be able to answer it. *Was it enough money to incite a murder?*

Julia spent the remainder of her morning phoning all the attendees of the pickleball potluck. She aimed to ascertain whether any of them had ever worked at one of the companies where Rudy Stephanetti had been employed. She had been surprised she had to remind several people she was investigating a murder and this was a lead police were following. *Why would anyone be upset by having to name where they had worked?* she wondered.

She also marveled at the way people's lives intersected. The expat communities in and around San Amaro were home, at least part of the year, to a few thousand people at most. Their origins spanned the United States, Canada, and Europe. Yet, within this limited sphere, her investigation had already unearthed five people who had attended the party or been at pickleball the day before the murder who may have known Rudy through working at the same companies during the same period.

It wasn't only Norm and Fran Webster, through their association with Pickleball Pro Gear, who had known Rudy—their connection was expected. What truly astounded her was the revelation of others, still lurking in the shadows, with a professional link to Rudy. *What secrets still remained uncovered?*

While speaking with Clint Brayer, she confirmed the dates of his employment as a cop in Saint Paul and queried him about his wife's employment during the same period. Clint was uncertain about the companies in which she'd worked the first few years of their marriage, so Julia wanted to speak with Anne directly.

Julia learned she wouldn't be back in San Amaro for four more days, as she was staying with their first great-grandson while their granddaughter and her husband were skiing in Utah. Julia started to make a reminder in her phone to call then. But Clint gave Julia Anne's cell-phone number and suggested she call now. "I don't want it to stall your investigation. Anne won't mind. She was a cop's wife for thirty-six years."

"You said something when we first talked. It's stuck in my brain. You stated you didn't believe Mr. Stephanetti's apology at the end of pickleball league play the day you asked him and his family to leave the courts. Can you say anything more about that? What didn't seem sincere about it?" Julia asked, as much out of curiosity as to potentially learn something from this veteran officer.

"I have a bachelor's degree in psychology," Clint said, prefacing his remarks and was about to continue, but was interrupted by an interjection from Julia.

"Oh? I do, too! Sorry, I didn't mean to interrupt, please continue."

"Great. It's an excellent background. I think it helps one to be a better cop. Anyway, about Rudy, there was no authenticity in his voice, his words, or his body language. Which is why I call him a narcissist. He was projecting an image of what he thought would impress people and said whatever he thought would get him what he wanted.

"In this particular case, I think it was to be liked and accepted by the group. Probably so he could manipulate us into letting him do what he'd wanted from the start . . . to be able to play whenever he wanted in his family unit. But I'm just speculating," Clint said. "In case it's helpful."

"Great, thanks, Mr. Brayer. I was curious what you based your comments on, and you answered my question. I'll give your wife a call about her employment."

From Anne, Julia learned she and Rudy worked for the same company, but not at the same time. Rudy had already left the company before Anne was hired. Julia was about to end the call when Anne surprised her. "A good friend of mine was working there during the same time frame as Rudy, though. I'll give her a call and see whether she remembers him. If she does, I'll call you back with her number. If it would help?"

Julia indicated it would be great.

When she was finished with Anne, Julia moved on to the last couple on her list, Dean and Sandy McLean. It was Dean who answered the phone, and, in his deep Texan drawl, he reminded her he worked for the bus service in Fort Worth for decades. When asked for the places Sandy had worked, Dean hesitated for a moment before naming Lone Star Compressors and Pumps as her employer for her entire career. Julia remembered Sandy saying she had stayed with the same firm until she retired. It was not a company on the list from Gloria, so she thanked him and hung up.

As she'd been on the phone, she'd made a list of companies where Rudy's employment had aligned with people on their list of suspects. She updated her chart of suspects with a new column labeled *Worked with Rudy*.

Julia had also received an email from the desk sergeant while she was making her calls, saying Ana Maria would be resuming her normal duties the following day. The gossip and speculation from online posts about the murder were dwindling. Still, Julia kept her friend busy for the remainder of the day completing a final report on the Facebook posts about the murder.

Julia recognized the pressing need for more research on the companies where Rudy had worked, yet the idea of diverting Ana Maria's focus for mere hours didn't seem like the most strategic use of her time. A sense of unease gnawed at Julia; an instinct told her something crucial was eluding her. But she didn't think Ana Maria was the person to help her.

A new plan took shape in her mind. She had someone else in her sights who might be able to uncover a missing piece of this intricate puzzle. She pulled out her cell phone, found her cousin's number, and dialed it from her desk phone.

"National Library, Alma Pérez speaking."

Julia was always surprised at how clearly someone thousands of kilometers away could sound on the phone. "Hey, Alma, it's Julia. How are you, and do you have a minute to talk?"

"Julia, what a wonderful surprise. I've been thinking so much about you since our time together last week. I'm fine and, yes, I have time to talk. What's going on with you?" Alma asked.

Hearing her cousin's voice brought a big smile to Julia's face. *Was it just a week since their time together?* she thought with amazement. "I got put on a murder case within an hour of being back at work. I can hardly believe it's been only a week, well, eight days, since I saw you. I'm doing fine, too, but I'm incredibly busy. All the witnesses and suspects in the case are English speakers, so my time is spread thinly across too many different tasks. While I'd love to chat, I'm sorry to say my call is to see whether you could help me with something. You being a researcher extraordinaire and all."

"Way to butter me up. What do you need help with?" Alma asked.

"I have a list of American companies and I need to know whether any of them changed their names between 1990 and now. You know, got bought out by or merged with another company, that kind of thing. I'm playing a hunch. I think one of my suspects is lying and telling the truth at the same time," Julia said cryptically.

"Hmm. I'm not sure how a person does both simultaneously. Maybe you can explain it to me sometime. But, yes, I can easily do the research for you. Send me the list of companies—email is best— and I should be able to get you the results in a couple of hours. Unless I get another assignment to be done immediately, of course."

"You are a lifesaver. Thank you. Here comes the email now. And when this case is over, I'd love to chat. Maybe we can share a long-distance glass of wine. Our conversations last week made a strong impact on me, and I'd love to keep it up. If you're interested," Julia said, feeling a bit vulnerable.

"I'd love it, Julia. They made an impact on me, too. It's a date. When you're not in the middle of a murder investigation, obviously. Okay, I got your email with the list. Shall I send my research results to this same email address?" Alma asked, bringing them back to the business at hand.

"Yes, perfect. Thank you. Love you, cuz. We'll talk soon."

Chapter Forty-Two

Ana Maria dropped her final report on Facebook posts potentially discussing the murder into Julia's in tray, saying she didn't know whether there was anything useful for Julia and Ricardo this time. Julia noticed as she retrieved it, the stack of papers was much thinner than Ana Maria's previous recaps. She thanked her colleague again for doing a great job gathering and analyzing the posts.

Julia began by reading the summary and analysis. For a while, some of the Facebook theories included the Christiesque notion that the entire Stephanetti family killed Rudy, or perhaps a crazed renter in the condos had. But now, apparently, the gossip machine had coalesced on the idea the son, Logan, must have murdered his father. Julia shook her head in disgust at people's ability to fabricate *facts* from pure speculation. *Still, they may be right,* she thought.

Even with this reduced number of pages in Ana Maria's final report, Julia wished she could skim it to see whether there was anything worth reading in detail, but her dyslexia made it impossible. Her brain was capable only of gleaning the content of written words by focusing on each word separately. It was laborious, but it was all Julia knew. She smiled to herself recalling when she'd taken a speed-reading class once, just before she started on her undergraduate degree. Over the two-day class, she had managed to improve her reading speed by a whopping three words a minute. Most of her cohort had improved closer to a hundred times Julia's number.

The summary instantly ignited a spark of curiosity in Julia. Her thoughts took an abrupt detour to the initial report Ana Maria had shared with her and Ricardo. That report had triggered a familiar yet elusive sensation. She had a nagging feeling something wasn't adding up. This new summary had her grappling with the same enigmatic sensation. Something in these posts was causing her internal alarm to buzz as if an elusive piece of this complex mystery was just out of reach.

With a persistent itch in her mind, Julia decided to delve into the raw Facebook posts, determined to decipher the source of her disquiet. Twenty intense minutes later, after revisiting Ana Maria's initial report and scouring the more recent posts, Julia found herself seated at her desk, grappling with the weight of her unshakable unease. There was something deeply troubling lurking within comments from both sets of data, something she was determined to uncover.

Both comments had been left on other people's posts, and while neither of them directly linked to the murder, they illuminated the most probable motive behind the atrocious crime. The first comment originated from Willie Platz in response to one of Wolfe Wagner's inflammatory posts. Wolfe had made a provocative remark, insinuating Rudy might have made advances toward someone's wife, concluding with the chilling notion Rudy got what he deserved. Willie's comment, in English, read, "Some women don't know how to take a joke." However, the translation software substituted "joke", *chiste*, in Spanish, with an enigmatic Spanish term, *adivinanza*, typically associated with a riddle or conundrum, giving it a subtly innocuous twist.

As Julia contemplated the original text, she unraveled a haunting realization. Her subconscious had instinctively grasped the true meaning when she read the Spanish translation, even before her conscious mind had fully processed it. The remark held a disquieting familiarity for her, one etched into her career. She had encountered these sentiments repeatedly, though often couched in different words.

It was a pattern she knew all too well—the undermining jokes and derogatory stories about women circulated among her colleagues, often in her presence. Those women who dared react negatively were met with mockery and belittlement, often using the same contemptuous sentence: "You just don't know how to take a joke." Julia sat at her desk, haunted by the resonance of these experiences, knowing intuitively they had deep roots in the case she was investigating.

The most recent batch of posts held a relevant and succinct response. Julia found it when reading the original English, full text of the messages. It affected her strongly. This one was a comment from Gretchen Wolfe. It had been made recently, but against the original "can't take a joke" comment Willie had made several days previous. Gretchen's comment echoed in Julia's mind. She had thought the same thing more times than she cared to remember. "Sexual innuendo taken too far isn't flirtatious, it's a form of abuse."

She was still trying to think through the implication of Gretchen making the statement in reference to Rudy's murder as she trudged up the stairs to their war room. As she hoped, Ricardo was finished with his interrogation duties. She raised the concern most present in her thoughts to her partner.

"Do you suppose she was speaking generally with her remark, or was it personal? Do you think she had more interaction with Rudy when they worked together than she let on?" Ricardo asked.

"We'll have to ask her. But her comment got me thinking about all the references we've heard about Rudy spending time with the admin assistants where he worked. I know women's rights are better in the States than in some other countries—Mexico being one of them—but I'm sure women still get sexually harassed in the States. I'm wondering whether Rudy was more than just a Lothario.

Perhaps he took pleasure in badgering women who didn't want to play his game. Remember what Karen Platz told us about Rudy at the party, something to the effect he stopped flirting with her when she flirted back."

Ricardo had already realized Julia was talking about more than just thoughts on the case. This was personal for her. She rarely talked with him about the difficulties she and her fellow female officers had with being victimized by some of their male counterparts. Julia would certainly never view herself as a victim. However, he got a new appreciation from this discussion of how difficult it might be to be constantly harangued with sexist comments. He would never put her on the spot with a direct conversation about it unless she initiated it, but he wanted her to know he was open to such a discussion should she want to bring it up.

"Unfortunately, there are more bullies drawn into police work than most of us want. I can't imagine how difficult it would be to bear the brunt of abuse on a daily basis. If our victim were that kind of abuser, it could provide a strong reason for the anger needed for such a brutal murder."

Julia gave a sad nod.

Chapter Forty-Three

When Julia got back to her desk, the message light was blinking on her phone. She keyed in the relevant numbers and retrieved two voicemails. One was from her grandmother inviting her to join her grandparents, her abuleos, for dinner that evening. She checked her watch and saw it was already an hour past her clocking-out time. She quickly phoned her *abuela*. Discovering she wasn't too late, she promised she'd join her grandparents in thirty minutes. After speaking with her *abuela*, she phoned the number of her second caller.

"Mr. Paul Fernell? This is Detective Sergeant Julia Garcia returning your call. You said you had some information for me from the evening of February twenty-four."

"I got the note you left taped to my door asking for a call. I just got back from a few days in Yuma. I *was* home the evening of the twenty-fourth, and there was more than the normal amount of activity. Lots of cars and people. Must have been a party, am I right? And I wasn't invited," Paul said in a jocular tone.

"Yes, there was a party. There was also a murder at the pickleball courts the same evening. I want to come and speak with you about what you may have seen or heard. Will you be around tomorrow morning, say about nine?"

"Oh. Okay. Yes, I'll be here." Paul Fernell suddenly lost his jocularity.

Julia lived on the same property as her grandparents, her *abuelos*, Juan and Elda. She loved them both dearly and was closer to them than her mom. She didn't have a bad relationship with her mother, but she and her dad had always been on the same wavelength. Her father understood her. And she'd adored him. She never had the same connection to her mom. So, when her dad died tragically when she was fourteen, she gravitated more toward her *abuelos* for support than her mom. Losing her dad broke her heart and made her teenage years difficult. Though Julia would probably have denied it, her dad's death left her hesitant to form any kind of deep relationship with men.

She stopped into her casita before going next door, dropped off her purse, and grabbed a bottle of brandy she kept under her sink. She rarely drank it herself, but her grandfather loved a tot after dinner.

The wonderful smell of her *abuela*'s cooking washed over her as she opened their door. She stood for a moment just letting it fill her with love. Because in her mind, Elda's cooking was an expression of pure love. Julia could tell just from the aromas, Elda had been cooking all day.

As she sat beside her grandfather, Elda set a steaming bowl of pozole in the center of the table and began ladling the fragrant soup into small bowls. Hominy, pork, cumin, and chilies had simmered for hours in broth to create the basis of what Julia thought of as the best comfort food in the world. A plate of sliced radishes, lettuce, onions, and more chilies plus wedges of lime provided all the toppings typically added to pozole upon serving. With her first taste, Julia almost groaned with pleasure.

Over their meal, they chatted about the delightful trivialities of her *abuelos*' life and the latest news of other family members—aunts, uncles, cousins—a normal Mexican family dinner. It was just what Julia needed, and she was glad she could tell them she'd spoken with her cousin, Alma, earlier in the day.

Once the kitchen was cleaned after their meal, Julia, clutching her brandy and two small glasses, climbed the stairs with her grandfather to the roof, as was their habit. Similar to most houses in San Amaro, the flat roof provided additional living space. Juan and Elda's held only a small round table and several mismatched plastic chairs, though some families used their roofs as additional living and sleeping space, since it hardly ever rained in San Amaro.

The pair spent a few minutes in silence simply savoring the warmth of the brandy and the beauty of the sunset. Then, as was also their habit, Juan asked about her latest case. Having been a policeman his entire working life, Julia's grandfather had retired from the position of station comandante. He was well respected by the current comandante, and Julia had no issue sharing her cases with her *abuelo*. He often provided excellent insights.

He already knew she was working on the pickleball-court murder, so she told him the latest details she and Ricardo had uncovered. Juan listened in silence with a deep sense of pride as she clearly laid out their interviews, the theories they were developing about motives, and how they had narrowed their suspect pool.

When she finished, Juan praised her work and her explanation of the case. He was thinking Hector Martinez, whom he had mentored as a new detective, must be delighted to have Julia and Ricardo working under him. Hector would make a good mentor.

"Do you have any thoughts about things we should be doing to get closer to uncovering the killer?" Julia asked, expecting he would give her some clever suggestion.

He surprised her by shaking his head. "Keep doing what you're doing, my dear. Your instincts are excellent. You and Ricardo make a good team. I know you'll solve it. You're getting closer every day," her grandfather said, raising his glass to her. "There's nothing I can think of you should be doing you haven't already thought of or done."

Later in the evening as Julia lay in her bed awaiting sleep, she was proud that her *abuelo*, whom she idolized as the kind of police officer she wanted to be, had said she was doing everything he would have done. Her desire to someday become the comandante herself might actually be possible. Her next step on her career path was to catch the killer of Rudy Stephanetti.

Chapter Forty-Four

Ricardo and Julia started their day by giving an update to Detective Inspector Martinez with their latest insights into the kind of person their victim had been. Martinez agreed their suspicions about Rudy's behavior toward women was the first motive they had that could explain the violence of the crime.

The motive appeared to exclude Logan as the murderer—until they considered the young man had also been the brunt of Rudy's bullying.

"If he were abusive and bullying to women, one of them might be pushed trying to get revenge. But are any of your female suspects strong enough to inflict the beating?" Martinez asked.

Julia answered, "Gretchen Wagner certainly appears to be strong enough, but I don't think she has a motive unless she lied to us about her time working with Rudy. Plus, I think this crime was perpetrated by a man. I can't see a woman inflicting either that type of beating or the final stabbing with the wooden handle, though a husband seems possible.

"How many brutally violent beating crimes are committed by women?" she asked rhetorically. "But, to be clear, I'm not yet ruling anyone out of the suspect pool based on sex. And, we have to remember, if the victim were not used to taking Valium, he may have been feeling its effects and therefore been easier to subdue. However, we have witnesses who saw two men, possibly in addition to Logan, in the vicinity of the courts near the time-of-death-window."

Martinez nodded and thanked the pair.

They left their superior and headed off to interview Paul Fernell.

The Fernells owned a condo near the one the Stephanettis were renting. Paul came to the door to answer Julia's knock. He was a much younger man than the majority of residents at The Oasis. Julia placed him in his mid-forties. He was tall and lean, clean shaven, and casually dressed in Tommy Bahama shorts and a Hawaiian shirt. His brown hair was thick but kept short in a brush cut. He was an attractive man, she thought. And, she noted as she walked past him at the door, he smelled good, too. Nice aftershave.

Once coffee had been poured, the three settled at the kitchen table, which looked out over the road and the golf course beyond. Julia reiterated the purpose of their visit and asked whether the man had met the Stephanetti family living a few doors away.

"I haven't met them, no, but I know the people you mean. I've seen them walking back and forth to the pickleball courts a few times."

"Oh?" Julia said with a note of surprise in her voice. "I'd have thought they'd go the other direction to the courts. Down to the left, rather than coming this way."

"Oh, no, there's a shortcut just to the right of my condo." Paul leaned toward the window to point out a walking path between his and the next condo block. "The path comes out almost right across from the west-side entrance to the courts. It's faster than taking the roads."

Julia shared this with Ricardo, and he scribbled away in his notebook. "You indicated on the phone yesterday, you were home the night of February twenty-four. Can you please tell me whatever you saw or heard? Please, don't try to edit anything. Sometimes, the smallest details can be the important ones."

Paul took her at her word and rambled on at length about the vehicles he'd seen going past in the early evening. Nothing stood out to the two detectives as being important. After a few minutes, he moved on in his narrative to events later in the evening. By the time he was finished telling his story, Julia and Ricardo wondered whether they might be getting closer to figuring out who had murdered Rudy Stephanetti.

Julia had received a text from Anne Brayer containing the name and number of her friend. Gwen Rowen worked at one of the companies from Gloria's list at the same time as Rudy. Upon being connected with Gwen, she explained the purpose of her call but found the woman was expecting her call and ready to share what she knew.

"Yes, I knew Rudy Stephanetti, though not well. We never worked directly together, but our paths crossed. He was working in marketing, I was in accounting. I was a CPA. Not Rudy's target audience, if you know what I mean," Gwen said.

"I'm not sure I do. Can you explain it to me, please?" Julia did not want to assume anything.

"Sure. Rudy had a reputation for picking on or trying to pick up administrative assistants. He mostly left the professional women alone."

"So, he liked to date clerical staff, women who worked for him, correct?" Julia needed to clarify what she was being told.

"Well, yes, but I'm not sure his goal was to get dates with the women he targeted. From what I heard from my friend in human resources, he seemed to get his kicks by humiliating and embarrassing women. He may have dated some of them, but I never heard that about him. From the stories I heard, he preferred the timid, shy, and insecure women, and apparently, he'd pester them mercilessly.

"I think it was a total power trip for him. It first came to the attention of HR when one gal he'd been picking on quit. In her exit interview, she admitted one of the junior executives—she didn't name Rudy as the perpetrator—would come to her desk and whisper inappropriate things to her several times a day. A couple of specific things she attributed to this man were being told he could smell sex on her and he could see her nipples getting erect when he came by.

"He denied the accusations completely, but the woman's coworkers confirmed Rudy would stop by the woman's desk frequently, though they never knew what he said. I heard there were other allegations against him, and then one day, Rudy just wasn't there anymore. My HR friend said he wasn't fired, per se, but I think they asked or forced him to quit."

"Do you know whether he defended his actions?" Julia asked.

"He concocted some ridiculous story about the whispers being gossip about other employees, claimed the woman invited his attention, and it was their little game. He argued it was all harmless fun," Gwen said.

Julia thanked her for her time and the insights she'd shared. Gwen's story confirmed the detectives' emerging understanding of Rudy's character, portraying him as a sexual predator who targeted vulnerable and timid women unable to confront or rebuke him. Julia remembered again Karen Platz's words: in effect, "When I flirted back, he lost interest." *Yes,* Julia thought, *he likes them docile and timid so he can bully them.*

While Julia was talking with Anne's friend, Ricardo was back at the dentist, getting the permanent crown to replace the temporary one from his previous root canal. When she got off the phone, she stared at the whiteboard list of suspects and their associated checklist of attributes, including who drove a Jeep and who had been wearing a Hawaiian shirt. She realized the board hadn't been updated with the idea the killer may not have needed to be tall and strong.

Next, she made a call to Gretchen Wagner and spoke with her about her comment on Facebook. It was not based on personal experience. Gretchen explained her younger sister had been among the first women in combat situations with the army. Gretchen's remarks were based on the sexual bullying she and her sisters in arms had faced.

Her mind drifted back to the other component she wanted to include in their murder suspects' list. Having a fairly large amount of Valium in his system could have made Rudy less able to ward off an attacker, and it was even possible he wasn't standing when the attack began. What if he'd been sitting on one of the benches or the ground? Julia set about updating the checklist. By the time Ricardo returned, he was sporting a new gold crown and had some ideas of his own after an hour in the dentist's chair with nothing to do but think.

Julia walked him through the information she'd used to update their murder board and what she'd learned from her phone call to Anne's friend, Gwen.

They started looking much more closely at the women with whom Rudy had worked. Their new working premise was his bullying behavior had pushed a husband to take revenge for his wife's suffering. Before they spent time exploring this new theory, Julia realized she needed to have a difficult conversation with Gloria. Surely she would know whether her husband was sexually bullying women with whom he worked. She checked her email before they headed out. Still nothing from Alma. A research assignment at work must be keeping her from getting back to Julia.

Chapter Forty-Five

Julia drove alone to the Stephanettis' condo. She was surprised when a middle-aged woman, not Gloria Stephanetti, answered her knock at the door. "You must be looking for Gloria," the woman said upon seeing Julia's quizzical expression. "I'm Marguerite Carmichael. Please come in. Have a seat. I'll get her for you."

Moments after Marguerite called her name, Gloria emerged from the master suite and joined Julia in the living room. "Marg, would you please bring us some iced tea and cookies?" Gloria asked her friend.

Julia was surprised by how much better Gloria looked. Her face had color, and her eyes no longer looked dull and lifeless. "Is this the friend you were telling me about? It looks as if her arrival has given you strength."

Gloria looked at Julia with an intensity Julia hadn't previously seen in her. "Yes, this is the woman I was telling you about. She arrived late yesterday, and having her here is wonderful." Marguerite came in with a tray of frosty glasses of iced tea and what appeared to be cinnamon-swirl sugar cookies. Next to cinnamon buns, they rivaled ginger snaps as Julia's favorite confection. She helped herself to two. Marguerite took a seat beside Gloria.

"Mrs. Stephanetti, I have some questions for you of a sensitive nature. Would you prefer to answer them in a more private setting?" As soon as Julia heard her own words, she was embarrassed at her seeming rudeness to Marguerite. "I'm sorry, I didn't mean to seem rude."

"There is nothing you can ask me I would not want Marguerite to hear. And please, call me Gloria." Gloria took the other woman's hand and gave it a squeeze. It appeared Marguerite returned the squeeze. Neither woman broke the physical contact. Both turned toward Julia.

"All right, Gloria," Julia said and paused while she thought about the best way to proceed. "With any police investigation, when we look at suspects, we are looking for means, motive, and opportunity: Did they have the capacity and capabilities to commit the crime? Could they have been at the place where the crime was committed at the time it occurred?

"There are several people here who fit those two requirements regarding your husband's murder. It's the third one, motive, with which Detective Sergeant Hernandez and I have been struggling. Recently, we have come to believe we may have found a motive strong enough to drive a person to commit such a brutal act. I need to know whether you think it's possible." Julia looked at the two women before her.

With her friend at her side, Gloria looked as if she could deal with anything. Julia continued. "Gloria, we have uncovered allegations of your husband repeatedly saying unwelcome and embarrassing sexually based things to shy and insecure administrative staff at the companies where he worked. Do you know anything about it?"

"Oh God!" Gloria covered her face with her free hand. "Sadly, I'm not shocked, Detective. I wouldn't say I knew about it directly. But I knew Rudy had a strong drive to feel powerful, to have power over people, especially people he considered weak or less intelligent than himself. He never, ever did it to me, or Brianna. Neither of us would stand for it. I admit I've had to act as a mediator between Rudy and others in the past. Rudy could be a bully. It's as simple as that."

"What about Logan? Did your husband bully Logan?"

Gloria's eyes hooded, and she looked suspiciously at Julia. "Logan didn't kill his father!"

Ignoring the woman's assertion, Julia continued in a firm, but gentle tone. "You said neither you nor Brianna would let your husband get away with trying to make you feel inferior. Did Rudy try to make Logan feel inferior?"

Gloria sighed. "Logan wanted to earn his dad's praise. And, yes, Rudy saw it as weakness. Theirs was a relationship fraught with tension."

"Were you aware your husband was asked to leave his job with one and probably more companies rather than be fired for his harassing behavior?"

Gloria looked at her lap for a moment, then took a deep breath, moved her gaze to Marguerite's face, then slowly back to Julia. "Yes, on some level I knew. And, God forgive me, I managed not to let it bother me." She held Julia's gaze. There was a look of defiance on her face.

Julia's mind worked overtime to assimilate this information and this new aspect of Gloria's behavior. It was almost insubordination, something Julia knew Rudy didn't tolerate, at least not from his children. A thought occurred to her, but she needed more information before she acted on it.

"You said the first couple of times we talked, Rudy frequently did his own thing, went his own way. I originally thought you accepted his behavior because you were trying to keep the peace. I'm starting to think his self-serving conduct also served you. Perhaps it allowed you, too, to live a secret life without reproach."

Gloria looked directly at Marguerite again. "I told you she was smart." Gloria then turned to Julia. "You're right, of course. Rudy and I lived separate lives except in our roles as parents.

"Marguerite and I have been lovers for almost eighteen years. We met when I was pregnant with Brianna. She was a nurse at the prenatal clinic I used. Rudy never knew about Marguerite, but I think he was aware of my preference for women. He and I had an arrangement. I looked the other way concerning his extramarital relationships, and he never asked me about any I may have had.

"I was young when we met and thought I'd grow out of my interest in other girls. He and I both wanted kids and wanted to do it within a marriage. I didn't have the courage to live openly as a lesbian, and Marguerite, bless her heart, was willing to follow me through it all. She, too, has moved each time Rudy's jobs took us to another city.

"Rudy loved to be a family man. At least, I should say, he loved to be seen as a family man. And, I believe he thought it made him look powerful to his friends. He could tomcat around on me and get away with it. I just thought he was pathetic. But he was a good earner. I was able to stay home with the kids before they started school, and we never wanted for anything. Plus, he could be charismatic and charming when he wanted to be.

"I know it must sound strange, but the relationship worked for us. The plan was to stay together until both kids left home. Then we'd split. Brianna was soon heading off to the Peace Corps and then university, and Logan moving on with a new coach and his own life away from Rudy and me. The plan was about to become reality.

"I no longer want to be in the closet about my sexuality. Marguerite and I have a plan of our own, finally." Gloria smiled. Julia realized it was the first time she'd seen the woman look happy.

"Well, thank you for filling me in. Would I be correct in assuming the surreptitious phone calls and texts you've been trying to hide have been from Marguerite?"

"Yes. That's right."

"When did you arrive here in San Amaro, Ms. Carmichael?"

"I got in yesterday. I managed to get a flight into El Centro, and then I took a couple of cabs and the bus from Mexicali. I got into San Amaro at about five thirty last night. It was a pretty easy way to get here, and I was amazed at how nice the bus was, much nicer than the ones in the States."

Marguerite rose and walked to a bench by the front door. She riffled through her purse for a moment, came back to the couch, and handed Julia the stubs from her flights and bus ride. Julia confirmed the dates and handed them back.

"Gloria, you previously told me Rudy and Norm Webster were on good terms. Were there any tensions between them when you saw them together here? Or between Rudy and Norm's wife? You know on the night of the party, Rudy fired Norm as a representative of his company, right?" Julia asked.

"No, I didn't know. I wonder why. But, no, I didn't notice any stress between Rudy and either of the Websters," Gloria said.

"Okay, thanks. Is Logan around?" Julia wanted to ensure he was still in town.

"No. He and Brianna are playing pickleball with Todd and Tiffany. Why do you need to speak with him?" Gloria asked, her mother-hen hackles starting to rise.

"No problem. Thank you for your help, ladies." Julia left, ignoring the question.

She hadn't seen Gloria and Marguerite's relationship coming but doubted it was relevant to their case. She was happy for one thing. The motive she and Ricardo had been theorizing held water.

Julia drove to the courts, parked, and got out of La Chica. She could see the four young people playing, confirming Logan was still around. She stood peering in through the main gate watching them play for a few minutes, just long enough for Logan to have seen her. Julia noted his next serve after seeing her at the gate crashed into the net. Clearly, her presence had some kind of an effect on him.

Chapter Forty-Six

Javier, dressed in jeans and a tank top, and Luis, in shorts and a T-shirt, were on their first undercover operation. Or, at least, it was how they described it to themselves. They had just arrived at the weekly swap meet at The Oasis. They were on the lookout for someone selling used comals. Unfortunately, Luis was about to realize, they should have talked through a plan about what they'd do if they found the stolen comals. Luis expected they would quietly take the seller to the station for questioning. As he would soon realize, Javier had other ideas.

The swap meet was held on a large sandy area of The Oasis just inside the main mountain-side gate. A portion of the space was set aside for parking, and the rest was laid out in similar-sized spaces marked out with white lime lines. Most sellers had their items laid out on tables or on the ground, though some had tents over their spaces. As the spaces were available on a first-come-first-serve basis, there was no organization of allotments. The vegetable guy was sandwiched between a table of used auto parts and a jewelry seller. No one seemed to mind.

The day had started slightly cloudy, but a breeze off the sea had successfully dispersed the clouds by the time Javier and Luis arrived and parked Javier's car. They didn't want to arrive in a police car. Luis was impressed Javier had such a nice car. A constable's salary wasn't high, yet he drove a bright yellow Challenger no more than five years old. The body had some minor damage here and there, and the upholstery on the driver's seat was torn and had been repaired with duct tape. Still, it made Luis slightly jealous. His own tiny hatchback was over twenty years old and showed its age.

Their path through the swap meet was serpentine, winding through the various rows of stalls where people were selling everything from food and freshly caught shrimp to old furniture, yard art, and used clothing. As they rounded the corner to the final row of tables and tent canopies, Luis caught sight of a woman sitting on an upturned pail surrounded by comals arrayed in the sand. He continued to walk at the same pace they had through the previous rows of tables.

Javier's sighting of the situation followed Luis's by no more than a second, but before Luis could react, his partner was running toward the woman at full tilt. It took Javier only a dozen strides to reach his target, and when he did, he grabbed her and pulled her to the ground. When Luis reached the pair, no more than a couple of seconds later, the woman was in handcuffs.

Luis was incredulous. His thought was if they found someone selling comals, they'd talk with the person to ascertain how she or he obtained them before accusing, let alone arresting, anyone.

As it turned out, when he had the time to inspect the comals on display, he discovered there were seven for sale, and one had a green-painted rim exactly as described by the first robbery victim with whom they'd spoken. It appeared they had found most of the missing comals. However, Luis wasn't prepared to assume the woman Javier was perp-walking to their car was the perpetrator of the thefts.

Luis began gathering the remaining comals and followed Javier to the car with them. They were heavier than he expected. On his way, he spotted a man and woman sitting at a table in front of one of the food-vendor stalls. On their table was the eighth comal. They were also in the process of wrapping up the remains of the biggest breakfast burrito Luis had ever seen. As he approached, the smell of eggs, chorizo, cilantro, and another aroma he couldn't name made his mouth water.

He stopped at their table and asked in Spanish whether they spoke Spanish. They each shook their heads. *"Por favor*, sit *aquí por un momento,"* Luis said, hoping they'd understand as he showed them his police ID.

He rushed to the car, stowed the seven comals in the trunk, told Javier what was going on, and headed back into the swap meet. One of the first vendors on the first row was a friend of Luis's, Arlo Anaya, a local fishmonger. He spoke English well. Luis conscripted him to help him communicate to the new owners of the eighth, stolen comal. Leaving his wife in charge of their stall, Arlo followed Luis.

Once the couple understood what was going on, they accompanied Luis and Arlo to the police car, where the comal seller was compelled to return the couple's fifty US dollars. Before Arlo left them to return to his stall, the American woman asked him whether he knew where in town they could buy a comal. After checking with the constables, he informed the couple none of the men knew of any place. Arlo suggested a shop near the Malecon where his wife bought cooking pots. Possibly, it would also sell comals.

Before Luis and Javier climbed into Javier's car, Luis guided Javier a few steps away. There he expressed his expectation. At the station, they would interview the woman properly before charging her with the crime. He argued she might be an accomplice rather than the actual thief, or there might be several people involved. And if they accused her immediately, they might not find any others involved. Javier acquiesced, eventually.

On the trip back to the police station, Luis phoned Inspector Martinez to inform him of the arrest they'd made of the woman they'd found selling comals at the swap meet. Martinez, in turn, found Ricardo checking email at his desk downstairs and asked him whether he'd be able to help with another interview. By the time Martinez had filled Ricardo in on the comal robberies and Luis and

Javier's recent apprehension of a suspect, the two constables and their suspect were at the station.

Ricardo was happy to help by leading the interrogation. Javier and Luis were less happy when they learned they would not have free rein to conduct the interview. But Martinez quickly disabused them of the idea they were ready for such responsibility. Neither had adequate experience to run the interview on his own. He instructed them to watch and learn.

Ricardo spoke with the two younger officers and got the details of how their investigation had proceeded and how they'd acquired the woman waiting in an interrogation room. When he entered the room with Luis and Javier, the woman looked more like a pile of disheveled clothes than a person. She sat, crumpled in on herself, staring at the tabletop in front of her. She didn't move as the three men took chairs across from her. Only when they were all seated did she lift her gaze toward them.

Luis turned on the recording equipment and introduced himself. Javier and Ricardo followed suit, and the woman, after some gentle coaxing from Ricardo, told them she was Esmera Badosa, aged forty-one, and provided an address in one of the poorer areas of San Amaro, where she confessed she and her family were staying while they were in San Amaro. That raised the question of where the woman actually lived. She then apologized for using the wrong phrasing and avowed she and her family lived in San Amaro at the address she'd just given them.

When Ricardo asked how she had come to be in the possession of eight used comals, she began to spin a tale the three policemen didn't believe for a second. *Her husband bought them at a market in Mexicali. He had dropped her and the comals off at the swap meet on his way back to Mexicali; she didn't know when he'd be back. Neither she nor her husband would ever steal.* And the lies continued.

Ricardo let her finish her story and deftly cornered her by saying they knew none of it was true. All eight of the items she was trying to sell had been stolen from homes in San Amaro over a few days the previous week. Luis pulled out the case files and the statements he and Javier had taken from the comal owners. He read the description of the green-rimmed comal stolen from the first victim and then produced a photo he'd taken of the same comal from the batch collected at the swap meet. Javier was fiddling with his phone at the same time. It caught Ricardo's eye, and he wondered whether the constable was looking for additional photos. But his attention was quickly brought back to the woman in front of them.

Esmera realized she couldn't maintain the artifice of her story and finally admitted she and her husband cased outdoor cookers under the pretense they were selling tortillas. When they found a comal they wanted, their two older sons would arrive on horseback late at night, slip into the person's yard, and retrieve it. Her cousin, who lived in Puerto Peñasco, told her there was significant interest from gringos for *properly cured* comals, and they'd pay well for them.

The woman's ability to fabricate stories so easily brought Ricardo back to the question of the address previously provided and prompted him to ask to see her CURP card. Short for *Clava Única de Registro de Población*, or Unique Population Registry Code, a CURP number is issued to each Mexican upon birth and acts similar to a Social Security number in the US or a Social Insurance Number in Canada. Luis was dispatched to use their police log-in for the CURP registry and Tax Administration Service to verify the woman's current address on file. When he returned, he announced her residential address indicated she came from the state of Chihuahua.

The woman tried to tell them her family had moved to San Amaro recently and just hadn't updated its address. But, by now they didn't believe her stories, and under Ricardo's interrogation, eventually she stopped lying.

Once the woman's truthful statement was taken, Javier and Luis were dispatched to collect the husband and sons. Ricardo left the constables to complete the final paperwork and returned to the war room to find out what information Julia's morning phone calls had produced.

Chapter Forty-Seven

Ricardo found Julia in their war room. He'd brought a couple of tortas from a market on his way to work because he had a plan. "Hey, Lucy, I brought us lunch today, because I have something I want to show you. It'll take about an hour. I think you'll find it interesting. Are you game?"

"Sure, why not? I'm still waiting for some information from my cousin. Whatever you have planned, it'll keep me from looking at my phone every two minutes."

Ricardo headed his truck in the direction of The Oasis. At first, Julia thought maybe he was taking them to the brewery for lunch, but he drove straight past it. A couple of minutes later, they entered The Oasis through a gate on the mountain side. The sign listing the communities accessed through that particular gate included *Centro Ecuestre* (Equestrian Center), and Julia had a notion of where they were going.

On the drive, Julia told him about speaking with Gloria and her concurrence their motive sounded probable. And she told him about meeting Marguerite. They agreed it filled in some blanks about Gloria and Rudy as a couple. Gloria seemed too self-possessed to be in a relationship with a bully without some other factors being in play.

Five minutes later, Ricardo pulled the car to a stop in the parking lot of an area that Julia had not known, until recently, existed in San Amaro. Ahead of her were about a dozen covered stalls and a series of corrals. In the largest corral was a group of about eight children and as many adults. Three of the kids were on horseback with an adult leading each horse. Beside one of the horses was the familiar face of Fran Webster. Julia didn't know the other two adults, though one was a San Amaro local whose face she recognized as a cashier at her neighborhood grocery store.

Fran Webster noted their arrival and said something to the third adult helping the young riders who spoke as they approached. *"Buenos días, oficiales, ¿Puedo ayudarle?"* (Can I help you?)

Ricardo answered. "Hi, we just came to watch. We heard about the work you're doing with local kids and came to learn a little bit more about it. I hope it's okay. I saw on The Oasis website you were having a class today."

The woman Julia recognized from her local market led the horse of the rider she was assisting over to the fence where Julia and Ricardo stood and introduced herself as Lucinda Aguila. She pointed out her daughter sitting on the fence and explained she had autism, as did all the kids there. She explained that her daughter, now seven, hadn't spoken from birth, until she was brought into the equine program.

"Senora Webster started this group. I never knew other people in San Amaro had a child with this disorder. Now we parents see we aren't alone here. Other families are dealing with the same situation, of having an autistic child. It has changed these kids' lives as well as the lives of each of our families. I volunteer to help, as do several of the other parents."

"This is wonderful," Julia said. "But please don't let us stop what you're doing. I'm delighted just to watch for a few minutes, if you don't mind."

"Of course. Watch. If you have questions, just let us know." Lucinda led her charges back over to where Fran was explaining an exercise she wanted the three riders to do. Lucinda acted as a translator, explaining to the riders and their assigned adult what was going to happen. Julia noticed Fran was wearing gloves. Tan leather gloves. Ricardo had noticed, too.

Julia and Ricardo watched for twenty minutes, during which the children rotated between watching with their parent or volunteer and riding. Julia knew from her psychology training that autistic kids often had a hard time following directions, yet these children seemed to be performing well their assigned tasks, simple though they were. She also noted the kids seemed to form a bond with their steed, another action not always easy for those with autism.

Before they left, Fran Webster strode over to where Julia and Ricardo were standing to see whether they had any questions about the class. Julia started by saying what a wonderful program it was, which brought a smile to Fran's face.

"Also, I couldn't help noticing your gloves. They're leather, aren't they? Do you buy them in Mexico?" Julia asked.

"No, I get them in the States. They're riding gloves. I still have a few pairs from when I ran the therapy program in Wyoming." Fran showed Julia a small brand on the strap at the wrist, which snapped to the glove to keep the gloves tight. It was a tiny horse's head. "This was the logo of my company."

"Too bad your husband doesn't have some. They might keep the thorns at bay when he's gardening," Julia said as casually as possible.

"He used to. He likely left them somewhere. Well, thanks for coming today. I should get back to the group."

She and Ricardo voiced their thanks and expressed, again, their astonishment at San Amaro having such a wonderful program.

Chapter Forty-Eight

Julia's message light was blinking when they returned to the station. When she'd listened to it, she turned to Ricardo with her eyes glistening with excitement.

"What's got you so happy, Lucy?" Ricardo asked before he had time to sit. "You look about to burst."

She showed him the list of companies where several of their suspects had worked at the same time as Rudy and filled him in on her subsequent phone calls. Finally, with the more mundane information she'd gathered out of the way, she shared the reason for her excitement and told him her cousin's research had possibly unearthed their first truly strong suspect with means, motive, and opportunity.

This time, Javier and Luis were in a squad car and back in uniform. The home they sought was in the poorest part of San Amaro. Luis turned the car onto a dirt road. The house they wanted was at the far end of the road, at a dead end. The dwellings they passed included tiny rusted, decrepit travel trailers from the 1980s and bare cinder-block cubes no bigger than four hundred square feet. Several places were stick-built homes constructed from patchworks of every kind of wood imaginable: bare plywood, fencing slats, particleboard, and, on one home, strips of wood from discarded pallets.

They were all hovels. And since there was no garbage pickup, if the homeowners didn't have a vehicle, they had no way to get their trash to the dump. Mounds of rubbish surrounded most of the homes and created drifts against fences, derelict cars, and houses. Scrawny, mangy dogs lay in the dirt of the street.

When Javier and Luis arrived at the address their comal thief had given them, two young children, a girl about ten and a boy about six, were the only people in the house. Neither was related to the woman they had in custody nor the husband and sons she'd claimed to have. The youngsters did, however, know the comal-stealing family. The girl informed them the father and sons had left no more than thirty minutes before.

Luis had a horrible sense of déjà vu. His eyes scoured Javier's face for any sign indicating he expected this. He didn't garner any clues from his partner. Still, this was the second time Luis was about to close a case and appeared to have been second-guessed by the perpetrator. Javier was the common denominator in both situations.

Every particle of Luis's being urged him to confront the other man, then and there. But he managed to curtail his instinct and instead lied. "I'm just going to give Ricardo a call and make sure we're at the right address. Will you keep an eye on the kids?" As he walked away from the house and Javier, Luis dialed a number at the police station. However, rather than calling Ricardo, he'd dialed Inspector Martinez. He quickly relayed his suspicion to his boss and made a request to which the inspector agreed.

"This is the right place. I guess we're going to have to come back later and maybe stake out the place. But right now, Ricardo told me we need to go back to the station," Luis said, continuing the lie, and climbed into the squad car. Javier followed him without any hesitation.

As they parked in the back lot of the station, Inspector Martinez materialized at the passenger side of the car. He stood so close Javier didn't have enough room to open his door, so instead opened his window and asked whether everything was okay.

"Both of you, give me your phones," Martinez commanded. "And unlock them first." Once in possession of the phones, he looked at the recent texts sent from Javier's phone. There was one to Marco Bustamente, Javier's older brother, sent at the time the constables and Ricardo were interrogating Esmera Badosa. It contained her address and the name of her husband with the admonishment: *Tell him I'm on my way to arrest him and his sons. Shake him down for whatever you can get for that information.*

Martinez tossed Luis's phone back to him and then pulled out a set of handcuffs. He opened Javier's door and affixed the cuffs to the constable. "Javier Bustamente, you're under arrest for selling confidential police information and aiding and abetting thieves. Constable Flores, please take him to the cells. When you've got him booked, grab Constable Cabrera and go arrest Marco Bustamente. He and Javier live together, so you can get his address from the desk sergeant."

Martinez turned back to Javier. "I'll be dealing with you myself, later."

Chapter Forty-Nine

Ricardo rapped loudly on the door for a second time. Finally, Sandy McLean opened the door, in a towel, her hair dripping on her shoulders. "Oh, hello, officers. Would you mind waiting there while I get dressed." Sandy pointed to a stretched-leather-topped table and four matching chairs on the veranda. "I'll just be a couple of minutes."

The pair took seats and waited.

It was closer to ten minutes before Sandy reappeared at the door, dressed in a T-shirt and shorts, and carrying a tray of ice water. This she set on the table before apologizing for keeping them waiting. "Now, how can I help you?" she asked, looking perplexed.

"When we spoke with your husband a couple of days ago, he told me you worked your entire career at Lone Star Compressors and Pumps, but that's not entirely true, is it?" Julia asked in a level tone.

"Well, I did work at the same place for my entire career, and I did work at Lone Star Compressors and Pumps, but I think what you mean is it wasn't always called Lone Star. Right?" Sandy scrunched her eyebrows over her soft blue eyes with a look of confusion.

"Yes, exactly. What was the company name when you first started working there?" Julia asked, not wanting to put words in the woman's mouth.

"It was called Oilfield General Supply Limited. Why does it matter where I worked and what it was called?"

"Rudy Stephanetti also worked at Oilfield General Supply Limited, didn't he, Mrs. McLean." It was not a question. Julia looked directly at Sandy with a piercing gaze.

Sandy's face had blanched at the man's name, and she dropped her eyes from Julia's intense look to her hands, which had been folded gently in her lap. Now they were white fists. "Yes, that's true."

"So, you lied to us when we first spoke and you told me you didn't know him." Julia again intoned the words as a statement, rather than a question.

"I don't remember you specifically asking me whether I knew him. I think you asked me whether my opinion of him was altered by his apology to Clint. And I told you it hadn't changed my opinion of him one way or another. Which was true," Sandy said with more backbone than Julia had anticipated.

"Mrs. McLean, please, let's not play word games with each other. I need you to tell us about your relationship with Rudy Stephanetti. Start at the beginning."

"I didn't kill him, no matter what you think." Sandy's voice cracked slightly as she said this. Then she stood. "Please give me a moment. I'm going to need Kleenex to get through this," she said as she walked into the house.

Julia updated Ricardo while the woman was gone.

When Sandy returned, she had brought a box of tissues, and her posture had changed markedly. She looked a ghost of the woman who had left them only moments before. Her face was gray, and her shoulders stooped as though she were carrying the weight of the world. She sat and turned her gaze to Julia. Her eyes were dull, lifeless. "What do you need to know?" she asked in a flat tone.

Julia realized this was going to be a difficult conversation. Not because she thought Sandy was going to lie to them again, but because she was going to tell them the truth. She steeled herself and realized she'd have to put her own experiences away so as not to influence the woman before her. "As I said before, just start from the beginning."

Sandy looked from Julia to Ricardo and then back to Julia. There was a pleading look in her eyes. Julia quickly realized the problem. "Mrs. McLean, through our investigation, we have learned Rudy Stephanetti could be *difficult* for clerical staff to work with. So, I can already imagine some of what your story will include. My partner doesn't speak much English, so he's not going to hear the details of your story. I will fill him in on your remarks once we leave. Okay?" Julia asked the woman. And then told Ricardo the plan. He quickly understood and nodded.

Sandy, too, nodded, but glumly, then took a deep breath. Her eyes flicked back and forth several times, not seeing anything, as she tried to think where to start and how to tell a story she'd never shared with a living soul. Eventually, she began.

"Dean and I had been married only a few months when I started work at Oilfield General. We were so much in love. We were planning to start a family in a couple of years. I had just graduated from secretarial college. He'd inherited his great-grandparents' home and had a solid job at the bus company. We felt on top of the world.

"I liked my job and the other women in the clerical pool, and I was good at the work. It was a joyously happy time for us. There were happy years back then." Sandy stopped and took a small drink of water. She replaced her glass on the table and sighed deeply before she spoke again. "Then Rudy was hired."

Julia and Ricardo waited, but it appeared the woman wasn't going to continue. Julia was just about to prompt Sandy to carry on, but just then the woman before them seemed to transform again. From some deep reach within, she gathered strength. She sat straighter, and her jawline firmed as she tensed her facial muscles. Julia had never seen her look so determined.

"He was an absolute bastard. A horrid bully. But I didn't know that at the start. He seemed nice. Charismatic. He was handsome, about my age, and was cheery when he was brought around to meet everyone. Oilfield General was not a huge company. There were fewer than two hundred employees back then, so everyone knew everyone. The secretarial pool had six of us and we worked in an area together, answering phones, typing, updating people's calendars, that kind of thing.

"Shortly after Rudy came on board, the company reorganized and assigned those of us in the pool to specific departments. I got assigned as the admin assistant to marketing, where Rudy worked. He was a low-level manager. It started within a few weeks of the reorg. We gals in the pool were a tight group, but everything changed when we were assigned out, for me, at least. We didn't have the comfort and security of being together.

"I don't know whether you know much about engineering companies, but eighty to ninety percent of the employees are men. Most of them are nice guys, but when they get together, they can turn into boys again. Rude boys. And none of the execs curbed such behavior. For the company celebration of Rudy's birthday, they had a stripper come to the office. Can you believe it!?"

Julia had to bite her tongue to keep from commiserating with her. She knew all too well how that type of thing could affect a person, but this wasn't about her. It was about getting Sandy to tell her story. "I imagine it was difficult," she said to Sandy with a small smile of encouragement.

"It was one thing when we gals were all together and some guy would make a rude comment. But when we got separated, we no longer had moral support from the crudeness." Sandy stopped talking and, again, appeared to be finished. She took another drink of her water and leaned back into her chair, looking at the table.

"I need you to tell me what happened, Mrs. McLean," Julia encouraged her.

"I know. This is hard for me. It was the worst time of my life, and it changed me. It almost destroyed my marriage, but worse, it almost destroyed me."

Julia could see in the woman's face she had returned to that time in her mind. She looked defeated, on the verge of tears. "I've never told anyone what I'm about to tell you." After a long pause, she began again. A single tear slipped from her eye and trailed down her left cheek. She did not wipe it away.

"It started with jokes, sometimes limericks. He'd stand behind my chair and lean over and say them quietly, almost in a whisper, in my ear. Close enough I could feel his breath on my neck. At first, they were harmless. Maybe a bit off-color, but not truly risqué.

"I was raised in a Southern Baptist home. You may not know, but it's a *very* conservative denomination. Dean and I continued to attend the same church until we moved here. Anything overtly sexual outside of marriage was taboo. I was always embarrassed when someone would tell a racy story. So, I blushed every time Rudy spoke his filth. Looking back, I think humiliating me was what he was aiming for.

"Then it got worse. He'd say personal things to me. For example, one time after a joke with a sexual undertone, he asked whether it had made me wet. My husband never even said those things to me. I was mortified. I didn't know what to do about it. I was embarrassed and angry, and I think he sensed it. He said something along the lines of *Oh come on now, this is harmless fun. Don't be a prude, it's unattractive and it's unnecessary. This is our little secret.*

"He gave it a rest for a few days after, and I hoped it was over, but it wasn't. When he started again, he was relentless. When I got some courage one time and told him to stop, he just asked me whether I enjoyed my job. *I can take it all away from you, you know. Make it so you won't be able to get a job anywhere in his town.* He was always so cocky and sure of himself, I believed he'd do it.

"I put in for a transfer to IT when I heard the gal working admin there was leaving, but Rudy quashed it. I believed I was trapped. I felt dirty. And, I was scared. I couldn't get over it. I was disgusted by his words. They made me feel sullied, but somehow, he convinced me there was something wrong with my reactions. I started to believe I wasn't a normal woman. But that wasn't the worst . . ." Sandy grabbed a handful of Kleenexes and began to sob.

Julia let her cry for a few moments and then placed a hand on her back and handed Sandy her water, encouraging her to take a drink and to continue when she was ready.

"The worst part was what it did to Dean and me. I got to the point anything sexual made me almost sick to my stomach. I got an ulcer. Every day I worried about what was wrong with me. He picked on me for a reason. I thought it was my fault.

"Then and for several years after, Dean would try to initiate marital relations, and I just couldn't. I believed I was so tainted, so soiled, I, I . . ." Sandy sputtered, let out a little mewl-like sob. "I couldn't . . . even make love . . . with my husband," she said through a storm of tears and sobs. "Rudy's abuse—I realize now that's what it was—tortured me for over two years. I tried to find work elsewhere, but Texas was in a slump, and Dallas-Fort Worth was hit hardest. People were being laid off. No one was hiring. I didn't know what to do. I even thought about suicide.

"Then one Monday over two years later, I got to work, and Rudy's office was empty. All his personal effects were gone. I asked around, but all I learned was he'd quit. I found out later he'd gotten handsy with one of the clerks in payroll and she'd filed a complaint.

"Maybe I was lucky all he did was verbally assault me. But"—Sandy paused and gathered herself up—"I actually think what I endured was worse. He was a bully, and I, whether because of my temperament or my upbringing, allowed him to bully me. I didn't see it that way back then. I thought it was all my fault. I thought somehow I'd invited his attention somehow. But I've come to realize I wasn't responsible for his behavior. He was just a jerk, a horrible, vile, misogynistic jerk."

Julia let Sandy compose herself before she moved the conversation along. "Did your husband know anything about what was going on with you at work?"

"Heavens, no!" Sandy said emphatically. "But he knew something was wrong. He tried to get me to talk about it, but I was convinced he'd be disgusted by me if he knew. I was terrified our marriage would end. Our relationship has never been the same since.

"It was several years after Rudy left Oilfield General before I could . . ." Sandy's shoulders shook as a new set of sobs overtook her. Julia was appalled at the devastation this telling of her past trauma wreaked on the woman. When the sobs subsided, Sandy spoke again. "It was years before I could have sex with Dean. And still sometimes, the horror I experienced from Rudy's abuse storms through my mind, ravaging me again when Dean holds me."

Julia made a conscious effort to immerse herself in Sandy's perspective, striving to comprehend how actions from decades past still wielded such an insidious grip on her life. Julia's memories of overt male bullying were impossible to ignore, but they were part of a collective barrage. They targeted all the women officers, not just her. While she couldn't fully empathize with Sandy, a sudden revelation nudged her toward a profound understanding.

As Julia reflected on the enduring scars of her father's death, she recognized the extent of her own trauma. She thought to herself, *Yes, I'm just as haunted by those memories today as I was back then.* Her resistance to forging meaningful relationships, she recognized, was less about preserving her aspiration to become a comandante and more about the lingering effect of her father's loss. The layers of her past unfolded, revealing the intricate tapestry of her emotions, a complex and often tumultuous journey.

Viewing Sandy's experience through this lens, it finally struck Julia with a bolt of clarity. She grasped the enduring trauma of a decades-old ordeal, how it could continue to torment the victim, as if she were still trapped in the same nightmare. Sandy remained ensnared by the horrors of the abuse Rudy had inflicted upon her so long ago. There was, however, still more of the story Julia needed to hear.

"Mrs. McLean, tell us about the night of the party."

"What do you mean? I told you about my time at the party. You can't possibly think I had anything to do with the murder."

Before Julia could reply, a red Ford pickup truck pulled into the driveway, and Dean stepped out of the driver's door. He took one look at Sandy and spoke in a gruff voice. "What's going on here?"

Chapter Fifty

Javier had been sitting in a cell in the police station for almost three hours when his brother, Marco, was brought in and placed in the only other cell. Each cell was eight feet square constructed of three cinder-block walls and fronted by bars. The brothers could not see each other, but they could converse. As he walked to his cell, seeing Javier, still in uniform, sitting in a cell shocked Marco. "What the hell!" he said.

Javier waited before speaking until the constables who had arrested Marco had closed the door between the cells and the rest of the station. "Did you get any money from that man?" he asked.

"Is money all you care about, Javi? We are in jail, dammit. What happened?" Marco asked.

"I think Luis must have ratted me out to Martinez. The little worm. Maybe I should have tried to cut him in for a share of the take. I don't know. I was going. . ."

Javier stopped speaking when the door from the station opened and Inspector Martinez and the station comandante entered the cell area. Seeing the comandante set Javier's spine atingle. *Oh shit,* he thought, *this is serious!*

"Good afternoon, Mr. McLean," Julia said when Dean approached them on the veranda.

"Afternoon, Officers." An air of caution surrounded Dean's words.

"We need you to come to the station with us. We have a warrant compelling a blood sample, and we need to get an official statement from you about your actions on the evening of February twenty-four. The truth this time. We have witnesses who contradict your previous statement." As Julia spoke, Ricardo stepped beside Dean and led him to La Chica.

Julia's pronouncement elicited a gasp from Sandy, and she jumped from her seat as though to stop the inevitable. "What are you doing? What's going on?" she asked of the police. Again she said, "What's going on?" this time to Dean.

"We are taking him to the station to get his statement *of the actual events of that evening*." Julia said the last phrase over her shoulder in Dean's direction. "You will have to make your own way to the station. Once the interview is finished, I will speak with you and let you know what happens next. You may have an opportunity to speak with him then." Julia joined Dean and Ricardo in her car. With the two men in the back seat, Julia headed to the station.

By the time Julia and Ricardo unloaded Dean McLean from La Chica and installed him in Interrogation Room Two, Marco and Javier Bustamente were already on their way to Mexicali in handcuffs in the back of a police van. Marco was subdued, but a low-grade anger seeped from his pores. His brother had all but promised him there was zero risk in the extortion plan in which he'd participated. Now here he was shackled and going to jail. If his hands were free, he thought he might throttle his brother.

Javier was also quiet, but he was plotting. He knew many officers on the Mexicali force; perhaps he could bribe one of them to let him and his brother go. In Javier's world, everyone and everything had a price.

Fingerprints and a blood sample had been taken from Dean immediately upon being ensconced in the interview room. Vicente hurried off to compare Dean's blood with the sample found inside the leather gloves worn by the murderer. While he was doing the analysis in his lab, Julia connected the recording equipment, invited Inspector Martinez to join her in the interview, and verified with Ricardo he had his translation software running and could hear them "loud and clear." She left Dean in the interview room with a constable while they waited for the blood comparison to be completed.

Eventually, Vicente provided Julia with his results.

Martinez, Ricardo, and Julia had spent the intervening time reviewing all their data in the war room. With a solid suspect against whom they could compare their amassed information, it seemed fairly certain he was their man, but all their evidence apart from the blood typing was circumstantial at this point. They had to wait for the final piece before speaking with Dean.

Julia had gathered all the relevant information onto several pages of a lined yellow pad of paper in preparation for the interrogation. When Vicente stuck his head into the conference room with his results, the three moved quickly. Ricardo returned to his desk and donned his headphones. Julia and Hector Martinez joined Dean, and the interview began.

"Mr. McLean, you are under suspicion for the murder of Rudy Stephanetti on the twenty-fourth of February of this year." Julia began the formal process and read him his rights. "We have evidence of blood matching yours inside a pair of gloves covered on the outside with Mr. Stephanetti's blood." It was a partial lie. The blood types did match, but DNA analysis had not been done to confirm the blood was his. "The gloves were found in a dumpster behind the pickleball courts where he was murdered. We have witnesses who saw you going to and from the courts at the time of his death. A small piece of leather from the just-mentioned gloves was embedded in the handle of the paddle used to kill Mr. Stephanetti. We also spoke at length this morning with your wife and think we understand your motivation, but we want to hear it from you."

"I lost those gloves. They were in the pocket of a jacket I pulled from the car when I left for a walk. They fell out somewhere. Whoever found them is likely your killer. Because it's not me," Dean said defiantly.

Julia shared Dean's answer with the inspector. He raised one eyebrow with an air of disbelief.

"None of what you've told us explains your following Mr. Stephanetti to the courts, or how he was found dead just minutes after you left," Julia said firmly.

"Oh, I went there all right. I figured he must be the reason Gloria had changed so drastically all those years ago. He was boasting about all his big, important jobs with their fancy titles, and he mentioned having worked at the same place as Sandy many years back.

"I followed him, and I did what I wish I'd been able to do back then. I punched him square on the nose as hard as I could. I heard it crunch. He squawked like a baby. He was sitting on the ground holding his broken nose and bleeding all over his fancy shirt when I left." Dean's eyes blazed as if he were a religious zealot, daring the unbeliever to disagree.

"I don't think you're telling us the truth, Mr. McLean. I think you followed him to the courts and confronted him with his abuse of your wife and then you put on those leather gloves, cracked his skull with the paddle so hard the paddle head broke from the handle. Then you beat him with your fists to within an inch of his life before finally ending it by stabbing him in the neck with the handle." Julia spoke calmly, but there was an intensity bordering on menace to her words.

"That's not what happened. But it sounds as if you think you've got it all figured out," Dean said with as much resignation as anger.

"Why don't you tell us what did happen, then."

"I already told you what happened. I was there, I punched him, and then I left. He was alive when I left. End of story. Whoever found those gloves is the person you should have sitting here. That's who killed the bastard."

Julia and Martinez spoke for a minute before Julia started again to try to get the real story from their suspect. They kept having him go over his story again and again. Where had he lost the gloves? When and where did he put on his jacket? Why had he skulked in the shadows if he didn't have a more nefarious plan than to just punch the man? The questions persisted. For hours. Dean's story stayed consistent throughout.

Finally, at eight thirty that night, Dean was taken to the cells. They'd try again tomorrow.

Inspector Martinez confirmed he'd try to get authorization to send both the glove and Dean's blood sample to Mexicali for DNA testing, if Vicente didn't have an alternative. If Dean was their killer, it was a step they'd have to take to get definitive proof it was his blood inside the glove. With a rush on it, they might get the results in a few days.

Chapter Fifty-One

Julia found Sandy McLean sitting on a hard plastic chair in the station foyer. According to the desk sergeant, she was already there when he came on duty at five. He'd given her a bottle of water, and she'd used the *baños* once, but otherwise she hadn't moved.

"Mrs. McLean, we are keeping your husband in custody overnight. We have the right to hold him for forty-eight hours without charging him. You should go home now and get some rest. Do you have any questions before you go?"

"You can't possibly think Dean killed Rudy. He wouldn't. He couldn't. He can hardly kill a fly." Sandy was panicking. Her eyes were wide and frightened.

"I need to accompany you to your home and gather the clothes Dean was wearing the night of the party. We need them for forensic testing. Do you want me to give you a ride home?" Julia asked.

"No, I don't," Sandy said angrily, then realized how rude she must have sounded. Her southern manners kicked in. "Thank you, though."

"You need to calm yourself before you drive home, Mrs. McLean. Can I get you some more water?" Julia admonished and asked the distraught woman before her.

"No, I still have some." Sandy took a deep breath and blew it out slowly through open lips, her cheeks ballooning in the process. She stood and straightened her back. For the second time, Julia watched the woman gather inner strength. "I'll be okay." She walked out the door of the station without a backward glance.

Julia wondered whether her bullying at the hands of Rudy Stephanetti had catalyzed Sandy's inner strength. She hadn't had it when he taunted and abused her decades before. If she had, things would have been different back then.

Julia gathered her car keys and Ricardo, and they followed the McLeans' tan-colored SUV to their home.

Sandy led Julia into her and Dean's bedroom and opened the closet. "Dean does our laundry. He always has. He doesn't cook but believes housework is the responsibility of everyone living in the house. He also does the dishes and trash. He even vacuums. I credit his parents. They had eleven kids. His mom made them all help. He's a good man, Sergeant Garcia. He's not a murderer!" Sandy said emphatically. Then more calmly but with an angry undertone, she pointed to Dean's clothes. "Take what you need."

Julia checked her notebook, trying to remember the clothes Dean had been witnessed wearing at the party. Finally, she found it. Blue jeans and a Hawaiian shirt. She could not find the shirt in the closet, though there were a couple of pairs of jeans.

"I believe your husband has a beige bomber-style jacket. Where would it be?" Julia asked.

"Our coats are in a different closet, by the front door."

Julia called out to Ricardo to look for the jacket, and moments later he indicated he'd found it. Julia continued looking through the bedroom closet and found a pair of leather sandals with what could have been blood on them and placed them in an evidence bag. With Sandy watching, she also riffled through their drawers, the laundry basket, and all the cupboards in their laundry area. Finally, she returned to their bedroom and took every pair of jeans and short-sleeved buttoned shirt in the closet. She had the sinking feeling Dean had destroyed the clothes he'd been wearing at the party. Vicente would have to test everything. Maybe they'd get lucky.

While Julia was gathering all Dean's clothes inside the house, Ricardo grabbed a flashlight from La Chica and searched outside.

There was nothing in their trash bins, their vehicles, or the garage. On the back patio was a fire pit. It looked well used and had two lawn chairs and a small table next to it. Among the ashes in the pit were a few charred shreds of fabric. He pulled on a pair of blue nitrile gloves and collected the contents of the fire pit into an evidence bag.

Back at the station, the forensic lab was empty, as expected. Vicente worked the day shift, and it was now almost ten at night. Ricardo and Julia locked their evidence bags in a filing cabinet in Inspector Martinez's office and headed home.

The next morning, the pair was waiting in the lab when Vicente arrived. They had retrieved the items they'd left in their boss's office. The evidence bags were now piled on the counter in the lab. Vicente's eyebrows shot up when he walked in and saw the pair and their mountain of potential clues. They requested he start with the leather sandals, the bomber jacket, and the bits of fabric from the ashes. And to report his findings from them before starting on the mound of clothes.

Julia had given Logan the names of two lawyers in San Amaro who spoke English well. As can happen in times of enormous stress, he had done nothing with them, instead preferring the ostrich approach to the situation. At breakfast, Gloria tackled the elephant in the room.

"Logan, you *need* to get in touch with a lawyer. I'm not suggesting it because I think you've done anything wrong, so don't give me that look. You need to know what your rights are here in Mexico. Maybe we need to contact a US consulate or something. I don't know . . . and neither do you. This could be more serious than we think. Please call one today so we can at least know where we stand. Please." His mother was not normally a forceful person. Logan took notice.

"Okay, okay. I'll call this morning." He didn't want to have to think about his dad's death. Talking with a lawyer would make it all too real. The idea of being convicted of murder in Mexico, however, was worse than the thought of having to speak with a lawyer. With a deep sigh, he grabbed his phone and headed upstairs to phone an attorney. He didn't want anyone else in the house listening to his conversation.

Chapter Fifty-Two

Dean McLean's appearance hinted at a night fraught with sleepless torment. His bloodshot eyes were nestled deep within the shadows of their sockets. The pallor of his skin, a sickly gray hue, served as an eerie canvas for his inner turmoil.

There he sat, perched on the bench, his head buried in his trembling hands. It was a moment of stillness, shattered only by the haunting echo of Julia's approaching footsteps. As if in slow motion, Dean's head rose, revealing his exhausted countenance, and his weary eyes locked onto Julia's presence, a silent testament to the storm raging within him.

"Mr. McLean, I wanted to let you know we have collected clothes, shoes, and charred fabric from your house, and our forensics expert is analyzing them now. If we find any trace of Rudy Stephanetti's blood on any of them, we will be formally charging you with murder. If you wish to amend your statement in advance, now would be the time." Julia continued to stand in front of the cell awaiting a response from their suspect.

Dean looked at Julia for a long moment. His response was to grab the blanket on which he'd been sitting and throw it over his shoulders as he lay on the bench with his back to Julia. She waited for another few beats before leaving the cells.

In the tense moments preceding their departure from the confines of their makeshift war room, Ricardo and Julia huddled together, their gazes locked onto the trove of evidence displayed before them. With furrowed brows, they meticulously reviewed every piece of information pertaining to both Dean and Logan. As Julia pored over her recorded notes, a disconcerting recollection resurfaced: Logan and Anne Brayer had independently claimed to have encountered a man accompanied by a husky or a dog of a strikingly similar breed just around the time when Logan had made his way to change his clothes.

The realization hung heavy in the air, its significance lingering like a dark cloud. Julia understood unearthing the identity of this mysterious figure with the dog could hold the key to discerning the veracity of Logan's account of events. Her fingers reached for her phone, and with a determined resolve, she dialed the number of Tina Vela. Was this connection going to unveil a crucial piece of the truth they so desperately sought?

"Hello, Mrs. Vela, this is Detective Sergeant Garcia. We spoke the other day." Julia intoned the last sentence with a slight upward inflection.

"Yes, of course, I remember you and your partner. How can I help you?"

"Have you seen someone walking a husky or some dog resembling a husky any of the times you've been out walking Charlie?" Julia asked.

"Oh, sure. That's Tivo, and he *is* a husky. I see his owner and him often, actually."

Julia tried to keep the excitement from her voice. "Would you happen to know Tivo's human's name? Or where they live?"

"I don't know the man's name. Silly, isn't it? I know the dog but not the person. But I know which condo they live in. It's almost straight across the twelfth hole of the golf course from our backyard. I can show you which one if it would help," Tina said.

"That would be great. I can be there in about fifteen minutes. If you're not busy, I'll come now?"

Getting an affirmative answer from Tina, Julia grabbed her keys. Ricardo was ready to go in another minute, and they headed out to The Oasis. Tina and Charlie met them at the door. Charlie had on his harness, and Tina had his leash in her hand.

"Sorry, I don't know the condo number, but I walk around there most days, so it's easiest for me to just show you, okay?" Tina asked.

As the three people and Charlie walked, Julia chatted with their guide. Julia learned Tina and Lorenzo would be in San Amaro only one more week, but they'd made an offer on a condo not far from the one they were renting.

Once Tina had pointed out the condo where Tivo and his person lived, she and Charlie headed back, leaving the police to do whatever they were there to do.

Julia and Ricardo, excited they might unearth new information that could catapult their case forward, waited at the door with pounding hearts. Their anticipation leapt when the person they sought answered the door. Julia disclosed their purpose, and the man, who introduced himself simply as George, led them into his living room. Tivo was lounging on the couch, so George pointed to a pair of chairs and sat with his shaggy dog.

Julia first confirmed George had been in San Amaro the evening of the party, and he and Tivo had been out walking. Next, she asked whether George remembered seeing a young man, describing Logan, on the evening in question.

"Yeah, I do remember seeing a kid about that age. You don't see many young people here normally. Most of us are old retired folks," George said.

"Can you tell me what he was wearing? Also, about when and where you saw him?"

"Let me think." George pulled out his cell phone and checked his calendar. "Right. I'd been out at the brewery with a couple of friends that evening. We stayed playing cribbage there until after ten. I took Tivo on our nightly walk shortly after I got home. So, it would have been sometime around eleven. I remember because we got back at eleven fifteen. My mantel clock chimes on the quarter hour. A single chime. It takes me about ten minutes to walk from where I saw him back around the golf-cart path to here."

"And can you describe to me where you saw the young man and which direction he was heading, please," Julia asked. She pulled out a copy of the condo-area map she'd given to the canvassers and handed it to him.

George studied the map for a few moments to orient himself to his condo's position and then traced with his finger the route he and his dog had walked. Finally, he pointed to a spot on the map. "This is where I saw him, and he was coming this way, toward me, fast walking. He scooted along the pathway here between these two condo buildings," George said, pointing again to the map.

A light bulb went on for Julia.

"Do you remember what he was wearing?" The route the witness had pointed out as the one the young man had taken was the way to the courts. If Logan were the young man George had seen, he had already passed the condo the Stephanettis were renting.

"The young guy I saw was wearing shorts and a flowered shirt, one of those Hawaiian shirts, you know. And sandals." A crackle of energy shot through Julia. This was the information they needed.

Logan had lied again.

Chapter Fifty-Three

Logan was again back in Interview Room One at the police station. Alone. He did not have a lawyer with him. He hadn't called one yet.

"Logan, you lied to us again. Here's the situation. You have the means. You're young, strong, and tall enough to have inflicted the slash on your dad's head. You could easily have inflicted the beating your dad suffered. You have a motive. Your dad was a bully, and you were afraid to tell him you had a new coach. And, you had the opportunity. You were seen at the courts during the time-of-death window, and you admitted to having been there.

"Now we have a witness who saw you heading to the courts, still wearing the clothes you initially wore to the party. Not the black clothing you were seen wearing near the courts later. And you were at the courts much earlier than you stated you were. I have everything I need to charge you with your father's murder, so you'd better start telling the truth." Julia spoke emphatically. The gloves were off now. There was an edge in her voice.

Logan immediately noticed the difference. He assumed a more erect posture. He was sweating, though it was not overly hot in the interview room.

"I'm sorry I didn't tell you everything at the start. I was afraid." Logan looked directly at Julia. He held her gaze as he continued. "I was afraid I couldn't trust you. I've heard horrible things about police in Mexico. As I told you before, I was sure you'd just arrest me without any proof. But I've seen that's not true. You actually are trying to find out who killed my dad."

"Then tell me the truth. What did you do during the time you left the party?" Julia asked, her tone modulated and even again.

Logan leaned forward, his forearms on the table. He looked earnest, but not scared, Julia thought. Then he began.

"When I left the party, the first thing I did was go home. When I saw Dad wasn't there, I headed to the courts, still in the clothes I'd spilled the beer on. I guessed Dad was there as soon as I saw the lights on over the courts. So I walked toward them. But because of the cloth they have covering the chain-link fence, I couldn't see onto the courts themselves. When I got close to the courts, I could hear voices. Dad and some other man. It sounded as if they were talking about some company Dad worked at a long time ago. So, I decided to come back in a few minutes. I hurried back to the condo to change. I needed to talk with Dad alone.

Julia reiterated Logan's story so far to Martinez. "Please continue."

"So, I changed my clothes. And by then, I realized I'd been away from the party far longer than I'd expected already. My thoughts were vacillating between just going back to the party without talking with Dad and going back to the courts. At first, I decided not to talk with him and headed back to Todd and Tiffany's. But partway back I changed my mind and jogged back to the courts.

"When I got there, the lights were out. It had likely been about ten minutes since I heard him talking with the other guy. But, since I hadn't seen Dad on the way, I thought maybe he was still there. I used my phone flashlight to look around. That's when I saw him then. Dead. It was so horrible.

"Everything else I told you, from the point of finding Dad's body, was the complete truth. The noise behind the courts, going back to the party. All of it is what happened." Logan took a deep breath and let it out slowly, his shoulders finally relaxing.

Julia had Logan go through his story again and again. He told it calmly with little change from what he'd just told them. She suggested he'd found a pair of gloves and used them to beat his father. At this Logan looked confused.

"What gloves? I don't know what you're talking about."

After the third time through his version of events, Julia and Martinez spoke again. Logan's story didn't seem to fit together coherently. They agreed he wasn't yet telling them everything. At his desk, Ricardo listened in and agreed with their assessment. Julia led Logan through to the cells and locked him into the one beside Dean McLean. Let him have time to think before having another go at him.

Chapter Fifty-Four

Julia had been ruminating on the blood-covered gloves in evidence ever since she'd seen Fran Webster wearing a similar pair less than twenty hours before. Since then, the momentum of the case had accelerated from plodding to warp speed. Two viable suspects were in their cells. One admitted to having the gloves but claimed they were lost the night of the murder. The other claimed to know nothing of the gloves. Still, they must further investigate the gloves. They might hold the key. Julia headed to the evidence locker.

What she found was disturbing.

She located Ricardo and told him what she'd discovered. They headed directly to Martinez's office.

Ricardo let Julia do the talking. It *was* her find.

"Sir, I know we have two people in custody already for this crime, but . . ." She paused before speaking again, hoping she was on the right track. She explained about the equine therapy program and Fran's gloves and the small brand of her logo on the inside of the wrist strap. Then she dropped the bombshell. The gloves in evidence contained the same small brand. It was covered over by blood, but when looked at under a magnifying glass, the indentation of the brand was visible. Norm Webster might be the murderer after all.

When Norm was brought in, he was placed in an interview room, where he was joined by Julia and Hector. The formal interview began when Ricardo texted Hector a thumbs up indicating he was ready at his desk.

"Mr. Webster, we have a pair of gloves in evidence covered in Mr. Stephanetti's blood. They are unique gloves, sir. They have a brand on the strap that exactly matches the horse-head logo on your truck. Your wife has a matching pair. What can you tell me about them?" Julia asked.

"Good Lord. I lost those gloves over a year ago. You say they were used in Rudy's murder? Wow!" Norm answered easily.

"There is also blood on the inside of the gloves. Would you give us a blood sample so we can rule you out as the killer?" Julia asked.

"I don't have to. I can confirm the blood is mine." Norm stuck his hand out and showed them a gnarly white scar along the side of his right pinkie finger. "It happened when I was getting ready to string some barbed wire fencing. I was just carrying the roll of wire out to the field. I didn't have my gloves on, and when I dropped the roll to the ground, a barb caught my finger. I wrapped a handkerchief around it to stanch the bleeding and then put on my gloves.

"Have your forensic guy run tests on that blood. He'll be able to tell you it's two years old. If there's some more-recent blood in there, too, it'll be your killer's."

Julia hadn't told him where the blood on the inside of the glove was found, but Vicente had reminded her only moments before it was in the little finger area of the right glove.

"Do you recall where you may have lost the gloves, Mr. Webster?" Julia asked.

"Last time I remember having them was at a Plumeria Club meeting. It could have been there, but honestly, I don't know. Kind of the definition of lost, don't you think?"

"We also have a witness who saw your truck in the pickleball parking lot within the time-of-death window. Your wife admitted she didn't know whether you'd gone out after you took her home after the party because she headed directly to bed. You were the last person seen with the victim when he was alive, and he had just fired you. We have everything we need to charge you with the murder."

"But you haven't charged me yet. I think it's because you know I didn't do it. So, test the blood for age. It's over two years old," Norm said in a calm, firm, lawyerly voice. "I didn't do it."

Julia and Hector conferred for a moment before Julia had the man tell his story in detail of the evening of the murder. Norm told them virtually the same story he'd told them the first time they spoke. He disputed the witness statement from Lorenzo Vela, saying people are always confusing his truck with The Oasis's maintenance trucks. Norm pointed out his truck was the same model and year as The Oasis's and the logos shared most of the same colors. At a glance, they could easily be confused.

The police questioned everything several times, but the man's story didn't change.

As the interview continued, Hector texted Vicente to find out whether he was able to analyze the age of the blood inside the gloves. Vicente texted back immediately indicating the police lab did not contain chromatography equipment, but he'd check with the commercial labs in town.

Twenty minutes later, Vicente texted back saying the Sangre-Lab on Calle Guadalajara had the needed machine and he was taking the glove in for testing. The results would be available tomorrow morning.

They left Norm Webster in the interview room with a blanket, a bottle of water, and a young constable stationed outside the door.

Logan was in the cell nearer the door to the rest of the station. He could hear movement in the cell beside him, but he didn't know whether the person was Mexican or American. The sensation of being in a cell was something he'd once tried to imagine after watching a TV series set in a prison. The reality was much worse than what he'd imagined. There was nothing there except a concrete bench, a rough blanket, a sink, and a toilet. After five minutes alone with his thoughts, he questioned whether he had the mental, emotional capacity to handle it . . . even overnight.

"Hey, you an American?" It was whispered so softly, Logan wondered for a moment whether he'd actually heard it.

"Yes." Logan was not whispering.

"What did you do?" asked the other man, softly.

"They are trying to pin my dad's murder on me. I was at the scene, and somebody saw me. He was already dead, but they won't believe me. I'm pretty sure I'm going to be sent to prison." Logan's voice cracked as he expressed his fears. The gravity of the situation overtook him. Not trusting the cleanliness of the blanket, he took off his T-shirt and sobbed quietly into it.

Whether the other man could tell he was crying or not Logan didn't know and didn't care, but there were no further whispers from the other cell. It seemed as if he wept for hours. Eventually, he crumpled into a heap on the bench and slept.

Chapter Fifty-Five

At eight the next morning, Julia, Ricardo, and Hector convened in the upstairs war room. Ricardo had brought doughnuts. And one cinnamon bun. They had three suspects in custody with compelling evidence against them all. They reviewed all the relevant statements from witnesses, the suspect's interrogation transcripts, and forensic evidence, and shared their interpretations of it. Ricardo was leaning toward Logan being the killer. In Julia's mind, it was most probably Dean.

Hector was undecided. "Until we get some better forensic evidence, I don't think we can make a solid case against any of them. Unless the results of the blood-aging test show Norm's blood inside the glove is fresh."

Julia debated voicing her thoughts about Dean. She pondered her own experience with male bullying and worried that her focus on Dean and Sandy might be clouded by her own experience. She couldn't honestly say it didn't.

When she finally spoke, it was with these things in mind.

"The type of verbal abuse Sandy experienced from Rudy can be insidious. To a person with little confidence or one in a subservient role, it can be soul destroying. I believe the effect of the depressive thinking one can experience when subjected to it over a long period could have brought her relationship with Dean to the edge of ruin.

"But I know Logan was a victim of Rudy's abuse, too, just in a different way. He isn't as emotionally strong as his sister, though his decision to hire a new coach shows a definite strength emerging.

Was it enough to make him strike out at his dad? I don't know. And did the first blow open a floodgate of pent-up animosity toward his dad? Playing itself out as the brutal beating and stabbing? Again, I don't know.

"I guess," she said finally, "what I'm trying to say is, at this point, even though I see two of them as possible killers, I'd put my money on Dean. I am not convinced Logan did it. And I think Norm is telling the truth about losing his gloves."

Since the station's two cells were occupied by Logan and Dean, Norm had been detained in the interview room all night. He was less than happy about it, too. At ten thirty, a few minutes after Vicente had given the officers the results of the chromatography test, Julia and Hector again entered the interview room and got a verbal blast of anger from Norm.

"Mr. Webster, we had to keep you in this room all night. We didn't have a cell available. However, the blood-aging test revealed the sample from inside the gloves is over two years old, as you suggested. You are free to go. I've already called your wife. She will be here shortly."

It took the man less than a second to bolt out of his chair and escape the room. Julia was planning to escort him into the foyer where there were chairs on which he could wait for Fran's arrival. But the man was outside in the front parking lot by the time she made it out of the interrogation room.

Before Julia had turned to leave the foyer, a young constable informed her that Logan was shouting for her. She headed back to the interview room; Hector was just leaving, saying he would be in his office. She told him Logan was asking for her.

Julia entered the cells first and Logan spoke at once, with pleading desperation. "Please, I need to talk with you . . . in the interview room."

Julia tried to get him to tell her what was going on, but the young man refused. His eyes darted toward the other cell as he tried to telegraph his concern for speaking in the cell.

When she and Ricardo were seated in an interview room with Logan, he finally spoke. "The man in the cell beside me, he's the one who was with my dad the first time I went to the courts. I recognized his voice when he was talking with me this morning. It's him. He must have killed my dad. Is he under arrest?"

"Do you have anything else to tell us, Logan?" Julia asked, ignoring his questions.

He didn't and was returned to his cell.

When Julia and Ricardo trudged back upstairs to tell Hector Logan's revelation, Vicente was waiting for them. He wore an excited expression, and his body was almost vibrating with anticipation of sharing his findings.

Chapter Fifty-Six

Vicente had found Rudy's blood on the beige bomber-style jacket from McLean's coat closet. There were no traces of blood on the shreds of cloth pulled from the ashes of the McLean's fire pit, but he was able to confirm some bits were denim and some contained a flower pattern. The dark stain on the leather sandal was blood, and it, too, matched Rudy's.

Dean McLean was back in the interview room Logan had recently vacated.

"You are officially under arrest for the murder of Rudy Stephanetti. It's time to tell the truth, Mr. McLean. We have all the evidence we need, but it may reduce your sentence if your statement indicates your cooperation. Remember, Mexico's legal system is based on the Napoleonic code. Here you are guilty until proven innocent.

"With the evidence we have, you will not be able to prove yourself innocent. This is your opportunity to tell your side of the story. Your statement will become part of your case before the magistrate."

Dean stared at his hands on the table for several minutes. Julia could see he was thinking, and so she remained quiet. When he started speaking, it was with resolve and resignation. He wouldn't let a young man pay the price of his crime.

"That bastard stole the only thing precious in my life . . . my sweet, gentle, fun-loving, passionate wife. After he got through with her, she was nothing more than a shell of the woman I married. She was broken in a place deep inside, and I couldn't fix it. Can you imagine how it feels to watch your reason for living disappear slowly in front of your eyes?" Dean asked, looking into Julia's eyes. Julia hadn't known the man could be so emotional. In their previous conversations, he'd appeared stoic to the point of apathy.

"So, you knew Mr. Stephanetti was badgering your wife at work? Correct?" Julia asked.

"No, I had no idea what was happening at the time. I thought maybe she was having an affair when she started to withdraw from me. But she swore she wasn't, and we have never lied to each other. Or so I thought at the time." Dean stopped and scrubbed at his face with the palms of his hands as though trying to wash away the memories. Then he resumed.

"The first thing I noticed was she wasn't interested in making love the way she'd previously been. She wasn't at all self-conscious about sex, and we had a full, wonderful relationship. Then slowly, she withdrew. I tried all the things she usually enjoyed. Saying sexy things to her while we were doing the dishes, kissing the back of her neck softly, that kind of thing, but it seemed to make her withdraw even more. I asked her whether something was wrong at work, but she tried to convince me everything was fine. She just wouldn't admit anything was different between us. I didn't know what to do.

"She got unconsolably depressed, and then I thought it was a brain-chemical thing. She started taking pills for it. But, they didn't seem to help much, as far as I could tell. They just made her withdraw more, in my view. It continued for almost three years. Then she started to come back a little. She was less depressed, more engaged with life, but she was still not the sweet, loving woman I married." Dean opened the bottle of water Julia had given him and took a long swig.

"And you say you didn't know it was Rudy Stephanetti who caused your wife's problems?" Julia tried to keep the incredulity from her voice.

"Right. I didn't know until she came home from pickleball one morning. As soon as she walked in the door that day, I could see she was right back in the same emotional state she'd been in during that horrible time.

"I said, 'You look as if you've seen a ghost.' She just nodded her head. Then she told me about the pickleball potluck that night and said she wanted me to go with her. I'm not much for social gatherings, and sometimes she goes to parties and things alone. She looked so sad, I agreed to go." Again Dean stopped for a gulp of water.

"Tell us what happened at the party."

"We got to the party about seven. There were a few guys there I know a little. One of them I know well, from the Plumeria Club, so I joined them in the living room for a while. About a half hour later, the Stephanettis arrived, and Rudy came and joined the same group of guys. He seemed like a self-centered prick to me. Sorry about the language. I didn't like him much.

"At one point, I looked back toward to kitchen area to see whether Sandy might be cajoled into leaving. I saw her then. She was standing in a nook between the living room and kitchen watching our group. She was white as a sheet and her face was — I've never seen her look that—she looked full of hatred. It was then I realized it must have been Rudy who had broken her.

"I asked him whether he'd ever worked in Texas, and he said he'd worked at OGSL. Oilfield General Supply Limited. Then I knew he'd done it. Whatever it was that destroyed my wife. He'd done it.

"I was so filled with rage, I wanted to kill him right there and then. I couldn't, of course. So, I just stood there. I felt so impotent. This man had destroyed the only woman I have ever loved. I could hardly breath, the desire to obliterate him was so strong. I know now what they mean when they talk about blood boiling. There was nothing in the world I wanted more in that moment than to see him pay. As though his death would erase all the years of sorrow he'd inflicted on her.

"When Norm and Rudy ventured outside with their cigars, I got the idea maybe I could get him alone somehow when he was outside. I saw a young guy, I think it was Rudy's son, leave the party, and I just headed outside after him. Told whoever was listening I was going for a walk on the beach. I grabbed my jacket out of the car because I had a pair of work gloves in one of the pockets.

"I did go to the beach in case anyone was watching me, but came right back a different way and stood at the end of the block in the shadows, just watching Rudy smoke. Eventually, he came walking toward me and then turned onto a path between the condos. I kept in the shadows and followed him. He walked into the courts and turned on the lights. Then he came back out, with a ball and paddle, and returned to the courts. As I saw later, there's a backboard there where a person can play against oneself.

"I heard him hitting the ball against it for a minute or so and then the sound stopped. I peeked in the back gate to see what he was doing, and he was just sitting on a bench. He looked a bit drunk, kind of slumped over." Dean said the last sentence slowly, in an almost trancelike state.

Julia had the feeling he was back on the courts in his mind. She didn't want to break the spell, so she simply waited for him to go on. A few moments later, he did.

"I marched in, then. I stood in front of him and told him who I was, Sandy's husband. I wanted him to know. I wanted him to feel scared like Sandy had. But, even after I told him the name of the company where they'd worked together, it took him a minute to figure out who Sandy was. He hadn't recognized her. Didn't know who I meant until I told him she had been an admin in the marketing department at OGSL. You know what he did? He grinned up at me and said, 'Oh yeah, I remember her. She was fun'.

"I just snapped. I grabbed his collar and stood him up. I punched him once. He landed on his face but slowly rose again and looked at me with the same smarmy grin. I grabbed the paddle and hit him as hard as I could. All the rage inside me was propelled into that strike. He collapsed and didn't get back up. I put on my gloves and straddled him, and punched him over and over. Anything to get the grin off his face. I just kept hitting him. I was in a blind madness. I couldn't stop."

Dean had been speaking with intensity. Reliving those terrible events. Now he'd stopped talking, and a heart-wrenching sigh escaped his lips. His body sagged against the back of his chair. He was pale now, ghostlike. His eyes, which moments before had blazed with madness, now were glazed and dull, focused on nothing. He started speaking again, a different man. A man face-to-face with the reality of what he'd done.

"Then the madness lifted. I saw what I'd done. He was hurt *real* bad. He was making a horrible, low, moaning sound. It was terrible. It reminded me of a cougar-mauled cow from when I was a kid. The cow made the same sound until my dad shot it to put it out of its misery. I saw the jagged handle from the paddle and put the man out of his misery." His tale of horror had been told. Finally, his eyes focused. He looked at Julia. She saw a shadow of the man who had started the interview.

"Apart from bugs, I'd never killed another living thing in my life before. I wish . . ." Dean stopped speaking. He looked at his hands as though they weren't his. He simply shook his head.

Julia wanted to know what he wished, but guessed she never would.

"Is there anything else you want to add to your statement, Mr. McLean?" she asked.

"No. Can I talk to Sandy now?" Dean asked.

Julia looked at the inspector and asked him the same question. He nodded. "Yes, I'll bring her in."

At the thought of facing his wife, he broke. He didn't weep. His face simply melted, as though all his muscles had gone limp. A single tear rolled down his cheek.

Outside the interview room, Julia phoned Sandy and asked her whether she could come to the station to talk with her husband. She said she'd be there in fifteen minutes. Julia relieved Inspector Martinez, saying she'd wait with Dean until his wife arrived.

When the desk sergeant phoned to say Sandy was in the station, Julia met her in the foyer. As they walked to the interview room, Julia told her Dean had admitted to the murder. Julia would give them five minutes to talk before he was taken back to the cells. Sandy reached out for the wall to steady herself. Her world had just dissolved.

Chapter Fifty-Seven

Julia stayed in the interview room with Sandy and Dean McLean. She had no desire to hear their conversation, but she had to. The couple sat across the table from each other as Julia had instructed them. They had five minutes, she'd told them. It was a heartbreaking meeting.

"I'm so, so sorry, my love," Dean said when a crying Sandy entered the room. "When you came back from pickleball that morning, I could see in your eyes and your slumped shoulders you'd regressed into the awful, horrible place you were in all those years ago when I lost you.

"Then at the party I saw the hatred in your eyes as you watched him. In the crush of emotions I experienced when I realized he had caused all the problems you had, I lost my mind. I just needed him off the planet, dead. In my madness, I thought it would make things better for us, for you." Dean shook his head sadly.

"I have regretted it every moment since you got in the car after the wretched party. The irony is when you got in the car to leave, I could tell, a weight had lifted from you on its own. I . . . . I didn't have to . . ." Dean struggled to find the right words. He failed.

Sandy took his hands across the table and just held them. The silence in the small room was overwhelming. Finally, she spoke. "That man has now ruined both of our lives. All I ever wanted was to be your wife and for us to get back what we had. And he has robbed me of the ability, twice now. I am sorry I could never talk with you about what happened to me.

"I believed I was so dirty I would never be clean again. I was afraid you'd leave me if you knew, somehow think it was my fault or I invited his attention." Sandy spoke through a downpour of tears.

"But when I watched him at the party, I realized what a cowardly bully he was. Every word out of his mouth was designed to curry favor, to manipulate the people around him.

"At the time, I thought there was something inherently wrong with me, something drawing his malicious attention and provoking his unbearable words. But after hearing him make such an insincere apology at pickleball and listening to him boast about his achievements and his family at the party, I finally realized. Manipulating and tormenting others, it's just how he operated.

"He tried to control everything with his conceit. As I realized it, all the power he'd held fell away. I realized he was just a scared little boy trying to feel less afraid by being a bully and controlling the people around him.

"I understand why you did it, Dean, but now I'm losing you just when I finally feel whole again. It's breaking my heart," Sandy said, crying even more. She blew her nose and hiccupped as she tried to dry her eyes.

"Did he ever *touch* you, Sandy?"

"He never did anything physical, no. His game was entirely psychological, and verbal. Sometimes I think what I experienced was worse than if he'd tried something physical. If it were physical, I would have had a case to take to human resources. He was so careful to whisper his filth to me only when no one else was around. It would have been his word against mine.

"In such a male-dominated industry, I was sure everyone would believe him over me. If he'd done something like grab my arm, I would have had bruises to show. Something, some evidence. Can you understand?" Sandy said, pleadingly.

"Sandy, I never stopped loving you. All I ever wanted was for you to be happy. I am so sorry I've ruined everything."

"Okay, folks, your time's up," Julia said through a lump in her throat. This case simply made her bone-achingly sad, and seeing the love these two shared through decades seemed to make it sadder.

As Dean was led out of the interview room by the constable who had been sent by Ricardo, Dean turned back to his wife. "Please, remember how much I love you, have always loved you." His voice was dripping with remorse.

Julia led Sandy from the room into the foyer of the station. "Do you have someone you'd like me to call for you? You shouldn't drive home by yourself. Or, I can get a constable to take you if need be."

"Would you please call Gretchen Wagner for me? She's a good friend," Sandy asked. Julia nodded and hurried to her desk to get the number.

"Mr. Wagner, this is Detective Sergeant Garcia. May I speak with your wife, please?" Julia asked the gruff man.

"What the hell for?" Wolfe asked in his usual rumbling-engine voice.

Julia was afraid he was about to disconnect and yelled. "Don't hang up! I'm calling at the request of Sandy McLean. She is at the police station and needs a friend right now."

"Oh, shit. Hang on." Wolfe loudly clunked the phone on the table, causing Julia to pull the receiver from her ear.

"Yes, this is Gretchen."

Julia introduced herself as the caller. "Mrs. Wagner, I'm phoning because Sandy McLean asked for your assistance in getting home. Her husband has just admitted to the murder of Rudy Stephanetti, and she is in no shape to be alone. Can you please come to the station and assist her?" Julia asked.

"Oh, my God! Poor Sandy! Yes, of course. It will take me about fifteen minutes to get into town. But I don't know where your police station is. Can you give me the address or directions?" Gretchen asked.

Julia assured she'd text the woman Google directions and returned her attention to Sandy. The desk sergeant had given her a bottle of water. Sandy was holding on to it as though it were a magic lamp, clutched to her chest. Perhaps she was hoping a genie could grant her the only wish in her heart. For this nightmare, all of it, to be wiped away so she and Dean could be the happy lovers they'd once been.

Ricardo joined her in the foyer and told her Dean was in the cells and would be transferred to Mexicali in two days. Julia relayed the information to Sandy as Ricardo returned to his desk.

While they waited for Gretchen's arrival, Julia outlined what would happen next so Sandy could prepare herself for the next steps. It did nothing to help the poor woman's anxiety. It pulled at Julia's heart as she thought of what the McLeans were facing.

Then she remembered the violence of the attack on the victim and had less sympathy. If the couple had simply talked with each other about the difficulty Sandy was experiencing, this murder would probably never have occurred.

The thought made Julia pause. *What important conversations was* she *avoiding?*

Chapter Fifty-Eight

While Julia had been waiting for Sandy to arrive, she'd instructed Lucia to bring Logan from the cells and put him in the interview room beside the one Dean was in. With Sandy and Gretchen now gone, she returned to speak with Logan. She informed him his dad's murderer had been charged and had admitted to the crime. The young man across from her gasped loudly and punched his fist into the air.

"Oh my God, I thought you were going to charge me." Logan took a moment to gather himself. Julia witnessed a scared boy disappear and a happy man emerge. "Did the guy say why he killed Dad? Do you know why he hated Dad so much?"

Julia gave him an abridged version of the torment Rudy had inflicted on Sandy and the effect on the McLeans' marriage. Through it, Logan was stoic, but by the end, he was also incredulous. He'd had no idea his dad was a bully to others than himself. Or that his dad could be so predatory. As he assimilated the information he'd just received, he appeared to gain confidence.

"Come on, let's take you home." Julia handed Logan his passport.

"Oh, hello, Sergeants, come in," Gloria said icily to Ricardo's knock at her door. Then she saw her son climbing the steps behind the officers, and her cool demeanor evaporated. She wrapped her arms around him and didn't appear to want to let him go.

"Gloria, we wanted to let you know we arrested your husband's murderer. He confessed this morning. I was sure you would want to know. And I wanted to bring Logan back personally."

"I hope you all understand we needed to interview Logan again because he'd lied to us again. And in hope"—she turned toward Logan—"you appreciate the importance of telling the police the truth. Our police training demands we treat people who are caught lying to us with suspicion."

Gloria's anger toward the officers thawed slowly as she took in Julia's words. After a couple of moments, she moved on from her resentment at the treatment of her son.

"Well, congratulations on finding the killer. Can you tell me who it was?" Gloria asked. Marguerite had joined her partner on the couch and looked as anxious as Gloria to hear the outcome of their investigation.

"It was Dean McLean, Sandy's husband. Sandy had been the recipient of Rudy's unwanted attention years ago when they worked together in Dallas. And she never fully recovered from the trauma she experienced. According to both of them, it destroyed their happiness and damaged their marriage." Julia wanted Gloria to know the reason, but at the same time didn't want to lay too much of the blame at the woman's feet.

Gloria got the message. She put a hand to her mouth, and her eyes welled up. "Oh, God. Oh, God!" Her body heaved with sobs. "Poor Sandy. And poor Dean."

Marguerite comforted her lover as she cried. "You never could control Rudy, my love. Even if you'd confronted him or tried to get him to change, do you honestly think it would have made any difference? This is not your fault."

Julia ached to provide her own words of comfort, but her role in this situation was not to placate. She'd given Gloria the information she was required to share. Her family and partner would fill the role of providing comfort.

Now she changed the subject. "Logan has his passport back. You are all free to leave Mexico when you wish. Logan, will you still be competing in the Palm Springs tournament? I know it's just a couple of days away."

"Yeah," the young man said. "I want to see how it is playing without Dad. Whether or not I want to continue playing professionally."

Gloria interjected, "We will leave tomorrow, if possible." Then she shifted to a different topic. "What happens to Rudy's remains?"

Julia walked the two women through the options for dealing with his body now that it could be released. It took them no time at all to agree on having him cremated in San Amaro. After a couple of phone calls, Julia let them know Rudy's ashes could be mailed to New Jersey. Gloria would have to complete some paperwork to initiate the cremation and handling of the cremains, but Julia promised to help her with the forms.

By the time Ricardo and Julia left, the cremation was organized. Gloria and Marguerite agreed to go to the station at eight the next day to complete the paperwork and then go pay the crematorium before they headed to Palm Springs.

When they got back into La Chica, instead of starting the car, Julia turned to Ricardo. "Doesn't it feel as if all the air has been sucked out of you when we finish a big case?" she asked him but continued before Ricardo had a chance to respond. "Maybe a better way to put it is I feel like a deflated helium balloon. I just feel flat, not actually depressed, just as if I've lost my enthusiasm."

"Yeah, I know what you mean. We've been going on adrenaline for a couple of weeks. You especially because you've had to lead almost all the interviews."

They sat for several more minutes while Julia filled Ricardo in on the final conversation between Sandy and Dean. She even admitted the sadness she felt for them. She didn't condone the murder or make light of its brutality. She simply needed to speak the words, to admit the emotional toll it had taken on her. And she knew Ricardo would understand without judgment.

Chapter Fifty-Nine

It was a beautiful spring afternoon in San Amaro. The desert was awash in color as palo verde trees with their bright yellow flowers and mesquite trees sporting yellow catkins vied with purple desert verbena and red ocotillo blossom sprigs for the most eye-catching appeal. Birdsong filled the air, and turkey vultures soared majestically against a cloudless sapphire sky.

As Julia drove, Ricardo hoped she was enjoying the view as much as he. But Julia's mind was on other things. Leaving the Stephanettis, Julia was quiet for a long time. As they drove past the venue for the blues festival, Julia was disappointed to see the stage was being disassembled. She'd missed the event for another year.

But topmost on her mind was the final interview with Dean and his and Sandy's last conversation. She had recognized in her own behavior some of the same mistakes the McLeans made. And she vowed to herself to be more open with the important people in her life.

Finally, she pulled the car over to the side of the road, and she turned in her seat to face Ricardo. He glanced her way and raised an inquisitive eyebrow. Did she need to talk more about Sandy and Dean? She surprised him.

"Ricardo, you are a special man, and I'm so glad you are my partner. I should say it more often, but I am grateful to work with you. I appreciate you took the time to find out about equine therapy and then took me there. It was a special thing to do.

"This case has got me thinking about how important communication is. And actually, now that I say it, I guess this thinking started on my week off in Ensenada before the case began. When people don't speak the truth to the important people in their life, the results can be loneliness and isolation, misinterpretations, and inappropriate actions. If the McLeans had just talked about what was happening to Sandy at work, Rudy's murder would probably never have happened." Julia's words throbbed with intensity.

"Or Dean might have killed Rudy then, instead of now," Ricardo said jovially.

Julia knew her partner used humor to lighten the mood. "Yes, that's a possibility, but I'm trying to make a point . . . about us." Julia spoke seriously and then wondered whether she was ready to have this conversation. Her nerve almost faltered, but she remembered the deep feeling of the connection after spending time with her cousin and the penetrating, probing discussions they'd had.

"I know you want our relationship to be more than just work partners. I do. We've talked about it before, and I admire and appreciate how you accept the limitation I put on our friendship. At this point in my life, my career is the most important thing for me." Ricardo opened his mouth to respond, but Julia stopped him.

"Please hear me out. This is hard for me, but too important not to say. I want to be clear with you. I truly value your caring, honesty, and goodness, and if I were actively seeking a long-term romantic partner, someone to spend my life with, it would be you.

"However, I'm not looking, and I need to communicate that honestly. It wouldn't be fair to either of us if I didn't express this plainly. I can't fulfill the expectations of a romantic relationship right now, and it wouldn't be right to keep you waiting for something I can't provide. I am sorry I can't be that person for you. I genuinely am. Do you understand where I'm coming from?"

Ricardo lost his jocularity. He took Julia's seriousness to heart. "I know all this, Julia. I understand how important your job is to you. The job is important to me, too, but I don't have the same aspirations as you," Ricardo said sincerely, then continued with a mischievous smile. "Good thing, too, because I'd absolutely become comandante before you if I wanted the job."

Then he smiled softly and became serious again. "It would be easier for me to move on if you weren't exactly what I'm looking for in the person to share my life with. I haven't met anyone I want to date, apart from you."

"Well, you should start looking, please. It would make me truly sad if you missed out on the family life I know you long for. Please don't let me stand between you and a full, rich life of the love you deserve."

Julia patted his arm and continued. "I didn't mean to make this all heavy. Truly, I didn't. I'm sorry if I did. I just can't be what stands between you and a happy life. Okay?" Julia asked.

"Okay. I hear you loud and clear, Lucy. And thanks for being honest with me. But, just for the record, you've never been *dis*honest with me. You've never led me on. I know how important your career is, and I admire that about you. Too bad you don't have a sister I could date." Ricardo gave her a sly look, then laughed. "Don't worry, I wouldn't do it even if you did have a sister. It would just be creepy!"

"Thanks, Ricky. You make it easy to talk about difficult things. Thank you! Shall we head back to the station so you can get your truck and enjoy the rest of the afternoon?" Relieved, yet sad, Julia put her car in drive and pulled back onto the road.

Chapter Sixty

Though the inspector had given them the afternoon off, there was still one thing Julia and Ricardo wanted to do before they clocked off for the day. First, they headed to the forensics lab and told Vicente they had arrested the murderer. After thanking him for his help figuring out the killer, Julia moved on to a more personal question.

"How is your grandfather doing, Vicente?" she asked.

"He has rallied this week. He is eating better and has a bit more energy. He is still ill. His cancer isn't in remission or anything, but the doctor switched his chemo drugs, and this new one doesn't make him as sick as the other one. So, we are celebrating. At this point in the cancer journey, one has to celebrate the small wins. Thanks for checking in. I appreciate it!" Vicente said.

"I've got a couple of phone calls to make when I get home. See you tomorrow, Ricky." Julia headed toward the parking lot.

"*Hasta mañana,* Lucy," Ricardo said.

Before Julia got out of the building, however, her cell phone rang. It was Inspector Martinez. "Julia, are you still at the station? I need you here now." There was no hiding the strain in his voice.

"I'm on the back stairs outside. I'm coming back in now," Julia said, heading toward Hector's office when she heard his voice call to her from the main floor. Ricardo was already there, also having had a terse, stressed call from their boss. Hector told them to follow him and headed toward the hallway leading to the cells.

"When Constable Juarez took Mr. McLean his lunch just moments ago, she discovered this." Hector led them into the prison area.

Horror awaited them.

Clad in underwear only, the body of Dean McLean hung, lifeless. He had fashioned a thin rope from his shirt, by twisting it tightly. This was tied around his neck as a noose. At the back of his neck, one leg of his pants was looped through the noose and knotted; the other pant leg was tied to the highest crosspiece of the cell bars. It wasn't more than five feet from the floor, but Dean had used his body weight to strangle himself by pushing his legs out on the floor in front of him.

There was blood dried on his face. The man had given himself a bloody nose and used the blood to write *I'm sorry* on a piece of toilet paper. It was hanging out the top of his underwear.

The words *Oh no* escaped Julia's lips without her even realizing it.

Dr. Serrano arrived just then and entered the cell with the dead man. After inspecting the situation, he turned to address the officers. He looked slightly pale but spoke with a strong, clear voice. "He managed to compress both the carotid arteries in his neck by balling the sleeves of his shirt within the noose at the spots where those arteries run. He would have lost consciousness in twenty seconds or less. Death probably occurred in under ten minutes, but he would already have been brain damaged by then."

Julia spoke again, this time intentionally. "When he spoke with his wife earlier, he was filled with remorse. I suppose I shouldn't be surprised, but I never suspected he'd do this."

"This is not your fault, Julia," Inspector Martinez said emphatically. "Of course, the comandante will have to do a custodial death investigation. And, Dr. Serrano will be doing an autopsy as part of the process, but I have observed all your interactions with Mr. McLean while he's been at the station, and you are above reproach. Please don't worry about this. And I still suggest you and Ricardo do as I suggested and take the rest of the day off."

Julia heard the inspector's words, but a heavy ache had descended upon her, each breath a burden. She stood stoically between Hector and Ricardo for a few moments, then shook her head, as though to clear it.

"I need to tell his wife," Julia said sadly. "I'll drive out there now, then head home. Thanks, Hector."

Ricardo asked whether she wanted him to come with her, but she declined. She needed to do this herself.

Gretchen Wagner was still at Sandy's house when Julia arrived. And it was Gretchen who answered the door to Julia's knock. Her face blanched when she saw Julia.

Julia delivered the news with as much sensitivity as possible. Sandy, already a mess from learning just a few hours before Dean had confessed to committing a brutal murder, simply crumbled at Julia's latest news.

Thank God Gretchen is here was all Julia could think. It was not Julia's responsibility or place to try to comfort the broken woman before her. And, she realized, her presence there was exacerbating the poor woman's grief. So, she left promptly, committing to herself to check on Sandy, through Gretchen, over the next few days. There was nothing else she could do.

Having fulfilled her responsibility, she headed home. But not before buying a bottle of wine on the way. Tomorrow, she'd embrace her role as a police officer once more. But for this precious night, all she yearned to be was an ordinary, vulnerable human being.

Epilogue

"Hi, Stella. It's Julia Garcia calling. We have apprehended the murderer of Rudy Stephanetti today, and, as promised, I'm ready to talk with you about this charity you want to start. I have a couple of days off coming up—can we get together this Saturday?"

Julia wasn't in the mood for casual conversation and ended the call quickly. She showered and changed into shorts and a T-shirt. She also wasn't ready to talk with her grandfather about the conclusion of this case. She needed some time alone to think it through. She made herself some soup and sat on her couch as the soup grew cool and then completely cold as she reflected on the last two weeks.

It had been an emotionally challenging case.

At seven that evening, as previously agreed, Julia placed a call to the one person with whom she wanted to talk. She was now lying on her couch, a glass of wine in one hand and her phone, on speaker, lying on her chest. Her call was answered on the second ring.

"Hi, Alma, I hope you have a full glass of wine. I have so much to tell you."

If you enjoyed Death in the Kitchen, don't miss the next book in the San Amaro series.

Go to MarnieJRoss.com and subscribe to follow the writing process.

Acknowledgments

I owe huge to thanks my beta readers Linda Wiggins and Cal Whedbee for their insightful feedback as this book took shape, and Tricia Sikes, my wonderful wife, who helped me in more ways than I can possibly list.

About the Author

Marnie Ross is an expatriated dual citizen of Canada and the United States now living permanently in San Felipe, Baja, Mexico with her wife and two small, rescued dogs.

Her passion for her adopted home and murder mysteries is the impetus behind the San Amaro Mystery series. If you want to learn more about Baja living and being an expat in Mexico while enjoying a gripping murder mystery, please sign up at, *marniejross.com*, and experience the adventure.